If We Do

If We Do

Quill & Flame
PUBLISHING HOUSE

Anna Augustine

Quill & Flame
PUBLISHING HOUSE

If We Do

Copyright © 2024 by Anna Augustine

Published by Quill & Flame Publishing House, an imprint of Book Bash Media, LLC.

www.quillandflame.com

All rights reserved.

No part of this publication may be reproduced, digitally stored, or transmitted in any form without written permission from the publisher, except as permitted by U.S. copyright law.

This is a work of fiction. Names, characters, and incidents are products of the author's imagination or are used ficticiously. Any similarity to actual people, living or dead, organizations, business establishments, and/or events is purely coincidental.

NO AI TRAINING: Without any limitation on the author or Quill & Flame's exclusive copyright rights, any use of this publication to train generative artificial intelligence is expressly prohibited.

To my brother, Andrew.

The reason that Emily loves the Beatles so much is because you could never stop singing, playing, and/or ranting about John, Paul, George, and Ringo for more than an hour back in 2020-2023. So, this one's all on you! I love you!

Prologue

Oliver

My cell phone buzzes as I step out of the conference room, all too eager for an excuse to retreat to my office. Usually, I don't pick up calls from unknown numbers, but the desire to vacate the hallway—and my mother—is massively overwhelming today.

I accept the call. "Hello, Oliver Markel speaking."

"Hello, Mr. Markel. This is Officer Sterling Howard of the Bloomingdale Police Department." The voice on the other end is deep, the background noise a touch chaotic.

My heart lurches into my throat and my palms go clammy. The only person I know who lives in Bloomingdale is my friend, Gavin Dangler. But why would the police be calling me?

"Yes, Officer Howard. How can I help you?"

The man is all business, but I can hear the note of sorrow in his voice when he says, "There's been an accident with Gavin Dangler. I'm afraid ... he's gone, Mr. Markel."

"Gone? Gone where?"

"He's ... he passed away."

"What?" I sit down hard in my desk chair, a shudder working through my body as nausea churns in my gut. "What happened?"

"Gavin and Brittany were in a car accident. A head on collision. We're fairly certain both of them died on impact." Officer Howard's voice is steady, and it helps me to keep breathing despite my heart's frantic pace and the fact that my mind feels like it just imploded.

An accident.

Died on impact.

Gone, gone, gone.

"It's a miracle that the baby is fine."

Everything freezes for the second time in five minutes. It's like a record screech from those old movies my nanny used to watch with me. Everything stops. Nothing but the heaviness of my breathing and the spinning of my office. "Baby?"

"Yes, their daughter? Charlotte? There was a note in Gavin's wallet that said you were his daughter's godfather and that if anything happened to him, we were to call you. We were also told by his lawyer that you were named the legal guardian of the baby, in the event of his and Brittany's passing."

"But—but—" *Nothing was supposed to happen to Gavin.* He was supposed to live to be eighty-three and have a busload of kids with his high school sweetheart and I was *never* going to have to take on the role handed to me when they asked me to be Charlotte's godfather. It was supposed to just be ceremonial, an honorary position.

No, no, *no*!

I moisten my dry lips with my tongue. "Well, I...I'll be there as soon as I can."

"She's in protective custody with a social worker. We can give you more information once you're here. How long do you think that will be?"

Bloomingdale is only a two-hour drive. I glance at my watch. "I'll be there by six."

"Good. Thank you for your promptness, Mr. Markel."

"Of course. Goodbye."

I end the call and then stare blankly out of the floor to ceiling windows.

Gone.

Passed away.

Accident.

Collision.

Gone. Gone. Gone.

Guardian. Charlotte.

I have to go. Pushing to my feet, I all but run out of the office.

I have to be there for her. Have to help.

That's the only thing I can do for Gavin now.

"I'm sorry, you're just not the right fit." I fight back a yawn. Charlotte Elizabeth Dangler is nestled in the crook of my arm and I'm struggling to focus on the applicants filtering through my front door. The last few nights have been sleepless. I need a nanny—one willing to be here by seven in the morning most days and stay through seven in the evening to get the little girl to bed. I don't know how to care for her. I have no idea what I'm doing.

Not for the first time, I wonder, *why did I say yes to being her godfather?*

I suppress a groan as yet another applicant waltzes in the door. Her black hair brushes her chin as she walks up to me. She certainly looks like a nanny. An oversized cardigan over a band t-shirt (is that the Beatles?), black leggings, and high tops. The upper half of her hair is pulled back in a short ponytail, and while I can tell she has on makeup, it's light and simple.

But she doesn't address me. Rather, her eyes are on the little girl in my arms.

"Hello. I'm Oliver Markel." I watch her as she studies the baby.

"This is Charlotte?" she asks, her voice barely above a whisper. She finally looks at me and I'm struck dumb. Her eyes. They're wet with unshed tears as she extends her application to me.

"Yes." I cough to clear the thickness from my throat and take the paper.

"May I hold her?"

I blink. This woman—whoever she is—is the first person to ask to hold Charlotte. Slowly, I nod, and the applicant scoops the little girl into her arms. The baby squirms for a minute before settling back with her pacifier bobbing. Her little hands are curled by her cheeks, and she looks angelic.

"Well, you're just an adorable little miracle."

I glance at the paper. *Emily Fitzpatrick* is printed in loopy, neat handwriting on the line. She's twenty-three and lives in the city of Cloverfield—only fifteen minutes from my house.

"Miss Fitzpatrick, why do you want this job?" I ask, dragging my gaze back up to look at her. She's swaying, rocking Charlotte, and smiling down at her. For a moment, my brain decides to loop that one horror movie where the nanny tries to steal the baby from the family. But I shake it away when Emily smiles at me.

"I love kids. I'm working at a preschool right now, but turned in my two weeks' notice...well, a week and a half ago. It's hard work. Exhausting, really, and I'm looking for something different. One of my roommates told me that this might be a good fit."

"Oh? And who's your roommate?"

"Susan Fenton."

My brows raise. I've known Susan since we were kids. We'd been friends for a long time when we'd both attended a private school in Nottingham—one town over from where we both now live in Cloverfield. She ended up attending the little community college in Cloverfield when she refused to go to the school her parents wanted her to attend for business and instead began paving her way into the baking world.

Which is more than I can say for myself, stuck in a job that I feel coolly indifferent to, at best, and hate at worst.

I tap the edge of the papers against the counter. "So, you care about the baby? That's the reason you want this job?"

Emily's dark brows furrow. "Shouldn't that be the *only* reason?"

I can't help it. Her sincerity has me smiling with a nod. "It should be."

"Were people coming here who didn't care about this sweet angel?" I see her arms tighten and her frown deepens.

"Yes, but they weren't offered the job." I look down at her list of references and past work. The preschool is pretty popular—I know it's the biggest and best in the tri-county area. That, plus her relationship with Susan has me saying, "I think you'd be the perfect fit for us."

An awkward silence falls over the kitchen and I clear my throat as heat rushes my cheeks. That came out…wrong. "I mean, you'll be the perfect fit for Charlotte. If you're willing to do a trial run the rest of this week to see if you enjoy working with the baby, then—"

"Mr. Markel, I already adore her. I promise you, nothing Charlotte throws at me will be worse than the preschool or any of my other babysitting gigs." She grins, her hazel eyes sparkling.

"Well…if you're certain."

"I am. That is, if you're offering me the job?"

Have I not? I retrace our conversation. My tired brain rebels with a dull ache behind my eyes and I finally give up. "Yes, I am offering you the nanny job."

"Excellent." Emily smiles and I swear it's brighter than the lights that hang overhead. "When do you want me to start?"

Chapter One

Emily

Four months later...

I am running late. To be honest, I usually always run slightly late but that's not good because if I'm late that means my boss—the young, almost-a-multi-millionaire hotshot, Oliver Markel—will also be late. And late is one thing he *can't* be.

"Darn businessmen," I mutter as I tromp down the stairs at the *unholy* hour of five-thirty AM. It is only Tuesdays when I *have* to be at the house by five-forty-five on the button so that Oliver can make it to the office by six-thirty for his weekly board meeting. He has an almost forty-five-minute commute. But since I'm not yet in the car for my jaunt to the outskirts of Cloverfield (who builds their half-a-million-dollar mansion in the middle of farm country?), it's likely I'll be five to ten minutes late.

"Keys, keys, keys," I whimper as I try to struggle into my sheep skin suede boots while digging through a purse that would make Mary Poppins proud, let me tell you! Amidst the gum wrappers, receipts, loose bits of paper, cracker crumbs, and lip balms, I finally locate my key ring that has approximately three keys and forty keychains.

Feeling a rush of adrenaline when my phone pings with a text, I shove my arms into my coat sleeves as I hit the automatic start my Nanna Jane gave me last year for Christmas. But, of course, instead of hitting the start, I press the panic button.

The screeching blare of my horn echoes across the frosty front lawn. I frantically press the button, but instead of stopping the alarm, the windows roll down.

"Of all the blasted—" I bite my tongue to keep more colorful language from spewing as I hurry outside, and fling open the car door. Shoving the keys into the ignition silences the alarm, but my hands are shaking, and I can feel the start of a headache already forming behind my eyes. "It's too early for this."

My phone's ringtone goes off.

Oliver Markel.

"Buckets!" I take a steadying breath before I pick it up. "Good morning, sir. Sorry, I'm pulling out of my driveway right now."

"Oh." His voice sounds gravelly. Sexy, even.

I emphatically shake my head at that. *Nope, absolutely not!*

To state the obvious, Oliver is every woman's fantasy. Successful. Rich. Drop dead gorgeous. Seriously, he could be a contender for *sexiest man alive* if he put himself out there more. But currently he's more than happy camping out in Cloverfield. Well, he does hop over to Highland to help run his parent's marketing firm. He's a genius with story-spinning. I even heard that he might have helped Tanner Bradshaw's publicist for a while.

But despite that, for whatever reason, the man is—and has been for the last four months I've worked for him—single.

A wail of pure anger rattles out of my phone, nearly rupturing my eardrum as I pull out of the driveway.

"Sorry! I know I'm running late. I'll be there soon." I tuck my phone between my shoulder and my ear.

"She's been doing this all night." Oliver clears his throat, and I can almost hear the desperation bleeding through the phone. "Her pacifier isn't working, she won't take a bottle, and bouncing isn't helping."

"She's been colicky all week." Another scream. "Buckets! She's ticked!"

A long pause ensues. I pull the phone back to make sure the call didn't drop. "Mr. Markel?"

"I'm sorry, but did you just say *buckets*?"

"Yes. I did." I speed a bit faster as I hit the lengthy stretch of backroad that no sane and/or sober person is on at five-thirty-seven AM. The *sun* isn't even up yet. "I can use more colorful words if you want. But I figured that—for the sake of your goddaughter—I'd refrain."

He clears his throat yet again. "I called Mother to tell her I'll be late because Charlotte is fussy, but please hurry. I really don't know what to do with her. You're the miracle worker."

There's something about the way Oliver says it—*miracle worker*—like he really believes I'm something special. That I really can help his goddaughter. It warms my frozen body enough to smile. "I'll be there in ten."

"Be safe." He pauses. "See you soon."

Oliver ends the call and I toss the phone on top of my bag. Every interaction I have with the man is ... strange. Though, I suppose getting saddled with a two-month-old baby girl after her parents died in a horrific car crash would make one a little odd. Not a situation most twenty-five-year-old guys find themselves in.

I break land speed records and reach Oliver's in about half the normal time. I'll probably get lectured by the hyper rule follower, but a child needs me. Who follows speed limits in cases like that?

Swinging my purse over my shoulder, I walk up the back sidewalk to the kitchen door. Frost crunches against the few leaves his lawn team failed to rake up yesterday. The low hedges that line the twisting sidewalks rustle in the cool breeze and I exhale slowly, watching my breath cloud in the early morning light. I move to the sliding glass door and unlock it with my key. I open it just far enough to squeeze through before closing it with a soft click.

I hear the earsplitting scream of a healthy set of lungs before I see Oliver through the large arching doorway that leads from the massively oversized kitchen into the white—yes, *white*—living room.

He's pacing between the large white leather *rocking* recliner and the white suede sofa. His bare feet sink into the white fur rug that covers the only nonwhite thing in the room—the oak flooring. White shiplap stretches between the floor to ceiling windows that look out over the rolling, hilly yard that's way too beautiful as it's accented by the rising sun. Joanna Gaines would approve.

I set my purse and keys on the enormous granite countertop and kick my boots under one of the chrome barstools. Shrugging out of my coat—which I discard next to my purse—I hurry into the living room.

"Did you try swaddling her?" I ask above the wailing.

Oliver turns toward me, and it's only then that I realize—he's not wearing a shirt. Oh boy. Shirtless Oliver is...distracting. Who knew how much his designer suits were hiding, despite them being perfectly tailored to his broad shoulders.

Okay, fine, I'll admit it. Oliver Markel is ripped. He's got a six pack—somehow, because for real, when does the man find time to work out? —and his biceps are...impressive.

I swallow as I meet his gaze, his green eyes twinkling as the morning light creeps above the horizon. Oh, he totally knows I am checking him out. Well, I refuse to be embarrassed. I can appreciate the work of art that is Oliver's physique just as I would a sculpture in a museum, thank you very much. There is barely any difference. Except for—well, Oliver has a nicer smile.

Clearing my throat, I hold my hands out and wave my fingers toward myself. "Tiny human?"

"Here." He hands me Charlotte all too willingly. She proceeds to scream loudly enough to make my ears ring.

Yep. There's a headache in my future today.

I snag her purple afghan off Oliver's shoulder as he heads for the massive staircase that curves up one side of the front entry hall. Hopefully when he comes back, he'll have a shirt on.

Shaking the image from my head, I spread a swaddling blanket out on the sofa and lay Charlie in the middle. She's a sweaty mess but swaddling usually calms her. Pinning one of her arms to her side, I wrap the blanket around and under her, quickly doing the same motion with the other side and then tuck the bottom up so she can't wiggle free. Throwing the purple afghan over my shoulder, I pick her up again.

"There we go!" I coo above her now softer cries. "It's my baby burrito!"

I hum a nonsense song about burritos and babies as I bounce up and down, trying to calm her. Scooping the pacifier off the glass coffee table, I pop it in Charlie's mouth. She smacks it between her lips. Tiny baby whimpers slip out as she heaves a shuddering breath and *finally* gives into sleep.

I sigh in relief. While I love babies, trying to keep this one happy when there's clearly no one who will ever replace her mom is exhausting.

Especially at six o'clock in the morning. I wrinkle my nose. This is one of the biggest downsides to nannying.

Although I can't ignore all the benefits: during work hours, I can go to my place to clean, indulge in Susan's extraordinary cookies, go shopping for an outfit for Molly's bridal shower, or swing by Sweeties for a cup of coffee. Of course, all of that is done with Charlie in tow. But it really isn't a bad gig.

"She asleep?" I turn toward Oliver, loving that he now has his white dress shirt on and is looping his tie around his neck. His navy-blue dress pants hug his legs—hello, thigh muscles— his blond hair has been tamed into gentle waves, and when he steps closer, his cologne wafts through the room. Man, he smells like a *man's* man.

I clear my throat before softly whispering, "Yeah. How was her sleep last night?"

Oliver levels a glare at the baby. "Horrible. The screaming you heard? Mild compared to last night."

"Ouch." I wince. "Sorry."

Oliver shrugs, but I can tell he's frustrated. I can't say I blame him. It's hard enough to be the actual birth parent of a wailing infant. At least then there are usually two parents and you *planned* to have the child. I look down at Charlie at that thought. Poor thing.

"I need to head out, but I'll be home earlier than normal. Do you want me to pick up anything for dinner?"

I eye Oliver. It's not the first time he's offered, and usually I say no. I don't want to come off as a leech. But...I have a feeling today is going to be a long one.

"Chinese sounds really good."

Oliver smiles, and I swear it's brighter than the sunrise. "Are you actually letting me buy you dinner, Nanny Emily?"

I roll my eyes. "It's the least you can do, *sir*, after foisting your screaming goddaughter off on me."

He chuckles as he grabs his suit coat out of the closet under the stairs and shrugs into it. "Your wish is my command."

The insufferable man *winks* at me before walking back into the entry hall and his office that's on the other side of the house. A few moments pass in which I settle myself into the rocking recliner and let my eyes drift close. Oliver's shoes clack across the marble entryway and the oak flooring before I sense him looking down at Charlotte and me.

"I'll be home around four," he says.

"Okay."

He shifts slightly. "You'll be okay with her?"

I crack one eye open at him. "Mr. Markel, I've been okay for the last four months. One rough day isn't the end of the world."

"Okay, if you're sure." He rubs the back of his neck and then nods. "See you later."

He's out the door before I can reply, and I shake my head. The man is strange. But it's never a dull day working for him, that's for sure.

Chapter Two

Oliver

I sit in my silver sports car for a moment. My knuckles are white as I grip the steering wheel, exhaustion making me want to call in sick. But if I do that, Mother will want me to visit the doctor and Dad will call me fifty times with questions he could easily answer himself, meaning I'll be just as tired—if not more so—than I am right now.

Hitting the garage door opener as I turn the key, I blast the heat, willing the car to warm before I start my commute to the office.

I'm not looking forward to work. Although, I rarely do. The office Christmas party is coming up in a week and a half. It's the event Mother always goes all out for. Apparently, this year we're renting a giant ballroom to host a fancy dance and dinner. Why is that bad, you ask? Well, because Mother is harping on me to come and bring my girlfriend—the nonexistent one I created five months ago to get my mother off my back about never dating. Oh, Miss Imaginary is gorgeous and hardworking. Plus, she travels a lot for work, so you know … she is conveniently always gone whenever my parents want to meet her.

But that excuse isn't going to work for this party. Mother is nothing if not persistent.

I sigh and back out of the drive, heading down the road as the local country pop station blares Hunter Hayes.

It's not that I don't want to have a relationship. I do. There just hasn't been anyone worth taking out for more than one dinner. Not a single woman I've dated in the last year *hasn't* gotten all tongue-tied around me because of my wealth. It's either that, or I got so nervous that I'll say something wrong, that I fail to say anything at all. And never mind the fact that anyone dating me is dating the now six-month-old baby girl Gavin left me when he and his wife died in August.

I merge onto the freeway, click my cruise on, and continue my commute without thinking. Mainly because I don't want to think about the fact that Charlotte is now mine, that Gavin is dead and buried six feet underground, and that there's no way I will wake up from this nightmare that's my life.

Unbidden, Emily comes to mind. She has been a pleasant surprise. The woman is so good with Charlotte, knows how to calm the baby down anytime she's fussy, and she's just so...natural with the little girl. Not for the first time a pang of jealousy hits me. I want to be good with Charlotte. I want her to like me someday. But a squirming little bundle who is only now starting to hold her head up for longer than a few seconds? I don't know what to do with her.

Plus, there's the nightly screaming. I'm about at my wits end with that. I'm half tempted to ask Emily to move into the guest room to help me with nighttime duty because I *need my sleep*.

Now, there's an idea.

My office building looms ahead of me far too soon. Gathering all my thoughts on pretty nannies, baby girls, and best friends, I shove them into their respective boxes and lock the lids. Work isn't the place to be thinking about those things. Unless, of course, Emily calls with an emergency. Then it'll be time for a full-fledged panic attack because, though that has yet to happen, it is quite possibly my worst nightmare.

I pull into my parking spot, gathering my briefcase and the empty travel mug (I always fill it up with the coffee provided at the weekly board meetings), and head for the revolving glass doors. The tightening in my chest that comes every time I step through them appears. I hate it, although I've had it for years. I know what causes it, but escaping isn't possible. So, I breathe in deeply through my nose and exhale through my mouth—demanding calm to enter my soul.

You've got this, I hype myself up during the elevator ride. The bell dings and my shoulders instinctively hunch with tension. With an exhale, I step down the hall and through the conference room door.

"Sorry I'm late." Every head turns to look at me with varying levels of disdain. I swallow the lump of panic and force my smile that makes people soften onto my face. "Charlotte had me up last night and was giving her nanny fits."

Sure, Emily was a little late today; but they don't need to know that. I'm not throwing an innocent to the wolves for no reason and me being uncomfortable isn't a good enough one.

"Yes, well." Mother clears her throat and I glance toward the head of the table where she sits, perched on her chair like it's a throne. She smooths her already immaculate golden blonde hair (which I inherited) while her eyes throw daggers in my direction. She pats the table in front of my empty chair. "Sit down, Oliver."

I resist the urge to roll my eyes as I plop in the leather desk chair and cross my arms over my chest. That earns me another glare from Mother. A look across the table at Dad reveals him reading a report, ignoring me completely.

It has always been this way. Mother and Dad, obsessed with Mother's marketing firm; me, getting dragged along. No brothers or sisters. I'm fairly certain I'd been an *oops* on their part, a hiccup in their perfectly planned lives.

But had that stopped them from dictating every area of my life? Nope! School? Private. College? University of Michigan—one of the top schools for a marketing degree. Job? Hired as one of Mother's team members.

Now, I am treated just like all the other employees. No favoritism here (although I am excellent at what I do, so I get a lot of the bigger clients). In fact, Mother and Dad are often the hardest on me. Sure, I helped Tanner Bradshaw's agent and publicist with his image, and that had paid really well. But since his early retirement, my parents have been even tougher on me to get some new clients for the firm.

I pick up my pen and shake it between my thumb and forefinger as Mother begins talking. I tune her out. It is mostly just the schedule of what needs to be done this week, and which clients we are trying for. I know it all already. This is all she talked about the other night at dinner when I took her and Dad out for her birthday.

Can this please be over? I feel my heart rate pick up. As discretely as I can, I suck in a slow, deep breath in through my nose, then breathe out through my mouth. The urge to click my pen hits but I continue to shake it. Shaking it means I won't get yelled at. Again.

"That should be it." Mother shuffles some papers on the table and jerks my attention from my breathing. "Any questions?"

There aren't any. She was thorough, as always.

"Good." Mother smiles. It's bright and inviting and just like mine. That fact makes it hard to swallow. I look so much like her. Act so much like her.

I am determined to be different, though. But can someone raised under an emotionless hand actually have feelings? I stifle a sigh as everyone stands and files out of the conference room door.

"Oliver, wait."

I flinch, hand on the door handle. *So close to freedom, gosh dang it.* I turn back toward Mother. "Yes?"

She studies me. "You look tired."

"I told you. Charlotte has been up a lot the last couple of nights."

Mom's lips pucker. "You could place her in the system."

"No."

She continues on as if I hadn't spoken. "Honestly, I don't know why you said yes to being her godfather in the first place."

We've been over this. Over, under, around, and through. There isn't anything more to say, so I repeat what I've already told her. "I won't put Charlotte in the system. I told Gavin I'd take care of her. You taught me to be a man of my word, right?"

Her lips twist and she doesn't respond.

"Exactly."

Dad stands a little behind Mother. He pushes his glasses up, his brown eyes turned down to the bundle of paperwork in his arms.

"Anything to add, Dad?" I ask. Sarcasm colors my words, blocking out the roar of my heart in my ears.

Dad looks up briefly and shakes his head.

I want to scream. It's always been this way with our family, and I *hate it.* Dad does whatever Mother says because not only does she run the firm, but she also runs the house. It doesn't sit right. Aren't marriages supposed to be a team effort? Shouldn't they be working together? But no. Mother is the boss and Dad is her doormat.

"I need to get to work."

"Fine." Mother shoos me out the door. "But don't be late to a meeting again, understand?"

What are you going to do, fire me? Strangely, the thought doesn't fill me with dread. But she won't fire me. Mother will berate me in front of the whole board, give me a good lecture in private, then deal me the silent treatment. But firing her son would make her look bad and heaven forbid we do that.

I plunk down at my glass-topped desk and swivel the chair around to stare out the windows. The sparkling city of Highland stretches out below. Though it's the neighboring city of Cloverfield and quite a bit bigger, I can honestly say that Cloverfield has more appeal. But who am I to say where my mother put her office?

I run a hand through my hair, not caring that it breaks up the gel and will likely ruin the work I put into it this morning.

My phone buzzes in my pocket and I pull it out to see a picture of Charlotte in her stroller. The text below says *getting some fresh air* with a heart emoji after it. From Emily. It produces a small smile. Though she never calls while I'm working, Emily often sends pictures of Charlotte throughout the workday. They make me feel more a part of the little girl's life. Makes me feel paternal.

That sends a shiver down my spine. I'm not sure I'm cut out to be a dad. But ready or not, here it is—in the form of a baby girl landing quite literally in my lap. The only person she has in this world is her bumbling, idiot godfather who doesn't know the first thing about raising a child.

Chapter Three

Emily

The morning went okay. Charlie woke up and took a bottle. After her diaper change, we went on a little walk. But ever since lunch, all Charlotte Elizabeth Dangler has done is scream.

And now I want to scream right along with the healthy lunged infant. My legs are on fire from squatting in a futile attempt to calm the colicky baby, but she only cries louder. My ears are absolutely ringing from the force. If I weren't a few weeks shy of twenty-four, I'd be venting my frustration the same way.

"Charlie! Please stop." Tears prick my eyes as I ease her from my shoulder to my arm, belly down so that the palm of my hand is pressed against her stomach. I've noticed before that it seems to ease the gas bubbles she gets on a regular basis, causing baby burps—and sometimes projectile spit up.

Still crying a bit, she squirms before producing the hoped-for burp. We both sigh in relief, and I let the few tears slide as she *finally* gives in to sleep again.

"Thank goodness." I ease into the rocker recliner and cover the little girl with her purple afghan. Her fingers twine through the holes of the blanket as she smacks her pacifier, her belly still against my arm.

There's something special about the moments of snuggling Charlie. My heart breaks for her every day. Her life has been tremulous in her short six months on earth; something I know all too well.

My current book—a mystery by the one and only Aria Jean Mcoyle—sits on the arm of the chair and I've only just settled into reading with the slumbering Charlie on my arm, when my phone vibrates on the coffee table. Normally, this wouldn't be that loud. But given the fact the table is glass and that the ceilings of Oliver's home are vaulted which causes every noise to echo ten times louder, the buzzing sounds like the bass on a bad set of speakers.

I stifle the desire to swear as Charlie stirs. Stretching out my foot, I manage to knock the phone onto the white carpet—because apparently Oliver never spills anything onto his floor, unlike me who has more shirts *with* stains than without—and scoot it to the side of the chair. Then, oh-so-carefully, I manage to reach down and grab it.

Oliver Markel flashes across the screen, making the urge to scream a thousand times more appealing. But in the interest of my sanity and the sleeping child in my arms, I settle for my alternate cuss word.

"Buckets!" I whisper before jabbing the accept button. "Yes?"

"Emily?" Oliver's voice is rich and soothing, yet still makes me want to punch something in my current state. "Are you okay?"

"Yeah, everything is just peachy!" I hiss.

"Peachy?" I can picture his gosh dang perfect brow arching in disbelief.

I roll my eyes. "Charlie is being colicky again."

"Is she okay? Do you need me to come home?"

"She's fine, Mr. Markel."

"Emily..." he draws my name out with a sigh. It's a battle we've been having since the day that I started as Charlie's nanny. He insists I call him *Oliver*, and in my head, I do. But when I'm talking to him—whether on the phone or face to face—it's easier and safer to keep things professional.

Would I call him Oliver if he gave up the push? Yeah. Because if I'm being honest, watching him get frustrated at me every time I call him *Mr. Markel* is worth keeping it professional. One hundred percent worth it.

"Yes, Mr. Markel?" I chuckle when he sighs.

"Thank you for everything you do for Charlotte."

I pause. What on Earth is he talking about? "You…pay me to do it?"

"I know." He sighs again, but this time he sounds tired. "But I also know it can't be easy."

He's not wrong. But it's better than working in a room full of three- to five-year-olds. I used to work in a state preschool—lauded one of the best in the tri-county area—and it was gosh awful. Now, with one little baby, workdays are a dream come true. Plus, her little life reminds me so much of my own. She and Oliver are both so lost and I want to help them as much as I can.

"It's truly no problem, Mr. Markel."

Like that morning in the car, there's such a long pause that I actually pull the phone back to make sure we're still connected. "Sir?"

"I'll be home in a couple hours with food. You still want Chinese?"

"Yes, please." I barely hold back my groan of excitement. "Orange chicken!"

"Okay. Orange chicken it is." There's another, shorter, pause. "What's your favorite dessert?"

"Nope, just dinner is fine. I don't want a dessert."

"For the love…" I hear something brush against the phone speaker and I can perfectly picture him roughing his hand over his face in exasperation. "Emily, let me buy you something sweet after you put up with Charlotte all day."

"Might I remind you yet again that you *pay* me to put up with her?"

I swear I can hear the man roll his eyes. "Yes, I do. And I am incredibly thankful for you swooping in and helping. So, if you don't tell me, I'll simply call Susan and ask her."

The thought of my boss calling my roommate and friend about my favorite dessert has a blush rushing into my cheeks. Sure, they apparently grown up together, but still! It's embarrassing. I'm thanking my lucky stars that we're over the phone.

"I like brownies and hot fudge sundaes," I admit, rocking the chair with my toes when Charlie begins to stir. "Basically, anything with chocolate."

"Good." He sounds entirely too smug. "I'll be home around four."

"Okay."

"See you then, Emily."

"Bye, Mr. Markel."

I hang up mid-sigh and can't help but smile. It's far too easy to wind him up and, for whatever reason, it makes me *very* happy to get him riled.

In the short time I've worked for Oliver, I've noticed that he gets stressed out super easily. He always seems on edge. Plus, I haven't seen him smile a whole lot. It's one of the many reasons I tease him so much because, holy cannoli, the man's smile is worth all the money in the world.

Charlie jolts, her nose wrinkling as she shifts against my shoulder. I begin rocking and thumping her bottom. Whenever anyone asks about the future—my hopes and dreams—I readily admit that I want to be a mom. I want to have a house full of kids, stay home, and take care of them. I tighten my hold on Charlie as I breathe in the scent of her shampoo. She smells decidedly babyish. Our world looks down on women who want this, but I think it's a noble desire. To rear children? Love them and show them that they're worth it? To be the support you never had?

I bite my lip and close my eyes. My heart aches for Charlie and, if I let myself actually dwell on it, for Oliver and myself, as well. In so many ways, all three of us are orphans—whether by death, neglect, or both. But I don't want to think about any of that right now. So I pick up my book and begin reading as I listen to the ticking of the numberless clock on the wall, the soft snores of Charlie, and the ever so subtle *swoosh* of the recliner as it rocks. And before I know it, the book has fallen into my lap and I'm drifting in and out of sleep.

Chapter Four

Oliver

I yawn as I juggle three plastic to-go bags full of stir-fried rice, sautéed veggies, and orange chicken. After the meeting with the board, I had a number of phone calls with clients. I hate them. Although, I hate video calls even more. Chills race down my back just thinking about them. Really, I need a job that *doesn't* involve people.

The tightening of my chest lessens when I slide open the door and step inside.

It's dark. Why on earth are there no lights on? I set the bags and my keys on the counter and move through the house. Nerves coil at the base of my neck when I don't hear anything. Where are Emily and Charlotte? Usually when I come home, Emily is in the living room with a book and Charlotte is either napping or bouncing in her exersaucer. But the living room is cast in the shadows of the setting sun.

I scan the living room and then I see them. Emily is in the recliner, rocking it with one foot. Her eyes are closed, a book in her lap while Charlotte's head is nestled up on her shoulder. The baby's pacifier wiggles as she sucks it in her sleep. Emily's cheek is pressed against the top of the baby's head, her arms cradling her like a precious treasure.

I stand there for a full minute. I can't look away even as pang of longing hits me. I want to be a man who comes home to a family. To see my wife curled up with our kids all around her. I really do. But something stands between me and that dream. A wall built of *not good enoughs* and *you're going to fails*. The thought of messing up anyone, let alone a woman or child, sends my thoughts spiraling. So, I do what I do best—I shove it to a corner of my mind to deal with later.

Pulling out my phone, I take a picture of the sleeping duo before flicking on the floor lamp.

"Emily?" I lay my hand gently on her shoulder, a confusing pang shooting through me at waking her up. She stirs but doesn't open her eyes. "I brought food."

One eye cracks open and she looks at me. Then her mouth falls open and her cheeks turn cherry red. She shivers as she sits up. "Oh! Oh goodness! I'm so sorry, Mr. Markel I didn't mean to fall asleep and—"

"It's fine. Really." I glance down at the photo of her and Charlotte dozing contentedly and I smile. "You two needed the rest."

"Yeah, well, she needs to wake up if she's going to sleep for you at all tonight."

That's … a sobering thought. "Okay, you wake her up and I'll get a plate ready for you."

"Thanks." Emily smiles wryly. "But I think you have the easier job."

I retreat to the kitchen and grab two paper plates, piling them with fried rice and orange chicken. I put some of the stir-fried veggies I grabbed for myself on one plate, then call over the renewed screams of Charlotte. "Want any stir-fry?"

"Sure!" she hollers back as she comes bouncing—literally—into the kitchen. Charlotte is cradled in her arm as Emily does what basically equals a squat with a fifteen-pound weight. "This looks really good."

"Glad you approve." I smile as I slide her plate across the island. "Let me take her so you can eat."

"No, you've been working all day and deserve hot food. Besides, I'm on the clock for another"—she looks at the microwave clock—"forty-five minutes."

"And you were here an hour earlier than normal." I shake my head. "Hand me my child, please."

It's weird referring to Charlotte as *my child*. In my head, she's still Gavin's baby girl. My best friend in the whole world who was taken tragically early. He was only twenty-seven. His wife just twenty-five. Gone. Just like that.

The day I got that phone call still haunts me. The voice of the officer rings in my nightmares. Nightmares that feature mangled cars, baby screams, and blood. So much blood.

I struggle to breathe as Emily rolls her eyes and hands Charlotte to me with a shake of her head. The little girl looks up at me with her big, brown eyes as her paci bobs. I smile and the tension leaves me. Somewhat. This is the first time in month she hasn't screwed up her little nose and wailed the moment I took her in my arms.

"You need to relax," Emily states as she hops up onto one of the barstools. "I think she can sense when you're stressed, and it freaks her out."

"Thanks for the parental advice," I say dryly.

Emily smirks. "I aim to serve. Now, let me eat so I can get her ready for bed and be out of your way."

"Why do you think I want you out of the way?" I stab a piece of chicken and pop it into my mouth.

Emily snorts, swallows, and wags her chopsticks at me. "I make you roll your eyes so much I'm surprised they haven't popped out of your head. You don't like me around."

Well, I can't deny that I roll my eyes, but I do appreciate Emily. She's the only one who seems to be able to get Charlotte to quiet when she's angry.

"Okay. Finished."

I blink. She...inhaled that food. Like, gulped it down so fast I'm surprised she doesn't have indigestion.

"Wow. You're a fast eater."

"Yeah well, I skipped lunch."

I'm going to berate her for that foolish idea, but a low rumble has me pausing. Charlotte grunts and then warmth spreads over her bum. But it doesn't stop there. Up the back of her diaper, onto her back. It hits my hand and I gag.

"Emily, please help." I sound pathetic, even to myself.

And she is absolutely no help. She leans over the counter and plucks one of the fortune cookies out of the bag. Cracking it open, she reads, "*Someone close to you will learn a new skill that will benefit all those near him.*" Whelp, sounds like you need to learn to change Charlie!"

I glare at her. "I will pay you fifty dollars to change this. The smell alone is threatening to make me heave."

"But see, I'd gladly give up fifty bucks to watch you both change and wash Charlie." She grins wickedly.

"One hundred."

Her brows hop up under her bangs. "One hundred dollars to change an explosive poo?"

"Yes. Please?" I'm pleading, but I can't seem to care. "I can't do this."

"You're going to have to learn eventually." Emily comes around the island and takes Charlotte, holding her under her armpits as she scrunches her nose. "You do smell, Charlie."

The baby giggles and shoves her hands in her mouth.

"You know, this could be why she was cranky. Constipation." Emily smiles at me but addresses Charlotte. "Come on, Charlie. Let's get ready for bed so Mr. Markel can eat without your stink in his space."

My eyeroll is epic for this one—perhaps a bit too large and little over the top just to see Emily smile—and level a mock scowl at Emily and say, "For the love, Emily! Please call me something else in front of Charlotte. *Mr. Markel* is far too formal for my goddaughter."

She turns for the stairs, calling over her shoulder, "Who's to say I don't have some *lovely* nicknames for you that I'm teaching her?"

"Nope! I don't even want to know."

She laughs, the sound echoing around my vaulted ceilings, and I smile. Making Emily laugh is a highlight of my mornings and evenings. I could easily get used to it.

And that, ladies and gentlemen, is a really dangerous thing.

Chapter Five

Emily

"Go to sleep. Go to sleep!" I bounce as I pace the length of Charlie's room after changing the explosive poop. She seems a touch less crabby, but whatever crankiness she's letting go of is oozing onto me. My calves and back ache, I feel two seconds away from a total meltdown, and all I want to do is go home and take a long, hot shower. But the wide-eyed baby in my arms stares at me like this is grand fun.

Oliver leans against the doorway, watching. Only the glow of the nightlight fills the space, casting him in the soft orangey glow that does nothing to improve my mood. Seriously, how is he allowed to look like a freakin' model when my hair looks like I jabbed my finger in a light socket, I have spit-up on my shirt, and my eyes probably have rings to rival a raccoon's under them? *His* green eyes glow even brighter in the dimness— *how?* —as they track me and his goddaughter.

I still can't believe he paid me an extra *one hundred dollars* to change Charlie. Heck, a little more begging, and I would have done it for free. Not much grosses me out after working in a preschool. Besides, there was something in his eyes. Something raw and panicked and ... I don't know. Vulnerable, maybe? I would have helped him in a heartbeat—but part of me wonders if that help means pushing him into the hard things. Charlie needs a dad. She *needs* Oliver. Does he even see that?

The little girl grunts as I continue to bounce around the room. I look down and her eyes are *finally* at half-mast, her pacifier slowing its manic wiggling in her mouth.

"That's it," I coo. "Please go to sleep, little lady."

With a shuddery sigh, her eyes close. I slow my bouncing and will slumber over her. *Please stay asleep.* After a few minutes I stop completely, leaning against the side of her crib as I stare down at her. She gets even more relaxed and after a few heartbeats, I lift her up and over the edge of the crib, settling her on her back with a blanket over her legs. I run a hand over her head, the soft strands of her brown hair smooth against my palm.

"You're a pro."

I almost yelp when I realize Oliver is beside me. I hadn't heard him move into the room, but as we stand shoulder to shoulder, staring down at Charlie, I am way too aware of him.

"You really are a great nanny. You know that don't you?" He turns to me, and I see that his eyes aren't just green. Around the pupil, there's a light hint of blue. Holy wow. His eyes are...stunning.

"Emily?" His brows have gone up under that annoyingly handsome piece of blond hair that sort of swoops against his forehead in that totally hot Superman way. Seriously, genetics were too kind to this man.

"Oh, yeah. Well, thank you."

He leans his elbows against the crib edge, staring down at the snoring infant. "You know, Charlotte's dad, Gavin, was young when he married Brittany. They should have had decades together. Instead, they had two years and then they went and died and left Charlotte behind. I wasn't thinking it would ever happen. Or if it did, it would be when Charlotte was a teenager. But no. She's a six-month-old screaming bundle of helplessness that I don't know what to do with."

It's not anger. Not really. No, I know what Oliver is feeling. Have felt it myself. It's the raw emotion of loss. Grief over his friend and what should've—or could've—been.

Feeling a tiny bit daring in the dark room, I lay my hand against his forearm. His body coils beneath my touch, but I don't pull away. A little over four months of working for him, and this is the most personal conversation that we've ever had.

"I know loss, Mr. Markel." *All too well.* "And while you might feel incapable of parenting Charlie, Gavin and Brittany clearly knew you'd love and care for their precious daughter. It's why they named you her godfather and why you're the perfect person to raise Charlie. And I promise that I'll help as much as I can. It's why you hired me, after all." I pat his bicep then turn for the door.

"Do you really believe that?" he asks, his voice the barest whisper.

I pause, my hand against the doorframe, and look over my shoulder. Oliver is still hunched over the crib, his chin tucked to his chest as he stares at Charlie.

"I do." I bite my lip for a second before continuing. "I can see that you care about her. And really, that's the biggest thing. No matter how hard it gets, please...don't stop loving her."

He looks up at me, but I'm already out the door, hurrying down the stairs and into my car before Oliver starts asking me the questions I absolutely do not want to answer.

● ● ● ● ● ● ●

It's late by the time I get back to my house—well, late is relative. For most of my roomies, any time after seven o'clock is late. After work, I ran and picked up some items from the store and it's around nine by the time I kick off my shoes in the entryway.

Lights flash from the living room, and I follow them to find Molly and Tanner curled up on the couch. Molly has her head tucked up against Tanner's shoulder, and he's staring down at her as she quotes *The Princess Bride* right along with the characters.

"Don't you both have work tomorrow?" I ask, plopping down on the far side of the couch. Because I'm not the one wanting to get between Molly and Tanner. That falls on Susan's shoulders—for whatever reason.

"Yep." Tanner agrees, his cheek dimpling as he smiles down at Molly, who yawns. "And practice!"

Tanner is the hockey coach for the Cloverfield Cougars, and he roped Molly into helping as the assistant coach. With them being newly engaged, the kids are being extra nice—both in the classroom and on the ice—hence Tanner's good mood. Well, that and Cloverfield has been on a winning streak which means a shot at the state championship. For a rookie coach, that's pretty amazing.

"Go to bed!" I jab my thumb over my shoulder and stifle a yawn of my own.

"Em's right. I should probably head home." Tanner presses a kiss onto the top of Molly's head. "I've got to make sure Kai got his homework done."

Molly's lips press thin. "How's he doing?"

Tanner sighs and shrugs. I look down at my hands, not able to handle the sorrow in Tanner's eyes. Kai Reynolds is a seventeen-year-old junior this year and until a month ago, he was living with his grandpa—the former coach of the Cougars. Coach Reynolds had cancer and succumbed to it about three weeks ago. His house was reversed mortgage, so once he was gone, Kai became homeless. He would have been sent into the system, except Tanner worked it out for the boy to live with him and his mother—Maria Bradshaw—until Kai knows what he wants to do.

That story pretty much perfectly sums up Tanner—he is a big old softy who will do anything for anyone, no questions asked. I didn't know guys like him existed outside of romance novels until he returned to Cloverfield and recaptured Molly's heart.

"Well, I'll see you tomorrow." Tanner cups Molly's cheek and presses a lingering kiss to her lips. Molly kisses back and I mimic gagging until they break apart with chuckles.

"I'll walk you out." Molly stands and twines her fingers with her fiancés as they head to the front door.

"No snogging one another!" I call out.

I turn my attention toward the TV. Miracle Max is trying to revive the mostly dead Wesley. Why does that feel like the perfect representation of my social life? Only *mostly dead*. I mean, I have Molly and Susan. I have Charlie. But it's Oliver that my mind keeps looping back to. If my social life is *mostly dead*, his is *totally dead*. The man is just sad. Emotionally, sure, but watching him shows me the raw grief deep down and makes my heart hurt. It seems like he hides away in his big ole' white house with the pristine everything and just...goes through the motions of living.

I've worked for him for months, and I've maybe seen an authentic smile one other time before tonight. Watching him smile down at Charlie at dinner—holy cannoli! The guy somehow is even more beautiful when he really, truly smiles. Like, don't look at him if you have heart trouble because you will have palpitations.

Wait, am I attracted to my boss? Holy buckets! No! No way! This isn't *Jane Eyre*, *The Sound of Music*, or ... or any other story with a nanny or governess! I'm not doing it. Absolutely not!

"Woah! Em, are you okay?"

I jerk back to awareness. Molly, nice and rosy cheeked with slightly tousled hair from her make out session with Tanner, stares at me.

"What?" I intelligently ask.

"Your lip is bleeding."

I lick my lip and, sure enough, I've bitten it enough to break the skin. "Buckets!"

"Buckets?" Molly smirks as she flops onto the couch beside me.

"Yes, I'm trying to make my vocabulary more child friendly."

"Noted." She eyes me. "So, what's the problem?"

"Problem?" I grab a tissue from the box on the end table and dab at my lip. "There's no problem."

"Sure there isn't." Molly glares at me. "Because you always gnaw on your lips when everything is fine with the world."

I sigh. Sometimes having perceptive friends is the *worst*! I don't want to tell Molly about my horribly improper thoughts about Oliver and how him taking care of Charlie makes my heart skip a beat. Because if I do, that means delving into my past—which is something I don't like thinking about. At all.

"Just some things with work."

Molly's eyes narrow. "What about work?"

"Charlie has been colicky the past few days. It's wearing out Oliver and me both."

"Hm." Molly studies me, her eyes squinting further as she pushes her glasses up the bridge of her nose.

"*Hm*? What's *hm* mean?"

"It means I think there's more to the story. But I'm not going to push it." She smiles. "Seriously, you seem happier now than you ever did working at the preschool. Charlie is lucky to have you."

I smile, but it feels strained. Yeah, I'm happy working for Oliver and caring for Charlie. But something inside of me is antsy. I'm ready for more. I don't know what that *more* is, but it's the same feeling I felt when working at the preschool and it went away when I started nannying for Oliver Markel. Now it's back—and back with a vengeance. But the really disturbing thing—the thing I won't let myself think about—is that it goes away whenever Oliver is around.

And that doesn't bode well for the nanny who's determined not to lose her heart to her boss.

Chapter Six

Oliver

I bolt upright in bed as a scream echoes down the hallway. With a groan, I flop back onto my pillows and rub both hands down my face.

It sounds like Charlotte is terrified. I wonder how much her baby brain remembers of the crash. I saw photos of the car. It was crushed like a soda can.

The words of the officer echo in my head, a content loop I'm determined to never forget. *It is a miracle the baby survived.*

I wince as another wail carries into my room. Oh, yes. My little miracle with the insanely healthy set of lungs.

"She's alive," I remind myself as I kick off the covers, shivering when the cold snakes over my bare arms. Shrugging on my robe, I pad down the hall to Charlotte's room.

She's so worked up. Her whole body is trembling as her screams pierce through the stillness of night. Tears trail down her chubby cheeks, making tears of my own appear.

"Charlotte. It's okay, baby girl." The words feel foreign on my tongue as I scoop her into my arms. She fights me for a minute, but I rub my palm against her back, willing her to calm down.

Emily's observation from dinner hits me. *You need to relax. She can sense when you're stressed, and it freaks her out.*

I take measured breaths as I try to stay calm.

But in my head chants the voice of doubt. *This is Gavin's job. Gavin's job. Gavin's...or Emily's.* Where is the nanny when you need her? Home, asleep in her bed. Which is where I want to be. Not with an irate and/or terrified infant I'm clueless how to calm.

I growl and Charlotte bursts into tears again.

"Sorry, sweetie." I sigh and begin bouncing the way Emily did earlier that night. I struggle to think of what else to do. Panic tries to claw at my throat, but then I remember one thing my nanny used to do for me when I had trouble sleeping.

She used to sing.

There's only one song I remember, the one Marian sang to me almost every night for the first seven years of my life. I feel hot—is it hot in here? —but I clear my throat and attempt to sing.

Lullaby and good night,
Thy father's delight.

I almost choke on the word. Marian sang *nanny's delight* to me, and while I'm not Charlotte's father, *godfather* doesn't have quite the same melodic rhythm.

Bright angels beside,
My darling abide.

Truer words have never been spoken—well, *sang*. Angels are the reason I'm here, holding the now whimpering baby to my ear as I hum the melody and frantically scramble for the next set of words.

Lay thee down now and rest,
May thy slumber be blessed.
Lay thee down now and rest,
May thy slumber be blessed.

I hum the tune to "Brahms' Lullaby" as I bounce around the room, occasionally singing the words. Every time I go to lay Charlotte down, she flails and clings to me. I grab the bottle that's sitting in the warmer and fall into the glider in the corner of her room. She sucks on it as I rock and slowly her eyes close.

Mine slide shut soon after, the song still on my lips.

● ● ● ● ● ● ●

"Mr. Markel?"

I sit up with a snort. Where...am I? Pale pink walls, lacy curtains, the smell of formula. I blink and glance down. Charlotte is cradled in my arm, an empty bottle against her chest. Oh no, is she breathing? I shouldn't have sat down with her when I was so tired! What if I dropped her, what if she choked on the formula, or what if—?

"Mr. Markel, you're fine, Charlie is fine. Calm down."

I look up into Emily's smiling face. "I could have killed her!"

"But you didn't." Emily shrugs. "It's fine to fall asleep holding her. She seems to like it, actually. And if it means you get some rest, it's well worth it."

"I could have dropped her or smothered her, or—"

"But!" Emily holds up a time out sign. "You didn't."

I stare at her. How is she so calm about this?

"Now, do you want to get her dressed this morning, or should I?"

I glance down at Charlotte. "She's still sleeping."

"Yes, but it's eight o'clock."

"I slept in that late?" I ask, dumbly.

"Yep!" Emily grins at me, her hazel eyes flashing in the dim November sunshine coming in through the window. "I got here at seven, found you and Charlie conked out up here, and decide to let the crankies rest."

"Very funny." I roll my eyes, glancing down at the still slumbering Charlotte. "What should I do?"

"Well, I want her to nap today, so wake her up." Emily smirks. "And you're late for work."

"Work?"

Shoot!

"I'm late!" I leap up and all but dump Charlie into Emily's arms. "Get her dressed!"

"Okay, yeah, sure. No problem!" The sarcasm is almost tangible in Emily's voice, but I don't have time for it. I'm already late, and Mother is going to kill me.

I run a comb through my tangled blond hair and call it good enough before throwing on the first dress shirt and pair of slacks I can find. Slipping into loafers and a suit coat, I grab my briefcase before flying down the stairs.

Emily is at the stove, stirring a pan of something that smells delicious. I pause as I grab my keys off the counter and watch her for a split second. She's humming as she stirs, Charlotte sits in her highchair banging a rattle against the tray and talking in baby gurgles. It's so...familial. Something I've never had—not once in my twenty-five years of life. My chest tightens, but I ignore it.

"I'll be home late," I say as I shrug into my gray peacoat. I pause. "If that's okay?"

"Yeah, go. Sorry I let you sleep in." She looks a touch disgruntled but whether that's at me or the situation, I really don't have time to figure it out. I'm already in hot water.

"Oh," I pause in the doorway. "You didn't get your dessert last night. There's brownies and hot fudge in the fridge and ice cream in the freezer."

Emily's mouth opens but I'm already out the door. Throwing my briefcase into the passenger seat, I speed down the empty back lanes of Cloverfield's countryside before merging onto the highway toward Highland and work.

The closer I get, the tighter my chest becomes. My fingers tap against the wheel, and I can't push away the panic. Mother is going to be irate. She'll threaten me. She's going to want Charlotte gone because it's interfering with my job. But I can't lose the baby girl. She's my one tie to Gavin, the one thing I can do for him now that he's gone.

No matter what, I'm not giving Charlotte up.

I park and walk—though I want to run—into the building and up to our floor. My hands are sweaty, my body coiled tighter than a spring. Perspiration chills me despite the warmth of the building as I walk past the cubicles and into my office.

Gasping breaths shake me as I set my briefcase on my desk and brace my hands against it. "You're fine, Oliver. Pull it together, man."

But I can't. I'm late. I have never been this late. If Mother finds out—

A knock interrupts my spiraling thoughts and my one and only friend in the office—Ethan Matthews—pops his head in. "You busy? Because I have some questions about one of my clients and…" He trails off when he gets a look at my face, his black brows scrunching and making his rectangle-framed glasses slide down his nose. "You okay, Oliver?"

"Yeah, yeah. I'll be fine." I wave away his concern as I hang my peacoat on the coat rack beside the door. "What's up?"

"Did you just get in?" he asks instead of answering my question.

My collar suddenly feels like it's choking me. I undo the top button. "Yeah. I was up late and then overslept." No use throwing my ward under the bus. Yet.

"Well, don't let your mother find out." He shudders.

"Yeah, I'm aware."

Ethan grins now. His smile takes up most of his face and makes his brown eyes almost disappear behind his glasses. There's something about that smile. Something truly joyful that makes you feel it in your very core.

His smile unravels a bit of the vice that's been clenching my lungs for the last hour and a half. I find myself returning it and gesturing to the uncomfortable gray chairs Mother chose to complement my office décor. "Come on in. What's going on with your client?"

We spend an hour or so talking about a particularly difficult case he's a PR rep for.

As we're wrapping up, Ethan leans back in his chair and steeples his fingers. "So why were you late?"

"I told you. I was up late and overslept."

"Yeah, but was it because of Charlotte?"

I run my hand through my hair and turn to look out the windows. Yeah, it is probably rude to turn my back to Ethan, but my head aches and I'm seriously tempted to cry—something I don't like to do at all, but especially in front of people.

"It was." Ethan sighs. "I know we're not probably this close, Oliver, but let me offer a solution: ask the nanny to move in. That's what a lot of people do with your...resources?"

I snort. That's a nice way of saying *that's what people do when they're filthy rich.* I'm not suffering by any means. But there's something about the idea of Emily *living* in my house. It's my sanctuary and if she lives there, she'll become a part of that. She'll be there morning, noon, and night. Is that even a wise idea?

But then again, I won't be the only one dealing with the screaming infant every night. I can't keep going this way. It's not smart. I'll either get sick or have a nervous breakdown. Maybe both.

"Perhaps. But I don't know if she'll say yes."

Ethan shrugs. "Then you find someone who will. You can't keep up this pace. It's going to kill you. You already look like a raccoon." When I give him a look, he runs his fingers under his eyes. "Coon eyes, man."

He grins and I return it halfheartedly. "I'll talk to her tonight about it."

And with those words, the vice is back around my lungs, making me dizzy with the force of it.

Chapter Seven

Emily

I watch the door slam shut and shake my head with a small smile. I forgot Oliver said he was getting me dessert yesterday. Warm fuzzies wash over me. Oliver really notices those around him and values them. I admire it, because try as I might, I can't always see *everyone*. But he does and he makes sure they're cared for.

"Although, I think that's why Daddy Ollie is so stressed," I say to Charlie as I give the scrambled eggs a final stir and dump them into a bowl. I pull the sausage off the back burner and lay it on top before hopping onto a barstool beside Charlie.

My phone rings right as I take a giant bite of eggs. The caller ID says it's Molly and I grin as I hit *accept*. "Aren't you at work?" I say around my food.

"Ew! Are you eating?" I can picture Molly wrinkling her nose.

"Yep." I smack my lips extra loudly. "What's up?"

"Are you free to go Christmas shopping and to the tree lighting this Saturday?" she asks.

I pause, thinking over my mental calendar. Lists tend to just stress me, so I catalogue everything in my head. "I think so. I might have Charlie, though. Oliver is running himself ragged. He overslept today. Although..." I pause. Dare I tell Molly this bit?

"Although...what?" Her voice holds a quizzical yet worried tone. She's the mother hen of us three roommates, and I love her for it.

"Well, when I got here, Oliver was asleep in the glider in the nursery, cuddling Charlie against his chest." Moisture fills my eyes and I shove another bite of eggs into my mouth.

Molly chuckles. "That sounds adorable."

"It was," I admit after I swallow. "But when I woke him up, he flew into a frenzy because he was late for work. He's been really uptight about his job recently."

"Does he have anxiety?" Molly asks, and I hear a squeak which I'm pretty sure means she's leaning back in her teal desk chair.

I shrug, realize she can't see it, and say, "I don't know. I don't really know anything concrete about him."

Molly hums. "But you'd like to?"

I scowl. "No. He is my boss."

"Hey, if my life can be a second chance romance, yours can follow the boss/employee trope. Oh! Or is this the forbidden love trope?"

"Neither! And absolutely not, my life isn't a romance novel."

Molly snorts and her voice goes a touch dreamy. "Mine is."

"Gross, Molly. Go do your work!"

She laughs. "So, I'll see you in town Saturday? Say around ten?"

"Sure. I'll be there one way or another."

"Good. I love you, Em. You know that right?"

"I do." I really mean that. Molly and Susan showed up in my life right when I needed friends the most. They surrounded me, supported me, and showed me what it meant to be truly loved for who you were, not what you brought. Going to Molly's for Sunday dinners while in college was often the highlight of my week. Being wrapped into her home with her brothers, parents, and grandpa showed me what it meant to be a family—flaws and all.

We hang up and I scoop Charlie into my arms. "Let's go to town today. What do you say, little one?"

She raises her hands above her head and stretches, making me laugh. This job is a joy. I love having freedom in my schedule and getting to watch Charlie grow and turn into a beautiful little girl.

"I just wish Oliver could see this the same way I do." I sigh as I strap Charlie into her car seat. Hoisting it onto my hip, I click off the lights, and grab my keys.

As I snap the seat into the base, Charlie looks up at me with her big brown eyes and smiles her toothless grin. Holy buckets, my heart melts. Why, I would gladly be her mom. In a heartbeat.

Nope! Not going there! Because that thought leads to wedding gowns, sparkly rings, and a certain man at the end of the alter who has blond hair, emerald-green eyes with a splash of blue, and a smile that could give the stoutest of hearts palpitations.

I slide behind the wheel, blasting the hot air as I turn onto the road. I take my time traveling down the back roads and let myself enjoy the winter sunshine as it glints off the light layer of snow. It's roughly twenty minutes later when we pull into the small downtown district of Cloverfield.

Now, to be completely frank, downtown Cloverfield consists of approximately eight blocks. The most notable shops include a couple antique stores, three different boutiques, Sweetie's—the best coffeeshop in the world despite the fact that I usually get their specialty hot chocolate—a small bookshop, and of course, the sandwich shop called Yellow Submarine that has the best melt-in-your-mouth sub sandwiches to ever exist (and yes, the Beatles pun makes me love them even more.) There are other smaller businesses, but these are the ones I frequent.

I gather Charlie out of her seat and situate her in the baby sling wrap. I face her out since she can hold her head up now and is an incredibly nosy infant. Grabbing my purse, I walk toward Sweetie's and blessed hot chocolate.

I'd forgotten that today was the day the town was getting bedecked with Christmas decorations—despite Molly reminding me of the tree lighting this Saturday. People bustle up and down the sidewalks, stringing lights along their marques and awnings while putting garland and greenery in the front windows. Christmas music blasts through the speakers and when "Wonderful Christmas Time" by Paul McCartney comes on, I can't help but dance a little down the street. I wave to Rick Pruitt—Molly's grandpa—who is standing on a lift several dozen feet in the air as he attempts to string lights on the sign to the Rink.

"Hey, Em!" I pause as Ryley Pruitt, one of Molly's brothers, runs over to me. "What are you doing in town?"

"Heading to Sweetie's for cocoa."

Ryley grins as he squats, hands on his knees to look in Charlie's face. "Hey beautiful girl!"

She grins and kicks her feet.

"Want to join us?" I offer as he straightens back up.

"I'd love to, but I have to help Gramps with the sign." He jabs his thumb over his shoulder. "He's stubborn and won't let me up in the lift."

I laugh. "What, a Pruitt? Being stubborn? I've never heard of such a thing."

Ryley rolls his eyes. "Hardy har har. Plus, got to keep him from murdering Owen."

The little punk of a teenager is leaning against the Rink sign, staring down at something on his phone with a scowl. He was one of two kids who tried to get Molly and Tanner canned back in October, and I still have trust issues with teens because of it—and it wasn't even me he blackmailed.

"Good luck with that," I encourage, heading down the sidewalk once more. I wave over my shoulder. "See you later, Ryley!"

"See ya!"

Ryley would probably be considered attractive, I guess, with his chocolate brown eyes, butterscotch hair, and a smattering of freckles on his nose and cheeks. His nose is crooked from being broken one too many times while playing hockey in high school and college. He's handsome in a rugged way.

But to me, he's like the brother I've never had. He teases me, pushing my buttons to get me riled up. He laughs with Molly and me, and I know he'll always come to my defense. It's comforting. The Pruitts are my surrogate family—always there despite knowing nothing of my history because I don't talk about it. If I did, then I'd have to deal with it. And I don't *want* to deal with it.

So, I hike my purse strap higher on my shoulder and push the lingering thoughts out of my head as I stride down the street with Charlie. We soon reach Sweetie's and the bell jingles merrily as I step inside. Sweetie Esperanza runs the shop. The little Italian woman is as feisty as she is kind and I love her to death. She's been attempting to teach me Italian, and I always try to have a new phrase to give her when I come in.

Her shop is cozy, with art and quote signs on the wood paneled walls. Today, the pictures boast holiday scenes and snow-covered landscapes while the chalkboard signs host cheesy Christmas puns and quotes.

"A merry Christmas to you, Miss Emily!" I turn to see Sweetie's nephew, Nico, standing on a small ladder as he writes "*God bless us, every one*" on one of the higher boards. His girlfriend, Natasha, holds the ladder.

"Merry Christmas, Nico, Nat!" I call as I walk up to the counter.

"And *un felice anno nuovo* to you, Sweetie."

"*Molto bene!*" She clicks her tongue and smiles first at me, then Charlie. "How is my favorite nanny and her *bambina* today?"

"*Favoloso!*" I say.

"You're getting quite good at those words, *mia cara*."

"I'm trying." I laugh. "I would like one venti candy cane hot chocolate, please." I can already taste the smooth chocolate, the minty goodness of the candy canes, and the fresh whipped cream on the top. Devine doesn't begin to describe it.

"Coming right up." She jots whatever abbreviation she uses onto the large paper cup and hands it to the barista before turning back to me. "You look tired today, *cara*."

"Charlie has been a tad colicky the past couple days." I smile and press a kiss on the currently subdued child's head. "But she's being good today."

"Must be hard for Oliver, *povero caro*."

I nod, suddenly at a loss for words. I've seen the struggle firsthand. And sure, he's trying to hide it, and he does a pretty dang good job, overall. But the fact that I found him conked out in Charlie's room at eight o'clock this morning—when he's usually pushing past me to head to work at seven—is proof he's struggling. He's drowning and is too stupidly stubborn to ask for help. Or maybe, like me, he's been made to feel like asking for help is admitting failure.

"Well, Emily. I'm sure you're just the person he needs. You're *una tata eccellente*."

I love this game we play. One of the many ways she's helping me learn her beautiful language. She'll say a short Italian phrase and I try to figure it out. *Eccellente* means *excellent*. That much is easy to figure out. But *una tata*?

"An excellent nanny?" I guess, blushing red from the heat of my jacket and the tiny human wrapped against my chest. "I'm not that great, Sweetie."

"Ah, ah!" She waves a finger at me. "But I think you are. You are exactly where you need to be, *una cara*. It was no chance that you walked into Oliver's life when you did, and there's no mistake that you've done wonders with a *bambina* who needed someone to love and care for her."

I smile, my eyes burning from her praise. Recently, I started wondering if I'm truly doing anything worthwhile for Charlie and Oliver or if I am hindering him from fully stepping into his role of dad. Sweetie's words are just what I need to soothe my frazzled nerves. "Thanks, Sweetie."

"Of course, *cara*. And here is your hot chocolate. *Cioccolata*."

"*Cioccolata*," I parrot.

Sweetie grins. "*Molto bene,* Emily!"

I laugh, wave to her, Nico, and Nat, and head back out into the brisk November air.

The bustle makes me excited for Saturday and the tree lighting ceremony. The local businesses all have unique ornaments showcasing their shops that go on the massive blue spruce in the center of town. It's like a giant bulletin board or billboards, only prettier. The city workers are hoisting it into place now in the middle of the roundabout. White lights have already been strung around its boughs, and it settles easily into the massive handmade tree stand placed in what is normally a pristine flowerbed.

"Oh Tannenbaum" comes to mind, and I hum it to Charlie as we haunt the sidewalks. I smile and wave whenever someone calls out my name, but there's something about melting into the background; watching everyone get swept up into the Christmassy hustle and bustle yet being outside of it yourself.

I stop by Yellow Submarine to pick up my favorite sandwich—an Italian meat sub that has freshly sliced salami, pepperoni, and pancetta on a cheesy bread with fresh mozzarella cheese chunks melted to perfection. Or *perfetto*, as Sweetie would say. I conveniently parked in the lot next to the shop earlier, so once I procure my food, I'm able to feed Charlie while munching on the best sandwich in the world.

My phone rings after my first bite. Unsurprisingly, it's Oliver's name that flashes across the screen. I sigh.

"Hello?" I say around my mouthful.

"Where are you?" he asks, sounding way beyond frustration, and bordering on enraged. This is new.

I swallow, running my tongue over my teeth to rid them of the doughy bread stuck to them. "What do you mean? Charlie and I went walking around town. We're heading back after I finish my sandwich, so she can nap. Is something wrong?"

"Oh." He sighs and I can picture him running his hand through his hair. "Sorry, I just came home early."

And he freaked when we weren't there.

"I'm sorry, too. I should have let you know our plans. And I usually do, but you just flew out of the door this morning." I replay his words. "Wait, you're home already?"

"Yeah."

"But you got in late to the office."

"Yep."

"You said you'd be late getting home. Why are you home already?" Suspicion leaks into the words. I can't help it. Oliver is an absolute stickler with his schedule. If he is late to work, he's late coming home. Early in, early out. This is a departure from the norm.

"I...well, I need to talk to you about something and couldn't focus on any work with it on my mind." He sighs again. "When will you be home?"

"I'm leaving now." My pulse spikes into hyperdrive—cue flashing lights across my vision like the *Millennium Falcon* racing across the stars.

"So, I'll see you in twenty minutes, then."

"Okay, Mr. Markel." I gulp.

"Bye, Emily."

"Bye."

I hang up and stare at my bookish wallpaper on my phone until it goes black. My sandwich is no longer appetizing. Am I about to get fired? My unhelpful brain lists about a million and one reasons Oliver might dismiss me.

Yet, he's thanked me profusely over the last couple days for all I've done for him and Charlie. And it truly seems genuine.

So maybe the conversation is about something else. But what? I haven't the foggiest notion.

Chapter Eight

Oliver

I pace around and around my kitchen island as I wait for Emily and Charlotte to get back. My hands go from behind my back, to combing through my hair, to being wrung in front of me. They're a reflection of the hamster wheel that's my mind. A mind that can't seem to decide if I'm going to ask Emily the question I called her home for: *will you move in and help with Charlotte?*

Groaning, I plop onto the bar stool. I already know that question will go over like a lead balloon.

Glancing at the stove clock, I see only five minutes have passed since I got off the phone with Emily. T-minus fifteen minutes until blast off—and whether the countdown is to my head exploding or to the idea actually taking flight, I have no clue.

My hands shake as I fill up the tea kettle. I need a distraction and brewing a cup of my favorite peach tea sounds about as good as anything. As the water begins to heat, I pull out the canister of loose-leaf tea. Yeah, I'm a tea snob. I'll admit it. But there's something soothing about scooping the right amount of tea leaves into the steeper and adding a dash of my favorite sweetener. Therapeutic, as I pour the hot water and make sure that the steeping time is just right. Relaxing, as I breathe in the earthy, fruity scent that takes me back to childhood and Marian setting me on the counter to watch her do the very same motions.

I blame her for my propriety in tea making. She abhorred bagged tea (although I'll use it in a pinch) and was insistent that sugar and cream belonged on the side. If she knew that I used stevia, of all things, to sweeten my tea, she would bop me over the head with a teaspoon and scowl very non-threateningly.

Gosh, I miss her. She was my nanny until my seventh birthday, when Mother could finally enroll me in the private school where I met Susan. Where academics became the most important thing in my life and where my joy vanished.

I sigh, pushing my eyes with my forefinger and thumb to ease the aching, and swallow back the swell of emotions threatening to overwhelm me. Latching onto the unwelcome feelings, I shove them into their boxes in my mind, locking them away and hiding the key. I need my wits about me if I'm going to ask Emily to move in.

Move in? I almost choke as the vice steals the air right out of my chest. This is a bad idea. Forget the fact that Emily will be a single lady living with a single guy (Mother will absolutely *die* if she finds out about it), but Emily makes me...happy. She makes Charlotte happy. And what happens when she meets some amazing guy and gets swept up into a fairytale? She'll get married and leave me alone with a toddler. That's what will happen. And I'll shrivel under that weight. Welcoming her into my home—my sanctuary—is inviting trouble with hazel eyes and a mischievous smile to cohabitate with me.

The crunch of gravel in the driveway reaches me and I have the inexplicable urge to bolt. Go for a walk through the woods and around the little pond in the backyard. Or to race my car down the country roads and just...breathe. When was the last time I was able to inhale fully? I can't remember. Feels like eons.

The door opens and Emily comes swirling in on a gust of cool afternoon air. She glances at me—a quick sweep of her eyes—before gesturing to the car seat in her hand. "She is half asleep. I'm going to lay her down then we can talk, okay?"

I nod once, unable to do more as I watch her hurry up the stairs.

It's fine. Asking her doesn't mean she will do it. It's just asking. No harm, no foul, right?

Wrong! Because I *want* her to say yes. Wait, I do? I want Emily to move in? No, because if she does, she could break both Charlotte and me. Right? Of course, right.

"Okay, what is it you wanted to ask?"

I startle and whip around so quickly I almost stumble.

Emily stands in the doorway, her arms crossed. She looks defensive and my throat closes off. I don't want her to be upset. Upset means she'll say no. She'll get all angry like Mother when I do something she doesn't like. Is Emily passive aggressive? I can't remember her ever being that way but—but—

I gasp but can't seem to catch my breath. "I-I..."

Words. What are they and where did they go?

"Sit down." Emily grabs my arm and pushes me onto a stool. My forgotten mug of tea sits on the counter, and she shoves it toward me before pouring a glass of water for herself. "You look like you're about to pass out."

Yeah, it sort of feels like that too.

I sip my tea. The smooth peach flavor settles my whirling thoughts and helps me to suck a lungful of air into my chest. One, two, three deep breaths and I clear my throat. "Sorry."

"Are you okay?" Emily takes a sip of her water, studying me like I'm an anomaly. Maybe I am. I'm far from a normal twenty-five-year-old, that's for sure.

I trace the lip of my mug with my index finger. "I have a question, and I know it's going to sound a tad presumptuous and maybe a little desperate."

Her brows shoot up.

I pause, cough, shift on the stool, and then look down into my tea. "I realized today that I can't keep doing life like I have been."

"I could have told you that."

"Yes, well." I smile but don't look up. My chest tightens as I cup my chin in my hand. "I want to ask you…and you don't have to answer right now, mind you. But well…"

"Spit it out!"

I drag my eyes up to her. Her arms are crossed again. She looks a touch pale. I curse softly, mad that I've freaked her out. "Will you move in and help with Charlie until she can sleep through the night?"

"Charlie?" Emily looks up at me with wide eyes, and I realize I've never called my little girl that. That's Emily's pet name for her. Maybe I need to find a special name for Charlotte.

"Yes, Charlie. Charlotte. My little girl who's sleeping upstairs and is about to drive me to a nervous breakdown." My voice cracks and I clear my throat again.

"She's your responsibility."

"I know. And I also know I'm failing." I rub my face.

Emily taps her fingers against the counter. The sound has my shoulders hunching up and the muscles in my neck tightening. She's not saying anything. Why? What is she thinking? Did I make a horrible mistake?

Her drumming fingers grow faster, more frantic, and I can't take it any longer. I slap my hand over hers, stilling the drumming and freezing us in place. Neither of us move, breathe, nor speak. It's like I've hit the pause button on a remote—capturing this strange yet perfect picture we make in my kitchen.

"So," Emily says, pulling her hand free after an agonizingly long second of us not moving. "You want to foist your responsibility onto me, is that it?"

I shake my head. "I will still be her primary caregiver. I just...I need help, Emily."

She bites her lips, studying me like I'm under a microscope and she's the scientist. "You need help?"

I nod.

"How would my role change if I do move in?"

"We'd have to figure that out. Which nights you would be getting up with her and which nights it would be me."

"So, it'll be both of us taking care of Charlie?"

I nod again.

"Would you want any other help around the house?"

"No more than what you already do."

Emily cups her chin in her hand. "You do realize that your housekeeper quit three weeks ago, right?"

"What?" I stare at her.

"Ms. Acklin quit." She gestures toward the fridge. "Have you not noticed the note?"

I hurry over to it. Sure enough, Ms. Acklin resigned. That little jerk didn't even give two weeks' notice and she's still been cashing the checks I've sent the last three weeks. I turn back toward Emily and ask, "Why didn't you tell me?"

"I didn't think it was important." She shrugs.

I grumble a curse under my breath and Emily's eyes widen.

"Sorry." I wince. "I just—"

"No. No, you're—it's...fine."

"Well, take the rest of the day off. Think about the offer. I really value your help, Em."

"It's Emily. I'm Emily to you." Her gaze narrows. "And I still feel like you're up to something."

My fingers rip through my hair. "I'm only trying to look out for Charlotte."

"This is for her?"

"Yeah. And my sanity."

Emily's lip catches between her teeth and she nods once as she pulls her purse strap over her shoulder. "Well, then. I'll see you tomorrow."

"Emily." I grab her arm as she begins to head out the door. I don't know what possesses me to do that, but she looks up at me, her eyes wary yet soft. Words fail me again and I force a smile to my lips. "Whatever you decide, I hope you know how much your help with Charlotte means to me. You really love her. I couldn't ask for a better nanny."

"Thanks." She steps back and I let my hand fall. She takes one last long, sweeping glance at me before beating a hasty retreat.

I slump over the counter, absolutely exhausted, and let the hotness in my eyes manifest into tears. I pillow my forehead against my arms and give into the grief that's been dogging my heels for months.

Chapter Nine

Emily

"The nerve!" I slam the door to the house and stalk into the kitchen where Susan is placing her trademark Christmas cookies with the buttercream frosting into tins for her pop-up booth at the tree lighting event on Saturday.

She barely gives me a glance. "You're home early. What's Oliver done now?"

"How do you know it's Oliver?" I ask, settling onto the yellow barstool and taking the proffered plate of broken cookies.

"If it's not Oliver, it's Charlie. Same difference, let's be honest." Her brown eyes study me before narrowing. "But this is definitely Oliver's fault. What'd he do?"

I mumble something that vaguely resembles the words, "Move in."

"What?" Susan's brows rise under her blonde bangs. "Sorry, it's the mumbling. 'You know how I feel about the mumbling'." She quotes *Tangled* and gives me a pointed look.

"He...well, he asked me to move in."

Susan drops her spatula. "He *what?*"

I wince. "Yeah. He asked me to live at the house and help with Charlie."

"That's insane, Emily! Tell me you said no!"

"I said I'd think about it."

"No! Absolutely not! You're not moving in with a single man *alone*." Susan shakes her head and aggressively scoops up one of the cookies.

"Tell me how you really feel, Sue," I grumble, snapping the head off a snowman who's missing his nose.

"It's stupid! That's what it is. You're not moving in with Oliver *freaking* Markel."

"But I'm not moving in *with* Oliver." I protest. "I'm moving in *for* Charlie. A lot of nannies live with their families."

"Yeah, but usually there's two parents and they're like twenty years older than said nanny." She cuts me a scathing glare. "You're only a year younger than Oliver, he's unmarried, and why are we talking about this? It's ludicrous! Stupid. Asinine. Foolish. Pick your adjective!"

"I get it. It's dumb." Anger surges in my chest and I shove the snowman head into my mouth before I say something I'll regret. After swallowing, I say, "But if it means loving on Charlie even more? Caring for her and her little heart? She needs someone at night who will snuggle her and comfort her, Sue. That's the real issue, right?"

"No." Susan slams an empty tin onto the counter and glares at a gingerbread man like he's Oliver and she's considering grinding him to crumbs. "The real issue is Oliver asking you to *move in*."

"Sue, seriously. It's strictly a business arrangement. And if it means I get to help Oliver, it's kind of worth it to me. Maybe I can get him comfortable with being a dad—being who he's meant to be. He's so good at it, but he doesn't trust himself. He's not used to being himself."

A feeling that is a little too familiar if I am being honest with myself.

"You can't fix him, Em." Susan sighs, hitting the bottom of her spatula against the counter. "But I think you might have already made up your mind, haven't you?"

"I want to talk to Molly."

"Okay. But be smart, my dear."

I nod, and scoot off the stool. "I have about an hour before school's out, right?"

Susan nods, counting her cookies before adding one more onto the top and snapping the lid shut.

"I'm going to go read for a while."

Susan nods again, already working on another tin. She's angry, but whether at Oliver or me, I'm not sure. With a sigh, I head up the narrow flight of stairs and into my room.

Painted white, it's covered with art from books I'd collected over the years. I'm a sucker for character art, and that's what a good number of them are. My dresser with the mirror on top sits against the hallway wall, while the wall next to my bed is one giant bookcase. Molly loves classic fiction, but my shelves are brimming over with mystery, fantasy, and romance. And the best books are a combination of all three.

I curl up in the corner of my bed, looking up at my favorite dark and broody fantasy hero whose picture hangs on my wall, and sigh. "What am I going to do?"

He just stares out over my domain—read: *room*—like the great warrior he is in absolute silence. Most unhelpful.

I grab my Aria Jean Mcoyle off my nightstand and flip it open. But the mysterious escapades of the main characters do nothing to rid my mind of Oliver Markel and the defeated look in his eyes. Isn't that a good enough reason to help? To move in and take care of Charlotte so Oliver can get sleep and have enough energy to meet his work demands Besides, maybe I can help him learn how to care for his little girl.

I let the book fall onto my chest and look up at a silver-haired elf warrior hanging next to dark and broody on my wall. "What would you do?" His cold blue eyes are staring into his lover's green ones as he pushes her flaming red curls out of her face. He is just as uncooperative as the broody dark hero.

With a sigh, I grab my phone. Opening my music app, I click on my moody music playlist and toss the phone back onto the nightstand. "Hold Me" by The Sweeplings comes on and I hum along to the lilting melody as I close my eyes and hug the still open book to my chest.

I must doze because the next thing I know Molly is flinging the door open with a shouted, "Oliver Markel asked you to *move in*?"

"Molly," I whimper good-naturedly. "I was sleeping."

"No time for sleep. Details, girl!" She flops onto the foot of my bed, bracing her hands behind her. Her honey brown hair falls over her shoulders with a gentle wave I envy. Her blue eyes study me, and I slap my hands over my face so she can't see the conflicting emotions in my gaze. Apparently, that's more telling than anything. Between my fingers I can just see Molly's mouth round into an *O* of surprise. "You don't know what to do."

"No. I don't. Because while the thought of helping Oliver out is great and all, I think..." I groan. "I don't know, Mols. I feel like it might be a dangerous thing to do."

"Oliver's dangerous?" Molly lurches up, her hands balling into fists like she's going to come to blows if Oliver dares to lay a finger on me—all five foot, three inches of her.

"No, not that way!" I groan and pull my hands down my face. "I like him. I think he's going to be a great dad. He needs some help in that department, though, and I want to show him how to love Charlie well. But what if my heart gets in the way?"

"Hearts tend to do that." Molly sighs, sitting back down and pulling a pillow into her lap. "There's no easy answer. If it's strictly business related, I say there's no harm going and staying until you can get Charlie's sleep schedule regulated. But if it could become something more..." She shrugs. "I wouldn't. Don't risk your reputation."

"I can see it going both ways. Oliver keeps pushing our boss and employee boundary. Not in anything untoward, but more in a *let's be friends* kind of way. But I'm also worried for Charlie if I say no. Because I have a sinking suspicion that he really is about to have a nervous breakdown. He needs more rest. He's killing himself with early morning work followed by long nights with a fussy child."

"Are you worried for Charlie or Oliver?" Molly laughs a bit. "I really can't tell, Em."

"I know." I blow a raspberry. "Well, I'll tell him it's for Charlie if he asks."

"You're going to do it then?"

Biting my lip, I slowly nod. "But I'm going to draft a contract with what is and isn't okay."

Molly nods with a small laugh. "Let's get Susan up here. She knows a lot of legalese from her parents."

I chuckle. "Okay. And Mols?"

She pauses in the doorway, throwing a glance over her shoulder. "Thanks."

"Anytime. My room will always be open. Well, at least until May."

I laugh. "I can't wait to spend all of Saturday with you. They were setting the tree up this afternoon when Charlie and I went wandering."

"I'm excited, too!" Molly props her fists on her hips. "You know, you should ask Oliver to join us for that. You know Tanner is going to want to grill him."

I laugh and nod. "Maybe I will."

Molly drifts out the door to corner Susan, and I hug myself, a weird sense of peace at the decision settling over me. I look up at my heroes and smile. "Thanks for nothing, guys."

They, of course, just look out over my room, quietly observing the craziness of the story that is my life.

Chapter Ten

Oliver

I'm attempting to settle Charlotte—who awoke at the lovely hour of 6 a.m.—into her highchair when Emily arrives the next morning. Little Lady, which I instantly decide is not the right nickname for Charlotte, arches her back and screams bloody murder. Being the mature adult I am, I want to follow suit.

Dumping her keys, purse, and coat onto the island, Emily steps to my side. "Need some help?"

"Please." I rub my face.

Emily scoops Charlotte into her arms and rubs her belly. "Good morning, *bambina*."

My brows furrow. "Since when do you speak Italian?"

"Since Sweetie has been attempting to teach me," she replies over her shoulder.

Alrighty then.

Emily easily gets Charlotte strapped in—the showoff—and then hands the little girl some of the sliced bananas I have on the cutting board.

"So…" Emily's lip is between her teeth, and she stares at Charlotte rather than me. "I made a decision last night."

Here it comes. The rejection. She's going to say no and then I'm back to square one with applications and interviews and seeing who Charlotte likes. Trying to find someone willing to live in a house with a single dude and a six-month-old baby. Oh, and there's also—

"I'll do it."

Wait, what now?

I stare at Emily, and I swear my chin is on the floor.

"Did I break you?" She laughs nervously.

"I—no, it's just—you're willing to—you're going to—?"

"Yes, to both. However—" She raises a finger then shoves a folded sheet of paper at me. "These are the terms and conditions I have for this arrangement."

I glance at the paper.

1. *I will have my own room with a lock on the door.*

2. *I will be allowed Sundays off. That will be one of the nights you care for Charlie.*

3. *Absolutely no romance is going to happen! I am not Maria from* The Sound of Music *or* Jane Eyre *(also you don't have some mystery wife in your attic...right?). Keep your feelings to yourself.*

I laugh at number three. I glance up at Emily, who's grinning at me, and shake my head. "No feelings, hm?"

"Nope! Or you lose yourself a nanny."

Well, that's a sobering thought.

"Do you really think I have a wife in my attic?" I ask, pointing to the line.

"The chances are never zero."

With a chuckle, I turn back to the conditions.

1. *Tuesdays, Thursdays, every other Saturday, and Sundays are your nights to deal with Charlie should she wake up crying.*

2. *Any breaking of the rules in this document will be met with me departing from the house, never to return.*

Below that is a suggested pay raise—not nearly enough for everything she does—and a place for me to sign. I grab the pen out of my suit pocket and sign without hesitation. Sure, some of the conditions are odd—like me not falling for Emily. The only reason I like her is she can keep Charlotte happy. That's it.

I hand the document over to the nanny who signs it quickly with her loopy signature.

"Good." She nods once. "I can move in on Friday, if I have some help."

"I did say you were only moving in until Lettie learned to sleep, right?" My nose wrinkles. Nope, still not the right nickname.

"Yes, you did. And Lettie?"

"I'm looking for a nickname for her." I gesture toward Charlotte. "It's a work in progress. But back to you moving in. How much stuff are you moving here? I have a bed and furniture in the guest room. It also has its own bathroom."

"I have a box of books that I'm planning on reading, as well as a lot of my winter clothes. Toiletries and things like that. Oh, and there's Fredrick."

"Fredrick?"

"My bearded dragon."

I chuckle. "I'll see if I can get the weekend off."

"Good! Because if you can, Molly wanted me to invite you to come to the tree lighting event on Saturday. We're going to wander around Cloverfield before it. I think Tanner is coming."

"Oh." That could be fun. The last tree lighting I remember going to was my sixth Christmas and the last holiday I celebrated with Marian. "Sure, I can probably go."

Emily smiles and, for the love, why am I noticing how bright it is? I'm blaming the stupid contract. There's no way I would have noticed how cute she is without the thought of falling for a nanny planted in my mind.

Because I'm not falling for the nanny, right? Of course, right.

● ● ● ● ● ● ●

I thump my briefcase onto my desk an hour later and stare out the window. Trepidation swirls in my gut. Mother isn't going to like this. Never mind that until Charlotte, there was never a time I took off work. Ever. I was a stickler for coming in, working eight to five, then returning home to eat, sleep, and do it all over again the next day.

But since Charlotte crashed into my life, I've taken weeks off. I had backed up PTO—no reason to take a vacation when there was never anyone to spend it with—but did that matter to Mother? Nope. And now with Tanner Bradshaw off my caseload, I actually have very little work. Eight to five isn't necessary. Plus, I have workers under me handling a lot of the nitty gritty. I can easily take off.

So why does asking for it make my head spin and my vision blur?

Trying to catch my breath—it feels like I climbed a dozen stairs and then did fifty jumping-jacks—I turn and head out the door and toward Mother's massive office. It's at the end of the hall and also has floor to ceiling windows, bookcases along the interior wall and equally uncomfortable gray chairs before her glass and chrome desk. Unlike my office, she has a sofa and coffee table off to the left, and Dad's desk on the right side of the room. On the shelves are the many achievement awards she's won for marketing campaigns. She's been responsible for many congressmen and women winning elections as well as getting governors into office across the US. She is ruthless, going after whatever goal is set before her with a tenacious spirit.

It makes her a great businesswoman. And a sucky mother.

The door stands ajar. Mother stares at the screen of her computer monitor. Her reading glasses are perched on the edge of her nose as she studies whatever document is pulled up. Taking another deep breath, I knock on the doorframe.

"Mother, can I talk to you for a moment?" I ask.

She glances up, her eyes that could be duplicates of my own raking over me. "What is it, Oliver? You know I'm busy with this campaign."

I resist the urge to sigh. It's been this way my whole life, and I don't know why I hoped it might change now that I have a kid of my own. They never had time for me, why should they care about Charlotte?

"I know, I just needed to let you know I'm taking tomorrow and the weekend off."

Her gaze narrows as she pulls off her glasses. "Why?"

Oh, boy this isn't going to go well. I shove my hands into my pant pockets so she can't see them shaking. "I asked Charlotte's nanny to move in to help me with her colic during the nights for the time being. I am about to have a breakdown and figured it was the best course of action."

"You're having the *nanny*—a single young lady—moving into your house. You, a single young man? Don't you know how that will look? We have a reputation to uphold, Oliver!"

My teeth clench as I nod. "I'm aware, Mother. But I need help. I don't really have a choice. Besides, a nervous breakdown also wouldn't be good for *your* reputation, would it?"

She ignores my barbed question. "You could give Charlotte up for adoption. That would be the kind thing to do, you know." She sniffs, as if the tiny orphan who lives with me is gum stuck to her shoe—an inconvenient speed bump in the road of going after what she wants.

"Gavin and Brittany left Charlotte to *me* and it's my job to care for her and do it well. I didn't come in here to argue about whether or not it is wise to have Emily move in. She is and that's all there is to it."

"What's the arrangement?" Dad asks, startling me. I hadn't realized he was in here until now.

"Yes, Oliver. Tell us." Mother interlocks her fingers and lays them, palms down, against her desk calendar.

"Arrangement?"

Dad comes over to stand behind mother. "Yes. What's she getting out of it?"

Mother's brow arches. "You?"

My nostrils flare as I struggle to control my temper. What even am I hearing right now? "Mother, that's disgusting!"

"You aren't an idiot, Oliver." Dad scoffs. "Surely you know what lengths a woman will go to in order to get what she wants."

"Is she sleeping with you?" Mother pushes to her feet, hands braced on her desk.

"She's not like that and neither am I." I shake my head. "I'm not having this conversation with you. None of this is your business."

"Is she the woman you're dating?" Dad asks now. "The one who always is on business trips? Were you lying about that and really having her watch Charlotte?"

"So what if I am?" I ask, tired of this conversation. "My personal life is my business, and if you two can't accept that then maybe—" I can't finish the sentence. My throat closes off at the mere thought of standing up to them. Of disappointing them despite never being good enough. With a growl of irritation, I shrug and storm out of the office.

I can't believe they would think so low of me. Can't believe they'd assume I'd do something so...sleazy! I care too much about the sacredness of marriage to even entertain the idea of sleeping with someone before we exchange vows. Care too much about love and respect to hurt anyone that way—regardless of what they are willing to do.

And with Emily? Ha, no! She deserves someone who has their ducks in a row, rather than ducks that are mixed in with geese, swans, and maybe even a crane or two as they paddle across a pond like they've had one too many shots.

Slumping into my desk chair, I rough my hand over my face with a groan. I want to go home. I don't want to deal with the stack of paperwork, the thousands of emails, the questions, the planning for the next PR move for the celebrity who hates that I plan everything from their appearances on TV to what they can and can't post on social media.

All I want is a little peace for once. Is that too much to ask?

Chapter Eleven

Emily

The next morning, I arrive at Oliver's with two suitcases in tow, as well as a box of books I've been meaning to read for...well, years for some of them while others are newer acquisitions. Listen, book buying is a completely different hobby than book reading. And this is a hill I'll die on, thank you very much!

It's almost seven. The time I get to Oliver's about every day, but the lights are off this Friday. When he came home yesterday, he said he took the next three days off—although he seemed a touch disgruntled and didn't really want to talk.

Now, the house is quiet. No lights. No sounds. I creep up the stairs with my box of books and set them on the guest bed in what Oliver said was my new room. I notice he somehow managed to move a bookshelf in here from...somewhere.

Dang it, that was a thoughtful gesture.

I turn and tiptoe down the hall to Charlie's room. Oliver is standing by the changing table, the lamp beside it turned on the lowest setting. Charlie is cooing and has her fists shoved in her mouth as Oliver stares down at her.

"Well, I'm going to attempt to change you, Char." He shakes his head. "Nope, not the right nickname, either."

She giggles as he unzips her jammies. Once he's freed her feet, Charlie stretches, throwing her arms above her head and giving a little baby grunt before her hands return to her mouth.

"You like that, Charlotte Elizabeth?" Oliver shakes his head as he jiggles her tummy with the palm of his hand, making Charlie giggle despite her full mouth. "Charlotte is an awful big name for such a little girl. Emily calls you Charlie. But I need a name that only I call you."

He falls silent as he begins to change Charlie. I should move. Leave. I didn't mean to eavesdrop. But I can't seem to get my feet to listen to my brain.

"I don't want to mess you up," he whispers, startling me slightly. He slides her arms into a little green romper. "What if having you here with me makes you a mess? What if I'm not good enough to be your dad, hm? Because your daddy was an amazing guy. He loved everyone and took care of anyone who needed it. He befriended the awkward freshman who shared his dorm floor and never gave up on him. Ever. Even when that awkward guy locked himself away in his room and wouldn't come out. How can that awkward freshman possibly raise Gavin's daughter, hm, Lottie Beth?"

My heart breaks a little at his words. How can he not see how he's *exactly* like Gavin used to be? He *sees* people. He cares so well. He loves wholeheartedly, albeit uncertainly at times. He'll be a great dad and he's trying so hard. Could that be the problem? Is he trying so hard to be perfect that he'll never live up to the expectations he's set in his head?

Deciding it's time to quit lurking in the doorway, I knock on the frame. Oliver startles, and I swear his head hits the ceiling, so focused is he on attempting to snap up the romper.

"Hey, I'm here."

"Yeah." He lays a hand over his chest. "So I noticed."

"What do you want for breakfast?"

"I'm good with whatever."

"Well, we should go shopping later because I know for a fact that you're fresh out of almost everything."

He chuckles weakly as he glares at the half-done up, very askew romper. "I can't even get Lottie dressed."

"Lottie?" I ask, feigning innocence.

"Well, yeah." He rubs the back of his neck. "Like I said yesterday, Charlotte seems like too big a name for such a little girl."

"Well, that's why I call her Charlie." I grin as I step to his side and deftly do up the snaps. Charlie kicks her feet the whole time and I glare at her. "No wonder Uncle Ollie was having a hard time!"

"*Uncle Ollie?*" Oliver asks, sounding mildly horrified.

"Yep!" I grin. "I figured you wouldn't want to be *Dad* to her. Not yet anyways."

"Try not ever." He looks a little green at the thought.

"Hey." I reach out and grab his hand, ignoring the flutter in my chest when he doesn't flinch away. "You're going to be a great dad to Charlie. She needs someone like you to love her. I would have loved to have someone like you in my life while growing up. I … well, I was pretty alone. For Charlie to have someone she'll be able to depend on for the long haul? That's the greatest gift you can give her, Oliver."

I squeeze his limp fingers before dropping his hand. "I'll go get started on breakfast, okay?"

He nods, his eyes on the ground as I hurry downstairs and into the kitchen.

I don't let myself dwell on what Oliver's fingers felt like in mine. While it hadn't been the world's greatest handhold, I still felt sparks shooting through me like I stuck my finger in a light socket.

After settling Charlie into her highchair and handing her a bottle, I begin breakfast. It's a dance I've perfected in the months working for Oliver. Place bread in the toaster but don't start it yet because cold toast? That's a no from me! Spin over to the stove and scramble the last of the eggs from the fridge. After that, put bacon onto a parchment paper covered baking sheet to make it perfectly crispy—a little life hack that came courtesy of the one and only Ryder Pruitt!

Fifteen minutes later, I'm at the finale, sprinkling cheese over the eggs, buttering the toast, and flipping the bacon over before sliding it back in the oven to cook a bit longer.

My stomach growls. *Hopefully Oliver gets down here soon.*

I start humming "Here Comes the Sun" under my breath as Oliver strolls into the kitchen. He's changed into a cream-colored Henley with a blue and brown flannel over it. The sleeves are cuffed up so I can see the insanely expensive smart watch on his left wrist and a thin leather bracelet on his right. My mouth goes a little bit dry as he pads over to look at the food spread out over the gas range top.

"It smells good in here." Oliver's voice is soft. "Why didn't you tell me you're a chef as well as a nanny?"

I snort as I pour some orange juice into what I think are actually bourbon glasses. "Because this is about the extent of my cooking prowess."

"Scrambled eggs and toast?" Oliver leans his hip against the countertop and crosses his arms, a smirk playing on his face.

"Hey! There's bacon in the oven! Don't ever forget about the bacon." Handing him a glass, I smile sweetly. "But nope, I was referring to breakfast food."

"Well, that's about the best food to be able to cook." Oliver shrugs.

"Don't say anything until you try it." I raise a brow. "I'm pretty sure my food is a travesty more often than it is a delicacy. Probably about ninety-nine percent of the time."

Oliver laughs. And holy buckets! It's low and rumbly and rough. His green eyes dance and though he ducks his head, the shadows of the kitchen do nothing to hide his smile nor the way it makes him appear twenty-five instead of the forty he has since day one.

But hot diggity dang. Somehow both looks work on Oliver. Weak-kneed Emily has activated and oh dear ... it's not a good thing.

I can't fall for my boss. The contract said nope to that! Stop it, Emily Jane Fitzpatrick!

Sucking in a sharp breath, I scoop the eggs, bacon, and toast onto our plates. "Here. Tell me what you think."

He saves the plate from crashing to the ground when I all but shove it at him. I turn quickly and hop onto a barstool, not wanting him to see my expression. I'm sure I'm redder than a tomato. Oliver settles onto the stool beside mine and takes his time cutting his bacon and mixing it with the eggs on top of his toast.

I shudder. "You're a monster."

"What? Why?"

"That." I gesture to his plate. "It's a travesty."

"Wait, I'm a monster because I'm putting eggs and bacon on toast?" When I nod, his eyes crinkle from the strength of his smile. "Emily, you can buy breakfast sandwiches with all of this on it. How is that any different?"

Gosh, his teeth are white. Shaking my head to rid myself of that intrusive thought, I turn my attention to my own plate. "It's different, Mr. Markel, because I made scrambled eggs, bacon, and toast—not a breakfast sandwich."

He laughs again and takes a large bite of his food. "Delicious," he declares around the food, smiling without his teeth when I wrinkle my nose.

"You're disgusting."

He swallows and runs his tongue over his teeth before saying, "Maybe I just enjoy riling you up. Besides, you clearly enjoy doing it to me."

I freeze. He can tell that? How? I thought I was being subtle—well, relatively so. But apparently not enough. I glance at Oliver, but he continues eating like there's nothing wrong with me teasing him. This can be our boss/employee dynamic, right? Sure. We'll say that. I relax and go back to my breakfast.

Charlie grunts, smacking the highchair with her chubby fists and talking nonsense. I smile over at her and hand her a teether from the freezer. It rattles as she shoves it in her mouth.

"So." Oliver wipes his mouth with a napkin and takes a sip of his orange juice. "Grocery shopping, right?"

"Yep. You can come with, or Charlie and I can go. You need quite a bit."

"How long have you been doing this for me?"

"A while. It's just kind of become one of my rhythms now. I don't mind."

He leans forward, suddenly looking disturbed. "Do you use your own money?"

"Yeah." I draw the word out slowly. "I eat the food in your fridge for pretty much every meal. So, I buy your groceries with my money."

He stares at me for a disconcertingly long amount of time. I really don't mind spending money on food, especially since Oliver barely eats at home and pays me a small fortune for watching one baby. Besides all that, it means I get to stretch my cooking ability without burning food *he's* paid for. A win-win in my book.

But clearly not in his. Oliver crosses his arms and sets them on the counter. "I didn't realize you were doing that. I mean, I knew you bought food, but I guess I didn't think about it being your money. I'm beginning to see there's a lot I don't think enough about."

"You'll learn. You've been a bachelor for, what? Four years? Or more."

He snorts, keeping his gaze on Charlie.

It hits me then. A pang of sympathy...or something akin to it. Oliver just sits, staring at the tiny human who now—for all intents and purposes—is his daughter. He's a dad.

He doesn't talk much about his childhood. And like I told Molly, I honestly don't know Oliver all that well despite being his nanny for months. I've been nosy before and searched all the rooms. The attic and basement, too. And I know for a fact that there aren't any memories—nothing that ties him to his parents. Oliver's past? It's a giant question mark to me.

"Can I ask a personal question?" I ask after finishing the last piece of bacon on my plate.

"Sure…" It's his turn to draw out a word. He gives me a side eye as he stands and stretches.

"Why aren't there any pictures of you and your parents in your house?"

Oliver freezes. He looks like a deer in headlights. Maybe I shouldn't have asked.

He begins moving again like he was kickstarted by a defibrillator. He takes his plate, rinses it in the sink, then places it in the dishwasher. All the movements are deliberate. Harsh. *Oh shoot, did I make him mad?*

As he closes the dishwasher, he asks, "Where's Lottie's coat?"

"Mr. Markel—"

"Emily." He turns, and his expression is once again shuttered, cold, and detached. "Where is Charlotte's coat?"

"Coat tree by the front door."

Oliver nods and heads off to find it.

I turn to the baby. "Your nanny has a big fat mouth, and she stuck her foot right in it this time."

Charlie laughs, slamming her toy into the tray with a gusto that brings a smile to my wobbly lips. Oh, to be a child again. Full of innocence and hope. I rub my face before hopping off the stool and scooping Charlie up. "Come on, Charlie. Time to go shopping!"

● ● ● ● ● ● ●

I pull the cart cover out of my trunk as I watch Oliver struggling to unbuckle Charlie from the car seat. Sometimes, I just take the seat in with me on the cart, but with two of us going today, I figure the cart cover is a better plan. It's padded and means Charlie can watch everything going on inside the store. She's getting to the point that she likes to watch the bustle, the people, and brightly colored items and signs in the store more than just the person pushing the cart. She is nosy, that's for sure.

Plus, watching Oliver fight the buckles is mildly amusing.

"Need help?" I ask.

"Nope." Oliver grunts and I think I hear a mumbled, "Buckets."

"Did you just say—"

"Yes, I did!" He leans out and runs a hand through his hair, ruffling the blond waves. Whatever funk I cast over him by asking about his parents has dissipated. Now his aggression seems to be targeted toward the car seat which he is currently pointing at. "That is next level buckle-age."

"Buckle-age?" I smirk, rubbing at my chin as I appear to think deeply. "Is this a new word?"

He scowls at me and crosses his arms. "It is now."

I burst out laughing, slapping my hand over my mouth when Oliver's frown deepens. "I'm sorry! You're right, car seats are hard."

Oliver's expression softens and he sighs as he leans against the side of my car as I pop Charlie out of her seat. "I just...I can plan a whole marketing campaign, spin Tanner Bradshaw's injury as some new adventure for him, crunch numbers, impress clients, make hundreds of thousands of dollars a week. But when it comes down to it, none of that matters as much as that little girl." He runs his hand through his hair again. "And I feel like I'm royally screwing her up."

"Mr. Markel—"

"Seriously. Please, Emily. Call me Oliver?"

My throat closes off and I shift Charlie in my arms as I swing the diaper bag over my shoulder. "I—"

"Emily?"

I jump and turn toward the voice. Susan is coming out the grocery store, a cart full of bags rolling in front of her.

Saved by the roommate! I breathe a sigh of relief and wave. "Hey, Sue! What is all this?"

"Ingredients to make even more Christmas cookies for the tree lighting tomorrow." She smiles wryly at me before turning toward Oliver and looking him up and down. Her smile flattens a touch. "I hear you're coming, Oliver."

"Emily invited me. It's good to see you again, Susan." He nods towards her as he shoves his hands in his coat pockets.

"I have to get Charlie inside." I shift, sensing the tension pulsing between the two, although not entirely sure why. I mean, Susan was against me moving in with Oliver, but she wouldn't treat him this coolly because of that. Would she? "Let's go...Mr. Markel."

I'd been so close to calling him Oliver. But it still feels ... wrong. He's my boss. I can't just go around calling him by his first name. Can I? I mean he asked me to, but still. It feels so wrong. Especially with me moving in. Calling him *Mr. Markel* gives me a buffer, a way to keep my distance. That's good right?

I head for the store and Oliver follows.

"What was that whole thing with Susan?" I ask.

"Awkward past," is all he says.

So it's not about me moving in—or at least not only that. Good to know.

A gust of warm air rushes over us as we step through the automatic doors. A blessed relief.

I hand Charlie to Oliver. "Hold her while I get the cart cover on."

He obeys, watching me stretch it over the front of the cart and snap it into place. It keeps the germs off the little girl while padding the sides, letting her play with toys, and look around as I shop. I strap her in and then gesture to the cart. "You want to push?"

Oliver nods and takes the cart. He's quiet. It's actually a bit unnerving. Usually, he keeps up casual conversation with me if nothing else. But the silence between us is deafening in the subtle ambiance of the store.

I start in the produce, getting salad, apples, and Charlie's favorite treat, bananas. Then I head for the bread. After that, the meat and cheese aisle.

I'm heading toward the breakfast cereal when Oliver grabs my arm.

"What?" I ask, turning toward him. *Buckets*! He's a lot closer than I realized. My nose almost whacks into his chest.

"That's…" Oliver's breathing is slightly off, and I can feel his hands shaking. "That's my mother over there."

"Okay, and?"

"Why is she in this store? In *Cloverfield*?"

He's panicking about seeing his mom in the grocery store? What am I missing?

"I don't know, but does it matter?"

Oliver finally looks down at me and whispers, "It might."

"Why?"

"Emily, whatever happens, please, please, please go along with it." He swallows, a gasp popping out as he exhales. He's having a panic attack. Does he even realize? He seems to be a million miles away. "And you need to call me Oliver. Please?"

"Fine, okay. I'll play along. But I want a full explanation afterwards about…this." I gesture to all of him.

He nods and grabs my hand. My mouth parts slightly when he twines my fingers with his. I jolt, his skin against mine shocking me like a cattle prod to the chest. Much more than in the nursery this morning because *he's* initiating it.

Holy cannoli. "Mr. Mar—Oliver, what is this?"

He doesn't respond. Rather, he starts down the aisle, pushing the cart one handed—which I shouldn't find impressive, but totally do. I grab a box of blueberry chex, honey-o's, and crispy rice cereal as we pass. With each box I add to the cart, we inch closer to the woman who is standing in front of the granola bars. But she's not moving. In fact, I'm pretty sure she's staring at us. Which is slightly—okay, no, *very* unnerving. Oliver is going to have a lot of explaining to do after this.

A box of oatmeal packets, a bottle of syrup, and then I'm sidling up to the woman. We could probably skirt around her but, unfortunately, I need the granola bars she is blocking—because of course I do.

"Excuse me," I say as sweetly as possible. "Can I just grab that box, there?"

She turns and—holy cannoli! There's no denying she's Oliver's mom. Her eyes are just as unfathomably green, like emeralds in the sunshine. Her hair is curled in perfect golden waves, her pantsuit is without a wrinkle, and her lips are pressed into a thin, disapproving line.

"Of course." Mrs. Markel looks over at her son. "Hello, Oliver."

"Mother."

"So, is this the mysterious girlfriend we have yet to meet?" Her perfectly plucked and obviously darkened brow arcs. "Not much to look at."

My mouth falls open, but I quickly snap it shut. She thinks I'm Oliver's girlfriend. Well, okay, then. I suppose this is what he meant by *playing along*. But…is he telling people he's dating me?

Oliver's grip on my hand tightens—whether subconsciously or in warning, I'm not sure. "This is Emily."

Mrs. Markel glances at the cart where Charlie is sucking on one hand while also having a pacifier wedged in her mouth. "Emily, hm?"

"Yes, ma'am." I try to tug free from Oliver's grip, but he won't let go. This isn't helping my suspicion that he's been telling people I'm his girlfriend. "We were just out shopping for groceries on our day off."

"I thought you were moving her into your house today, Oliver." Her tone is icier than the air outside—and it's in the single digits.

Oliver's shivers, like the chill radiating from his mother's voice is affecting his body's temperature. "We are after this. And even if I wasn't moving Emily in, Lottie had me up last night, so I would probably have called in sick today anyways."

"*Lottie*? You mean *Charlotte*?" His mother sniffs. "Oh, Oliver. I shouldn't be surprised you've sunk to the juvenile use of nicknames, of all things. Charlotte is a perfectly acceptable name."

"It's too big for such a little girl," he defends but I watch him shrink in on himself. His head ducks, his eyes drop to the handle of the cart, his shoulders cave forward.

"Whatever." His mother waves a hand in clear dismissal, then turns her piercing gaze on me. "But you didn't answer me. Are you, Emily, the *nanny* or are you Oliver's girlfriend?"

"I—"

"Because if you're the girlfriend he hasn't bothered to bring around in the last five months of dating, I'm curious as to why? What's your aim? Why are you moving in? Is it so that you can seduce—"

"Mother." Oliver cuts her off. "Emily is Charlotte's nanny and if I'm dating her, that's no concern of yours."

Hm. Clever sidestep.

I turn to him and force a besotted smile to hide my irritation. While he didn't come right out and say he was dating me, he certainly alluded to it. My jaw tightens as I grind my teeth. When he'd told me to go along with whatever his mother said, playing his fake girlfriend wasn't quite what I had been expecting.

Though, he is clearly cowed by this woman in front of us. As for me, the thing I detest most in the world is a bully and a person who belittles others for the fun of it. His mother? She's the biggest bully I've encountered in a while, which means I don't like her. At all. So, I'll keep playing along as the fake girlfriend. For now.

I wrap my free hand around Oliver's forearm and lean my head against his shoulder. "Oliver is just the greatest, Mrs. Markel. You must be so proud of him."

"I—"

"He's kind and thoughtful. He's gentle, sees people as they really are, and he is such a good guardian to little Lottie." I smile at her, unable to hide the bite in it that I feel in my chest. "He grew up well, despite everything he had going against him."

Her mouth falls open and, although I don't have the granola bars, I say, "Come on, *Ollie*. Let's go find the ice cream."

I've clearly shocked the poor man by my declaration of praise and maybe with the nickname as well, because he follows me without a murmur. We reach the ice cream aisle before I step away, shaking with anger.

I'm angry at the witch of a woman who is Oliver's mother, though we'd barely talked. Yet I know I despise her. Absolutely loathe her for how she's browbeaten Oliver into the shell of the man I've seen the last four months.

And oh yeah, you better believe I'm mad at Oliver for putting me in that position in the first place! Honestly, why did he think it was a good idea to pretend I'm his girlfriend? For one, it's a total disregard of the contract. Secondly, as if someone like him would ever date someone like me!

And maybe I'm a teeny-weeny bit mad at myself, for lashing out and feeling so protective of the man at my side especially since I have no right to be. Because even though I'm certain I'd do it for anyone, Oliver isn't mine to defend. Sure, I know he's special. He's really an extraordinary person. But he isn't mine.

Honestly, I don't know who I'm angrier at for certain. But what I *do* know is that I want to understand Oliver Markel. Really and truly comprehend him and his life. If that means going along with this charade to confuse his mother—and likely myself and my stupid heart? —then fine. Because it's clear that Oliver is hurting, and if there's one thing I can't walk away from, it's someone who's a broken mess.

Chapter Twelve

Oliver

For the love, *why* do I always seem to stick my foot in my mouth? I should have warned Emily that Mother might think we're dating. But when I saw her standing in that aisle, the tight band of nerves wrapped around my chest, and I couldn't think. Couldn't speak. And now I have an irate nanny dragging me past the frozen pizzas and burritos until we're in front of the ice cream.

Once there, Emily's whirls on me, jabbing a finger toward the far end of the aisle we're in. She hisses, "What the heck was *that*?"

"Mother assumes you're my girlfriend." My words are surprisingly calm considering inside my head, there's a hurricane colliding with a tornado. It even has all the sirens to go with it—whooping and screeching so loudly that I can't think straight. All I know is that I broke one of Emily's rules and now she's glaring at me like I'm the biggest moron to walk the earth. And it's quite possible that I am.

"I'm *not* your girlfriend!" She flings her arms wide, still whispering. "Rule three, remember? No feelings toward the nanny. Besides, what is she going to do when she discovers it *is*, in fact, a lie?"

"I have no feelings beyond friendship, Emily. As for Mother, she never has to know it's fake."

"Ha." Emily scoffs rather shrilly. "She's going to figure it out eventually. Don't you have some elaborate office party thing in a few weeks?"

I slowly nod. The office party from Hell, that's what it is. Honestly, if it wasn't mandatory, I wouldn't go. The whole thing is straight out of an introvert's nightmare. Glitz and glam, uncomfortable clothes, all manner of coworkers throwing themselves at the boss's son trying to score a little more cash or a few extra favors. I hate it.

"And that right there is when she's going to find out this," she gestures between us, "is a bunch of bologna." She turns to survey the line of Ben & Jerry's ice cream options.

"What do you mean?" I ask, pushing Charlotte's cart further up so I'm standing behind Emily. I can see her reflection in the glass and she's practically shooting lasers out of her eyes.

"You asked me like a week ago to stay late to watch Charlie for the party. Although, I suppose that's not as big of a deal now that I live at your place—but moving on!" She shakes her head and steers back to the topic. "I'll be watching Charlie, and you'll show up without a date, and poof!"

"Poof?"

"The clock strikes midnight, and your mom will know we're," she gestures between us again, "a bunch a crap."

"But she already knows you're the nanny," I point out.

"True..." Emily squints at me.

"So why can't you go to the party with me? We can find a sitter for Lottie, and you can pretend to be my girlfriend."

"Seriously, Oliver. Fake dating? That never ends well."

"Doesn't it?" I lean my forearms against the cart handle.

"No! Someone always catches feelings and then the person without them leaves a trail of heartbreak in their wake." Emily pulls a container of brownie batter ice cream out of the cooler along with cookie dough.

"But you had me sign a contract. Therefore, I can't catch feelings, or I lose my nanny." I shrug. "Besides, this is just to get Mother off my back about not having a date in years."

She rolls her eyes. "Oh, great. I love being a means to an end."

"It'll be fine, Emily. I promise."

With all my other dates, I'd been so terrified of messing them up that ... well, I had. Whether it was spilling my drink in her lap, nearly setting myself on fire when my tie knocked over a candle, or running into a server and getting a whole bowl of cream of mushroom soup down the front of my suit, each date had a horrible ending.

But with Emily, I already feel completely comfortable. No shaking, sweaty hands. No screeching halt in my thoughts. No stumbling over my words. No, I'm perfectly calm which is odd, but not unwelcome.

"I'm your employee, Mr. Markel. I won't risk losing my job taking care of Charlie because you need someone to cover for the fact that you can't get a date."

I wince at that. "I can get a date."

"Oh?" Her brow arches. "Then let me help you find someone. I matched up a few people back in my college years." Her nose scrunches up and I wonder if it's because of her offer or if those matchmaking schemes hadn't ended well.

"I'll pass. Besides, few women like the idea of an instant family." I smirk despite the tightening in my chest at the thought of someone hating Charlotte.

"Fine." She huffs a breath. "It's their loss."

"But I *would* really like to take you to the party. You'll definitely shake up the dullness of my coworkers."

Emily grunts and marches back toward the frozen pizzas. Well, guess our conversation is over.

We do a bit more shopping in silence before heading toward the checkout lanes.

"What are they like?" she asks as we move to one of the shorter lines.

"And we're talking about…?" I hand Charlotte her pacifier when she starts to whine.

Emily steps into line and looks up at me. "The Christmas work parties."

"They're ostentatious. Flashy and fancy. People who mostly hate each other pretending to get along for a night." I can't explain to her my gross dislike for these forced events. Or that the thought of having her there makes the tension in my neck release. "But the food is amazing."

"Well, that's good." Emily laughs as she begins to set the groceries on the conveyor belt. "Because for being such a highly demanded marketer, you're really not making me want to go, Oliver."

I freeze, looking at her as she continues to set things up on the belt. She called me by my name. *Oliver.* She finally said it. Not for cover, not in that saccharine sweet way she said it to Mother. She simply…said it.

Why does that make my heart flutter, just a tiny bit? And causes my hands to grow clammy? Woah, that's not good, but I can't think about that now. No, I need to finish getting the items rung up and—

Charlotte begins to cry. I look at her, my eyes widening as she lets loose another wail. Not here! In the middle of the store where people turn to stare. I gulp, willing Charlotte to silence even as my body freezes, paralyzed in the face of a decision.

"Well, pick her up!" Emily shoos me with her hand. "I'll pay and bring these out while you get her a bottle in the car."

"I really think you should—"

Emily raises a brow. "You need to learn. She's six months old and you're bigger and stronger than her. I think you'll live."

Yeah, maybe physically I'm stronger, but the jury is still out on mentally and emotionally. I feel like balsa wood—thin and easily fractured. One slip, and I'll splinter in two.

But I obey the nanny. No, not just *the nanny*. Emily. The woman who somehow is sensing my pain, my hesitation, maybe even my panic. And she's being so good about it. Kind yet firm.

Yet, she doesn't want to go on a date with me. Why does that rankle? Who is this woman? Most women would love to go to some fancy party and earn my affection, but Emily is pushing me away.

Interesting. Has she been doing that all this time? Keeping me at arm's length for a reason?

That's a problem to work through later. Right now, I need to get my wailing goddaughter to the car.

I bite my lip as I carry Charlotte through the sliding door and to the car. Deftly, because this is one area I have gotten fairly adept at, I change her diaper. Then I hand her a bottle as I snap up her romper. I'm grinning triumphantly when Emily comes out of the store with the cart.

Together we load the car. Emily secures Charlotte in her car seat—something I'm avoiding so I don't crush my tender pride right after the diaper change and romper victory—then we set off for my house.

It's strange, riding in the car with Emily. Because as she turns on her favorite music group—the Beatles, apparently—and sings wildly off-key to "P.S. I Love You", I'm struck by how comfortable I am with her. I can tease, poke, and share my struggles with her, all without fear of judgment. I enjoy being around Emily. She is my friend.

And that thought brings no small amount of fear to me.

Because if I'm relying this much on her now, what will happen when she inevitably moves on like everyone else?

● ● ● ● ● ● ●

"What do you want for lunch?" Emily asks after we've unloaded and put away all the groceries.

"I don't care." I'm feeding Charlie some smooshed bananas but turn at the question to see Emily with her head in the fridge. One hand rests on her hip. She looks for all the world like she belongs here, in the massive and mostly-unused-by-me kitchen. My chest tightens.

"What about a frozen pizza?" She pulls a pepperoni pizza from the freezer, and I nod. The stove beeps as she sets the oven to preheat then turns toward us. "Okay. Nap time!"

I exhale and gesture. "All you, Miss Nanny."

"Nope. It's your turn." She grins as she waltzes over to the video baby monitor and clicks it on. "I want to help you learn to be a dad."

Oh, the dreaded *D* word. I audibly gulp and Emily chuckles.

"You can do it."

"I just got the freaking romper snapped; I don't know if I'm ready for nap time." I push out my lower lip, the action feeling slightly ridiculous for a grown man.

The ludicrousness increases tenfold when Emily snorts. "Oh my gosh, please don't ever make that face again!"

"Why, it made you laugh, didn't it?" I freeze, smile on my face but my body is telling me to run. Why, of all the moronic things to say, did that pop out of my mouth?

But Emily doesn't seem to notice my hesitation. She simply laughs again and nods. "That it did. Although that's not getting you out of nap time duty."

"What will?" I ask as I get a wet rag to wipe up Charlotte's sticky face and hands.

"The breakfast dishes."

I look at the big farmhouse sink. The morning's dishes are stacked within, not to overflowing but still full. There's the scrambled eggs skillet and the bacon pan. My nose wrinkles at the thought of the grease from the pan. I hate certain textures on my fingers, and bacon grease is one of the worst. And it doesn't wash off easily.

A glance at baby girl shows her eyes already drooping closed so I scoop her up. "I'll put Lottie to bed."

Emily nods. "I thought so."

"What's that supposed to mean?"

She throws her hands up in surrender. "It means I know you."

I roll my eyes and head for the stairs. "Not as well as you think!"

"Then teach me," she throws back.

I pause at the base of the stairs and look over my shoulder. I can just see the stove, where Emily is unwrapping our pizza to put in the oven. Longing hits me, sure and solid, in the chest. I want this. Banter and family and sticky fingers and laughter and ... everything that makes a house a home.

But those dreams are a long way off. With a shake of my head, I start walking up the stairs, determined that I will get Lottie to sleep.

Chapter Thirteen

Emily

I grab two cans of root beer from the fridge and set them on the counter. My face flushes when I think about what I'd said to my boss.

"I know you!"
"Not as well as you think!"
"Then teach me."

Grabbing the pad of steel wool, I begin to scrub the egg pan with gusto, hoping that I didn't just ruin this job. I love my job. I love Charlie and really love taking care of her. But I meant what I wrote in the contract—I'm not interested in falling in love. Because holy buckets. Oliver is...a lot. Like, *a lot* a lot. He's thoughtful and kind, but he's a total train wreck when it comes to caring for Charlie. He's scared. I want to help him, but *can* I really help with this?

Also, is it just me or was he flirting?

Listen, I'm fully aware that I tend to...project. Rather frequently, if I'm being frank. When I feel uncomfortable, it seems like everyone else around me feels the same way. Sad, or scared, or mad? Same deal. And I know enough about myself to know that it's usually only the negative emotions I project. When I'm happy or calm or excited, I often feel like everyone around me is annoyed with me. Because my emotions are *big*. I don't do things by halves. Rather, it's all or nothing.

Is it wrong to have big emotions? I don't think so, but I know the projecting part is not okay. I can't project my uncertainty about whatever Oliver and I are into this weird relationship. At least, weird for me. I've got to either fess up or bury it.

And right now, burying seems like the easier option. Especially with me living here and ... fake dating? Why on earth did I agreed to *that*? Because that was a dumb move. Dumb with a capital D.

I finish the egg skillet and set it on the drying rack before turning to the bacon pan. It is slimy and gross, something I knew Oliver would hate. In the past, I've seen him pale whenever he gets some of Charlie's food or formula on his hands. When he washes them, he thoroughly dries every drop of water off, and I've yet to see him put lotion on. He's a texture avoider—which I understand. A lot of kids in the preschool I worked at hated textures, going as far as not wearing certain materials because they would panic in them. I don't think Oliver is that bad, but with his hands, he is.

"She's asleep," Oliver says, scaring the bejeebies out of me. His socks make his steps silent, and seriously! Do the stairs not have a single squeak in them?

"I'm just finishing up this pan and then I'll get the pizza out." I force a smile, willing my heart to settle—which might have more to do with being *alone* with an insanely attractive man than the scare.

But no! We're not actually dating, and I am absolutely not going to fall for Oliver Markel.

"I can dry, if you want." He grabs the towel off the hook that's mounted to the side of the cabinet.

"Sure." I draw the word out. Honestly, it's a bit weird to all of a sudden see Oliver so invested in domestic life. He's basically been living at the office the entire time I've worked for him.

"What?" He raises his brow at me.

Oops. I had stopped scrubbing to stare at him. Because that's totally normal behavior.

"Sorry." I turn back to the pan, having no excuse for why I was staring.

He moves to put the skillet away, but I can still feel his eyes watching me. He seems to know where everything is located in the house—which is also a little surprising, because I've never seen the man touch the stove or any of the cooking utensils.

He turns toward me. "Why were you staring?"

I bite my lip as I rinse the bacon pan then scrub it with fresh soap and the dish sponge. "I was wondering...well, it's sort of a personal question."

"Ask it." Oliver leans back against the counter so he can better look at me. Not at all disconcerting—and sexy as heck.

But he's not just attractive. He's kind, thoughtful, takes care of his best friend's baby girl, is a hard worker, and he listens. But his looks sure make people do a double take. Well, they make *me* do a double take.

"Why—" I swallow the lump of panic in my throat. "Why are you taking such an interest in being home all of a sudden? I mean, you got me to move in, and now you're doing the dishes. I've never seen you in the kitchen. And I know Charlie's been fussy in the four months you've had her, so why didn't you have me move in right after you got her?"

He rubs the back of his neck. "Oh. Okay, wow. Not where I thought you would start."

"Sorry! You don't have to answer." My interest is piqued, but I won't push. I rinse the pan and set it in the rack before drying my hands. Grabbing the cardboard tray, I finagle the hot pizza onto it and plunk it on the island. Then I fish a bag of baby carrots out of the fridge and potato chips from the pantry. "Lunch is served!"

"You haven't let me answer, Em."

I freeze. He's called me that a couple times and I've brushed it off. But this time...only those I trust call me *Em*. The people I know will always be there. And Oliver isn't one of those people. Not yet and maybe not ever.

"I'm Emily, please." I smile woodenly. This is going to tick him off, isn't it? I'm going to lose my job and he's going to rip Charlie away and make me go crawling back to the apartment with my roommates. Susan's, *I told you so,* will be epic and I'll be humiliated. I'll have to go beg for a job from the monsters who run the preschool. My hands shake as I turn to hang the towels back up and wipe down the counter.

"Sure. Sorry." He clears his throat, and I can hear him as he settles on the stool and begins cutting the pizza. "So would you like an answer to your question, Emily?"

Most people would add a tone to my name, making it clear that it's stupid for me to set such a boundary. But not Oliver. I turn to see that he's served me two slices of the meat lover's pizza and is watching me, waiting for me to reply to his question.

I slowly sink to the stool. "You're not mad?"

"Why would I be mad?" His brow hops up.

"Well, I thought you'd want an explanation."

"About why you don't want me to call you *Em*?" When I nod, he laughs a little. "You don't owe anyone an explanation for your choices, Emily. If you don't want people to call you something, or you don't want to do something with someone, you can say no. That's allowed."

"I know that," I snap, a touch irritable. I think about agreeing to fake date him. There didn't feel like there was an out with that one. Not that I looked very hard. Because, holy cannoli, but the idea of dating Oliver—fake or otherwise—has a lot of appeal to it.

"Do you?" His brow quirks again and I scowl. He raises his hands in surrender. "Okay, fine. You understand. Now, back to me."

"A much safer topic," I mumble as I pick at a piece of bacon.

Oliver chuckles. "So, you asked me why I'm coming home earlier than before and worrying so much about Lottie now, four months later."

"Yeah." I crack open my soda.

Oliver stares at his pizza. His eyes flick back and forth like he's reading a page of a book. "Because I want to be worthy of raising her."

I wait, not wanting to break the tension hanging over the kitchen as he shakily inhales and exhales.

"I never expected to end up with her. Gavin and Brittany were young and full of life and excitement. One drunk driver took all that away. Took them away from Lottie. And now here I am, single and clueless about how to raise a baby. I guess four months ago, I was panicking and I just ... I shut down by throwing myself into work and trusting you with the day-to-day stuff."

I snort. "You called all the time in the evenings. My roommates gave me a hard time about it."

He smiles sheepishly. "It took a lot to learn how to care for her basic needs. Bottles and diapers weren't my strong suit."

"You adapted remarkably well." I admit with a little chuckle.

"Yeah, well, that's thanks to you. And recently..." He scowls at his plate. "Well, she's *not* going into the system."

Okay, there's definitely more to *that* comment than can be unpacked in one lunch.

"But what changed?"

"Well, I'm still stressed. Hence you moving in." He smiles "But...I also feel like it's time. It's time to learn more. I'm not treading water like I was those first few weeks, trying to keep my head from going under. Yeah, I'm exhausted because of Lottie's ... what did you call it?"

"Sleep regression."

"That!" He points at me as he nods. "But I'm ready for the long-haul and to be her...godfather."

"Mr. Markel—" I smile when he glares at me with a *seriously* look on his face. "Fine, *Oliver*. You know, it's okay to let her call you *dad*. You're going to be her surrogate father—the only one she's going to remember."

"That's what scares me." His throat bobs and he pushes away his plate. Crossing his arms, he leans them against the counter. "I'm not qualified."

I laugh. "You're more qualified than a lot of parents."

"But am I the *right* one?" He looks at me, his green eyes a fathomless depth that sucks me in for a minute. Buckets...I want to understand this man. To help him see that he is *exactly* who Charlie needs.

"You're the one Charlie has." I rest my hand against his folded arms. "And I know that you love her, Oliver. You're someone who will adore her as she grows, someone who will be there for her all of her life, and you won't back away when things get hard. I mean, you haven't so far. You've given her a chance to thrive and flourish. Hiring me was your way of taking care of her when you could have walked out and handed her to the system." My voice cracks and I lean back, emotion thickening my throat so I can't say more. I don't even know if I'll be able to eat.

"Thanks." He looks at his food before he picks up his pizza and begins to nibble at it. "So, what do you normally do in the afternoon?"

A subject change. I can live with that. Besides, I have more answers than I did fifteen minutes ago.

"I read. Or watch a movie while I fold laundry."

"I still can't believe you do chores for me." He tears a hand through his hair and legit *growls*. Holy buckets! That's something protagonists in books do, not real-life men! Although, I guess fake dating happens more often in books than in life—yet here I am!

I draw myself up on the stool, though he's still a few inches above me. "Like I said before, it's *fine*. I'm going to keep doing it, so don't push it. Charlie loves the sling and most days she takes two or three naps. I can get laundry, grocery shopping, and cleaning in because let's be real—reading and watching TV only goes so far."

He glowers—yeah, scowling as his face legit seems to darken *somehow*—and jabs a finger at me. "You're not a housekeeper. You're a nanny. Besides, you barely bartered for a pay raise at all when you agreed to move in here."

"Because it was more than fair seeing as I *live* here now. So as a housemate, I can help take care of the *house*!"

"Emily—"

"Oliver!" I laugh, and even I can hear the sharpness to it. "I'm not taking *no* for an answer! You need help, this saves you money, and I *enjoy it*!" I jab him in the chest, and holy cannoli! His chest is *solid*. "Stop making me feel bad for helping you."

His mouth snaps shut hard enough to hear an audible *click* of his teeth hitting together. "Fine. I don't like it though!"

"Noted and ignored." I grin and turn back to my food. "Let's finish lunch."

Chapter Fourteen

Oliver

I can't wrap my head around the fact that Emily has been taking care of my house. She seriously doesn't mind washing my dirty socks? She enjoys doing dishes and sweeping and dusting? And she has definitely changed my sheets and remade *my bed*.

Geez, why does that thought send butterflies through my chest? Why does Emily taking care of my home and child make me blush redder than a poppy?

It's not because I have free labor that enjoys cleaning up my mess. That's not it *at all*. In fact, that makes me see red. I'm definitely slipping a bonus into her next check for it on top of the pay raise she added to the contract. That's the least she deserves.

But it's not the labor, not fully. It's the *love* she shows to both Lottie and me. It's that Emily is considerate enough *to* take care of my house. She cares about my life, about making my house a home, and taking care of my baby girl. She came bursting in at the lowest, darkest moment and was a light. And now...

I shake my head as I place our plates in the dishwasher. Emily sets the glass container with the last two slices of pizza into the fridge. Rinsing out the cans, I throw them into the recycling bin before slowly turning to Emily. "What are your plans for this afternoon?"

"Well, I need to unpack, but that can wait for later." She shrugs. "Want to watch a movie?"

"Which one?"

Her lip pops between her teeth and she won't look at me.

"Oh no. What movie?" My voice sounds...happy. Lighter than it has in a long time and full of excitement to see what this crazy, wonderful woman is going to put me through next.

"I would love to watch *How to Lose a Guy in Ten Days*." Her eyes slowly drag up, laughter in their depths. "Or maybe *While You Were Sleeping*? Oh! Or what about *Leap Year*?"

"Those are all fake dating stories." My mind screeches like a record, stuck on the fact that she wants to watch a movie that kind of, sort of relates to the predicament I got us stuck in.

But another part of me is panicking. Thinking about fake dating Emily while she lives in my house is a recipe for disaster. Watching her care for Charlotte and doing all the things that a mother does...that a wife does? Heat curls in my stomach and I find my eyes flicking over her face, landing overly long on her lips.

Nope. Stop it, Oliver!

Emily crosses her arms and leans her back against the island. A smirk plays around her lips. Lips I can't stop looking at. "I'm impressed you know that. You watch romcoms?"

Oh, *shoot*!

The truth is...yes, I have watched romcoms. An unhealthy amount of them. And no, I don't have a mother who would have watched them with me. Nor a sister. It was all me. Because when I'm dejected or freaking out about my nonexistent love life, I'll pop in a romcom and get whisked off into the lives of Jack, Ben, Declan, and whatever other unfortunate male gets wrapped up in the whacky shenanigans the females of said movie rope them into.

Have I ever told another living soul this?

Nope.

Am I admitting that to Emily Fitzpatrick?

Apparently!

I clear my throat three or four times, unable to form words.

Emily laughs. "Cat got your tongue?"

I sigh and run a hand through my hair. "Okay, fine. I watch romcoms. I enjoy them. And I've even seen some of the classic romance shows and movies, thank you very much."

Emily's hazel eyes sparkle as she clasps her hands under her chin. "*Pride and Prejudice*?"

"Yeah. And *Anne of Green Gables*."

She squeals and then pretends to swoon over the island. "Seriously. Just when you couldn't get any hotter—" Emily slaps her hand over her mouth before slowly straightening. She mumbles something through it and turns a pretty shade of pink.

"I'm sorry, what was that?" I cup my hand around my ear. "Did Emily say I was hot?"

"Nope, that wasn't supposed to come out." She covers both cheeks with her palms and retreats toward the living room. "Movie time!"

Interesting. Maybe I *will* be able to get her to go to the Christmas party with me. We'll have to see. Because the thought of having to admit to Mother that I made up a girlfriend makes me want to lie yet again and get hit with a mysterious sickness to get out of going.

Emily ends up picking *How to Lose a Guy in Ten Days*. She plops onto the couch and crosses her legs. I settle next to her and stretch my arm across the back of the white sofa. I could brush her shoulder if I wanted. The shoulder that's currently bare, as her scoop-necked t-shirt has slipped to one side. I lick my lips and curl my fingers into a fist. Emily laughs at the ridiculous antics of Andie and Ben, and I find myself watching her more than the movie. Her face is so expressive and far more entertaining than the plot line. She leans over her crossed legs, elbows on her knees, her eyes aglow from the light of the television and her large smile.

Gosh, she's beautiful. I mean, she always was, but there's something in Emily I hadn't noticed before, something I can't fully put a name to, that's more captivating than any external feature.

When did it appear? Was it there when she started taking care of Charlotte? No, it was later than that. Today? No...no, it started when I came home that day to her napping in the recliner with Charlotte. She was so relaxed. Loving Lottie like she was her own.

She loves so well. That fact alone makes me want to get to know her better, to understand what's going on inside her mind. I want to serve her like she's been serving me without me even knowing it. She goes through life with a smile, but there's a host of information she doesn't share. It's there in subtle things. Small passing comments and actions that can easily be missed if you blink. I know this woman is deeper than she appears—and I want to explore the very depths of Emily Fitzpatrick's heart and soul. Sure, she's full of sunshine and roses, but I sense clouds around the glow, thorns beneath the flower.

"That was so good." Emily leans back as she clicks the TV off, jarring me out of my thoughts. Her hair tickles my forearm and I gulp back the desire to pull her closer.

"Yep," I say right as a scream ricochets down the stairs.

Emily leaps up, taking the stairs two at a time with me following at a more subdued pace. When I reach Charlotte's door, Emily is holding the baby against her shoulder, bouncing and trying to stop the tears. "It's okay, sweetie. Hush, Charlie. I'm here, and so is Daddy."

I swallow, watching the scene. Good gosh, this is ridiculous. I don't know Emily well enough for these emotions to pull on my heartstrings the way they are! But when I think about the future, why is Emily always there? Spinning Charlotte in the air, wrapped in my arms, holding a newborn in a hospital bed, calling me *daddy* in front of the kids?

Stop it, Oliver Tate Markel! Don't indulge in a fantasy.

Because that's exactly what it is. Emily may live in my house, but she does *not* belong to me. At all. And she never will.

I clear my throat and Emily looks up, smiling in the waning light from Charlotte's window. "Want to change her?"

"Oh, no, she's happy with you—"

"Oliver!" Her free hand pops onto her hip and she glares at me. "Come on. Where are your big boy pants?"

I snort in disbelief. "*Big boy pants*? I'm not a preschooler."

"Then don't act like one." Her chin juts out and I scoff a laugh at her audacity. The woman is infuriating but also irresistible—a dangerous combination for a man who's lived a normal and boring life alone for far too long.

"Hand her over." I gesture for Charlotte the way Emily did a few days before, cupping my fingers toward myself with a small smile.

She grins like I've handed her the moon and lays Charlotte in my arms. The little girl stares up at me, her big brown eyes unblinking as her pacifier bobs in her mouth.

Gosh, I love her. I love her so much and yet feel so incredibly incapable of the task ahead of me. Eighteen years; that's how long I have to raise Charlotte into an independent human being. And it terrifies me.

"Oliver?" I blink and look up at Emily. She's moved a bit closer and her eyes flick over my face. "Are you okay?"

"Yeah." I clear my throat when it comes out as a croak. "I just...this is kind of hitting me all over again."

"What is hitting you?" Her voice is barely above a whisper.

Holy cow, is it hot in this room? It feels really warm for almost December in Iowa.

"That I have to raise Lottie. Be her dad."

"Haven't we already had this conversation? You're going to be a great dad. You love her, Oliver." She sways a bit closer, and I swear I forget how to breathe. What is going on? Why am I noticing how close the *nanny* is to me?

She's just the help. I grimace at that thought. I sound like my mother and that's the last person I want to imitate.

The doorbell rings, breaking our revere.

"I—" Emily clears her throat and looks away. "I'll change Charlie. You should probably answer your own door."

"Yeah. Yeah, I'll do that." I practically shove Charlotte at her before hurrying down the stairs.

I hurry to the front door and when I open it, I'm surprised to find Ethan standing there.

"Hey, Oliver!" He grins as trepidation washes over me.

"Ethan. To what do I owe this surprise visit?"

Ethan grimaces. "Your mother asked me to stop by. Something about this"—he holds up a manilla folder— "and to make sure you were alone?"

I sigh, shoving my hand through my hair. Whatever is in the folder, it most likely could have waited until tomorrow. Which means...

"This is about her seeing Emily and me at the store, isn't it?"

"Hey, man! I have no idea. She cornered me on my way out of the office and since I like my job, I decided to obey her."

Mother is nothing if not...tenacious.

"Come on in, Ethan." He steps in and takes off his coat and shoes as I call up the stairs. "Emily! One of my coworkers is here with something from work. I'll be in my office."

"Okay! I'm going to feed Charlie and then I'll bring you something to drink."

"We're fine."

She doesn't respond so I gesture for Ethan to follow me into my office. It's a spacious room, with built-in bookshelves on either side of a large bay window that sits behind my wooden desk. This room I designed myself—meaning no white or chrome. At all. It's all dark wood, old golden light fixtures, and green drapes. Dark academia for the win.

"Wow." Ethan looks around as he takes a seat in one of the leather wingback chairs that sits in front of the mahogany desk. "This is different from your living room and work office."

I chuckle. "It represents the difference between my mother and me."

Ethan laughs and hands me the folder. "So, Emily is the nanny?"

"Mhm," I hum, tapping the folder against the desk edge.

"And she's moved in?"

"Yep."

He pauses. "Oliver, your mother came storming into the office today and said...well, she was screaming at your father and said that you're dating Emily? The nanny? And she's living here?"

I loathe lying. For one thing, I suck at it. For another, trust is important to me. I don't trust my parents and I hate that I don't—and while I've been lying to them about a fake girlfriend, that's for my own self-preservation. But with the rest of the world, I make it a point to be open and honest as much as possible.

And that means lying to Ethan isn't an option, so I shrug. "Kind of."

"How do you kind of date someone?" Ethan's black brows scrunch together, a divot forming in his forehead. "Unless...is she a fake girlfriend?" When I don't reply Ethan slams his hands on the arms of the chair. "Dude! She is! You're fake dating your goddaughter's nanny! And she's living in your house?"

I shush him, although I don't know why. Emily and I both know we're fake dating and now, so does Ethan. Everyone in the house is aware we're not dating for real, but, hey! I want to keep it on the down low. Especially since I'm beginning to really dislike that it's fake.

Wait, what?

Do I actually want to date Emily? Like, for real and not as a ruse?

Nope, I can't think about that. For one, if it ends badly, I'll be out the only other person who loves Charlotte as much as I do. Secondly, the thought of dating anyone scares the crap out of me. And thirdly, there's that stupid contract I signed.

I shove a hand through my hair and manage to nod.

"Woah! Dude you're pretending to date the nanny to keep your mom off your back! That...that's wild."

"Yeah. And now she's living here too."

Ethan props his chin on his thumb and first finger, resting his elbow on the chair arm as he studies me. "Is that smart? Because not to be the bearer of bad news, but your mom is having a conniption at the office."

"I'm twenty-five. I can run my own life."

"Yeah, but it's more than just controlling *your* life. Your parents love giving off the illusion of perfection. Having you *date*"—he does an air quote— "the nanny who is living in your house? That's ruining their perfect façade."

"Even more of a reason to do it," I mutter, sinking back into my leather desk chair. "But the only reason I asked Emily to move in was for Charlotte."

"So not to...you know? Put the moves on her?"

I glare at my friend. "You sound like my mother."

"Rude!" He chuckles but waits for me to answer the question.

"No. I'm not making moves on her. In fact, she's made it abundantly clear she's not planning on dating me. Ever."

"Noted." Ethan leans forward, elbows on his knees. "Okay, so what's in that file?"

"You mean you haven't looked through it?"

He lays his hand against his chest. "How dare you accuse me of such a thing! I would never stoop to such a level."

I raise a brow at him—because Ethan Matthews would absolutely have opened it if Mother hadn't taped it shut on all sides—and he chuckles.

I grab my letter opener and slice the tape. Opening the file, I scan the document, my anger mounting with every word.

Adoption agencies willing to take Charlotte Elizabeth Dangler.

My jaw tightens as I skim over the agencies' names, not interested in the slightest.

Families looking to adopt a baby girl.

My fingers ball into fists as I *do* read the names that Mother managed to acquisition.

"Unbelievable." I fling the file across my desk. "I can't believe her audacity! After I said no, Mother still went and dug up names of adoption agencies and families to foist my goddaughter off onto."

A gasp snaps both mine and Ethan's heads to the door. Emily stands there, murder on her face. Charlotte is propped on her hip while she holds two sodas in her other hand. I'm a bit concerned she's planning on chucking them as her flinty gaze bores into me. "Your mother did *what*?"

Chapter Fifteen

Emily

Okay, so listen. Getting wound up quickly is my trademark and being easily excited is part of my charming personality. But when I hear Oliver say that Mrs. Markel is trying to force Charlie off to an adoption agency, I about lose my ever-lovin' mind.

"She absolutely cannot do that!" I march into Oliver's office, completely ignoring his co-worker's open-mouthed gawking. I cradle Charlotte in my arm and wag my finger at Oliver. "I will not let you give up this baby girl, and if you do, I'll take her and adopt her myself! Hasn't she been through enough?"

"Emily—"

"No! No, I don't want to hear any excuses, Oliver! You're not allowed to give up on her. You can't. Gavin trusted you to raise her and she needs you."

"Emily!"

"What?" I gasp in a breath of air, far too close to tears for the current situation. Why am I so worked up?

I wince and look away from my boss. I'm worked up because this whole situation hits a little too close to the bruised part of my heart I hide from everyone. The side of me that's afraid of being left behind. Again.

Oliver stands and takes Charlotte from where I've propped her on my hip. He doesn't step back as he grasps my elbow with his free hand and says, "I'm not giving up on Charlotte. I never planned on it, and besides...I don't want to. Yeah, I'm scared. Yeah, I need a crap ton of help because I don't know what I'm doing. But I'm not letting her go into the system, or to a family I don't know. She's my responsibility and one I don't take lightly."

"But the papers your mother—"

"Were *all* my mother's doing. Not me. Never me."

I draw in a shaking gulp of air and smile sheepishly at Oliver's coworker. "Sorry about that, Mr...?"

"Matthews. Ethan Matthews. And hey, I understand. Mrs. Markel is frightfully forceful in her business dealings, so I can't imagine being related to her nor trying to live your own life with her hovering around."

Oliver laughs mirthlessly. "Yeah, it's no picnic."

I bite my lip. "So, it was your mother's doing. Got it. But what are you going to do about it?"

Sinking back into his chair, Oliver picks up Charlie's hand and lets her little fingers wrap around his index finger. He absentmindedly rubs his thumb over her knuckles as he stares off into space.

"I have a plan," he says at last. "But you're not going to like it."

Oh dear, I'm not? But seriously, Oliver only has to look at me and I'll do whatever he wants. I'm already fake dating the man, for crying out loud. What's the worst idea he can come up with?

"Hit me with it." I plop into the free chair beside Ethan. He keeps swiveling his head to look at Oliver and then me, but I'm trying to ignore him. He's cute—with dark brown hair and brown eyes—but he's not at Oliver's level of drop-dead gorgeousness. Although Ethan has freckles. I've always had a thing for freckles.

"So, the plan." Oliver clears his throat, drawing my attention back to him.

"Yes, the plan. What is it?"

"Well, we're already living together." Oliver clears his throat again and drops his gaze to Charlie.

"You're not telling me anything I don't already know." I cross my arms.

He doesn't acknowledge my sass. "Mother knows we're dating, per say. So, the plan is, we go to the Christmas party and…" Oliver blushes and, holy cannoli, how have I never noticed how cute he looks with rosy cheeks? Because I would have remembered Oliver blushing, surely. This is a brand-new development.

"Emily?" Oliver's staring at me and I realize I've completely spaced out.

"Sorry, what?"

"The plan is to get engaged at the Christmas party," Ethan helpfully supplies, making Oliver's whole face turn beet red.

"Absolutely not!" I launch to my feet and shake my head. "Holy buckets, Oliver, why on Earth would you think that's a good idea?"

"Holy buckets?" Ethan murmurs, but both of us ignore him.

"See, I knew you wouldn't like it, but hear me out. Please?"

"Listen, I'm already dating you." I put dating in air quotes. "And I'm living in your freaking house! But if we get engaged, people are going to talk."

Oliver waves away my concern. "They're already talking. What's a little more gossip?"

"Oliver...this is getting...this is getting into dangerous territory." I swallow the rising panic. Yeah, I've been attracted to the man since the day I walked into the nanny interview. And yeah, I've been trying for months to squash that attraction. Ergo, getting fake engaged is the last thing I should be doing, right?

So why am I even entertaining this idea?

"Look, I even have a ring." Oliver pulls out a little black box from one of the drawers on his massive desk.

"Oh, so you're just keeping rings around now. In case of an emergency proposal?"

"Yeah, because there's a line of women who want me." He grins. Holy buckets of cannoli, why does he have to be so stinkin' adorable?

"Um…pretty sure half of the female employees are interested. Single and otherwise." Ethan volunteers and that does nothing to calm the surging emotions in my chest. What is *this*? I have no right to feel protective and jealous of Oliver. He is my *boss*!

Oliver levels a glare at Ethan. "This was my grandma's ring. She gave it to me before she went into the nursing home because she was afraid Mother would simply sell it."

"Oh," I say weakly. A family heirloom. He's going to give me a family heirloom in two weeks when I agree to be fake engaged to him.

No, no, no! He's not because *I'm* not doing this. This is asinine. "What's the point?" I ask.

"Point?"

"What's this plan going to do?" Besides make me emotionally attached to a man I most certainly shouldn't become emotionally attached to.

"Keep Mother's claws away from Charlotte," Oliver states.

And there it is. The only reason I might be willing to do this harebrained scheme. For Charlie. It most certainly will not be for Oliver or the way my heart chokes me every time he halfway smiles in my direction. "But what happens when she finds out this is all fake? That I'm not your fiancé and that I really *am* just the nanny?"

"By then I hope I can juggle it all and she won't have a leg to stand on."

"And if you can't?" I press.

Oliver stands, hands Charlie to Ethan—who doesn't look like he knows the first thing about babies—comes around the desk and up to me. Way too close up to me. He opens the box and holds up the ring. It's a pretty gold band with a heart-shaped diamond. It catches the lights, rainbows dancing in its depths. It's stunning.

Staring at me the whole time, Oliver slowly slips the ring up my ring finger on my left hand.

Call it what you will—God, fate, destiny, or some other cosmic force—but the ring glides easily over my knuckle. An absolutely perfect fit.

Oliver squeezes my hand but keeps me pinned in place with those deep emerald eyes of his. "Well, look at that."

"It fits." I lick my lips. Why am I so nervous all of a sudden?

"Is this a yes, then?" He wags his brows—again, something reserved for fictional men because I've never seen a real guy pull it off before without looking creepy, yet Oliver makes it work—and tugs me closer. "In two weeks, we're going to be engaged?"

"I guess so."

"Wow, you sound so in love." Ethan chimes in, startling me. I forgot he was here.

I step back. "I'll work on it."

Oliver chuckles and gestures to his desk with the papers strewn across it. "You apparently convinced Mother, or she wouldn't have had that thrown together."

Glaring at the manilla folder, I cross my arms. "I'm making one thing very clear, here and now, Oliver Markel."

His brows hitch up.

"I'm doing this for Charlie."

"Okay." He shoves his hands into his pockets.

"And I'm *not* going to fall in love with you."

"Okay," he says again.

I nod once, scoop up Charlie, and make a strategic retreat. My heart races in my chest as I hurry into the kitchen. Charlie stares up at me, her big brown eyes questioning. I'm shaking. I shouldn't do this. But I am. I gulp. This is dangerous. Because when Oliver said *okay* it really sounded like he meant *we'll see*. And that's not good for me and my heart which I'm determined to keep caged. I don't need to get shoved away again. If anyone's going to do the shoving, it's going to be me.

For your heart's sake, keep Oliver at arm's length. Always at arm's length.

Chapter Sixteen

Oliver

"Well, she's fun." Ethan crosses his arms and leans back with a smirk. "I can see why you're smitten."

"I am not smitten."

Ethan chuckles. "I'm sorry, my dude, but you are. You won't even *look* at any of the women at work. Why are you proposing to this one?"

"It's an act. It's not real." But even as I say the words, my chest tightens at the lie. Because...dagnabbit, it's realer than I want it to be. I like Emily. She's been here when no one else has. She's cheering me on in fatherhood—something I never really expected to need. She's caring, kind, quick to laugh and tease. She's got a zest for life unlike anyone I've ever seen, and yet...

There are walls. I can sense when she slams the door on a conversation we're traveling towards. There are layers to Emily Fitzpatrick. And I've never wanted to peel back anything more in my life.

Ethan rolls his eyes. "Mhm, okay, sure. Whatever you say, man."

I pluck at the buttons on my Henley. *Yeah, whatever I say.*

This relationship needs to stay firmly in the *friends* category. Or better yet, *professional*. I can't go falling in love with the nanny. I can't and I won't.

Ethan's voice rings in my ears, *Mhm, okay, sure. Whatever you say, man.*

I look down at the ring box. A sinking sensation curls in my stomach.

I am in so much trouble.

● ● ● ● ● ● ●

Ethan and I chat for a bit about more work stuff, keeping far away from the topic of Emily and the engagement ring she still has on her hand.

We might not bring it up while talking, but my mind is in an infernal loop.

My ring.

On her finger.

It's like a primal part of me is claiming her. She's *mine*. My woman, the woman I want by my side for the rest of my life.

Ridiculous. Because I *don't know Emily*. She could be...anyone. I might wake up one morning and discover I hate the way she chews, or the way she cooks, or even the perfume she wears.

No, not that last one. I'll never grow tired of the perfume she wears. It smells like a snickerdoodle—all vanilla and cinnamon and sweetness. Just like Emily.

For the love, this is really not good. Not good at all.

I walk Ethan to the door. "Bring the paperwork for that client to my office Monday, and I'll see what I can do."

"Thanks, Oliver." He shoves his hands in his coat pockets and glances over my shoulder. "And for the record, I think you two would actually be a really good couple. You know, if you do end up falling in love."

He winks—the little punk—before turning and heading for his car.

"What does he know about love?" I mutter as I close the door. Rubbing my chin with my palm, I stalk toward the kitchen.

Music is going and I lean against the doorframe and watch as Emily, holding Lottie on her hip, spins around the kitchen to "Ob-La-Di, Ob-La-Da" by The Beatles. Every time there's a *brah* she hops, earning a deep belly laugh from Lottie.

The song ends, and I clap. Emily turns, her eyes widening before she chuckles sheepishly. "Sorry, did we bother you?"

"No, not at all. Ethan just left."

"Oh, okay. What would you like for dinner?"

"Actually, can I join the dance party?" I step into the kitchen and toward the girls.

Emily bites her lip. "Sure. Let me find a song."

She shoves Charlotte at me. I cradle her in my arm as I peek over Emily's shoulder. "How about a Christmas song? One we can jump to. I haven't heard her laugh like that."

Emily twists, looking over her shoulder at me. "She hasn't really laughed like that for me before, either."

"You must be pretty special then, Emily."

Her eyes flick over my face before she turns back to her phone. Soon, "What Christmas Means to Me" blasts through the house speakers. This is the Pentatonix version, and I freestyle it around the kitchen like Charlotte and I are on *Dancing with the Stars*. Certain parts, I hop, making Lottie giggle and I can't help but laugh with her. Her brown eyes sparkle in the lights. Her cherub cheeks dimple, her toothless smile lightening my soul. Moments like this are why I'm fighting Mother. This laughter and light in this little girl's eyes are worth every bit of stress. She's feeling loved in a way I can honestly say I've never felt—not by friends and certainly not by family.

The song ends and I'm gasping for breath. Emily laughs, her eyes aglow with...something. Joy? Admiration? Just...happiness? I don't know but I want to keep making this expression appear, it's better than the disapproving scowl she's been giving me lately.

"That was fun." Emily laughs, tucking her short hair behind her ears and clearing her throat. "But seriously, what do you want for dinner?"

"What do you think, Lottie?" I hold her up under her armpits and she shoves her fist in her mouth and squeals. "Yes, I think that's a splendid idea. Chicken nuggets and mashed potatoes."

Emily laughs again, shaking her head as she heads to the fridge. "With left over green beans."

I wrinkle my nose. "If you insist."

"I do." She turns from setting the bag of nuggets beside the stove. "What do you say to getting a Christmas tree tomorrow or Sunday?"

I pause after latching Charlotte's highchair tray into place. Not once in my life have I ever set up a Christmas tree. Part of me doesn't want to tell Emily this fact about myself. It's embarrassing. What parent refuses a Christmas tree to their one and only son? My parents, that's who.

"Oliver?" Her hand lands on my arm and I flinch. "What's wrong?"

"I've—I've never had a tree before."

She freezes. "Never ever?"

I shake my head. "My parents were allergic."

"But...not even a fake tree?"

I can't look into her eyes. Can't see the shock and disappointment I know will be there. My childhood was far from normal. I can't even say it was even in the range of peculiar. It was just sad. Sad and depressing.

When I don't reply to her, Emily sighs. "Well, then I'm just going to have to teach you about Christmas decorating, too."

I turn toward her. "No, Emily, it's really fine."

"It most certainly is *not* fine!" She fists her hands on her hips. "We're going to have a real Christmas here, Oliver Markel, or my name isn't Emily Jane Fitzpatrick."

"Is it?" I smirk as I hop up onto the counter, letting my feet dangle a few inches off the ground.

"Is what?" She's turned her back on me as she places two dozen chicken nuggets on the tray. She sways a bit, like there's a mystery tune floating around the kitchen that only she can hear.

"Is your name Emily Jane Fitzpatrick?" A traitorous thought jumps in my head when I catch sight of the ring still on her finger. I want to come up behind her and drag her to my chest, wrap my arms around her, and press a kiss right behind her ear. I choke on an inhale and hurry over to the sink to gulp a glass of water.

For the love, what is going on with me?

"You alright there, Oliver?"

"Yep," I croak. "Just dandy."

Dandy? What am I, an eighty-year-old grandpa?

Emily chuckles. "Okay. But what do you say about the Christmas tree?"

"Sure, how about Sunday? We could pick up lights and ornaments in town tomorrow."

"Oh yes!" She claps after she slides the tray into the oven. "They have fun ones in town! Several businesses make specialty ornaments for the holidays too!"

Her enthusiasm is contagious, and I smile. "Well, I'm looking forward to it."

My eyes snag on the ring. I want her to keep wearing it, but it will raise all sorts of questions tomorrow. Questions we can't have until the Christmas party.

3) Absolutely no romance is going to happen! Keep your feelings to yourself.

Too late for that. Way too late.

Chapter Seventeen

Emily

I'm getting ready for bed when I notice I'm still wearing Oliver's ring. Dang it, I forgot I had it on. How, I don't know. It just...it feels right. I take it off and look at it. The sparkly diamond, the cool gold band. It's beautiful—and absolutely what I would have picked out on my own.

With a muttered swear, I turn and head from the bathroom into what is now my room. The walls are painted a pale blue. A white quilted bedspread with tan accents is already pulled back, ready for me to tuck myself in. The book I'm reading—an epic fantasy with all the brother vibes—is on the nightstand along with a cup of tea. I need to hurry and get this ring to Oliver before my drink goes cold.

I step out into the hallway, only mildly self-conscious of my Christmas PJs. With red, white, and green flannel bottoms and a long-sleeve tee that says *Jingle All the Way*, they're not my most embarrassing of jammies, but they are close.

I knock on his door, and I hear a muffled, "One sec!"

Shifting my weight, I wonder what the heck Oliver will say. It's not like we're even a thing. But somehow it hurts to hand this ring back to him. But eventually I will have to. I'm not his, and he isn't mine. At all.

The door creaks open and Oliver leans against the frame with his forearms. Holy cannoli! He's missing his shirt. Again. If he was distracting on Tuesday, it's only worse after three days of getting to know him better and watching him soften to Charlie. The man is *fit* with a capitol *F*. My mouth goes dry, and I hold out my fisted hand where I'm clutching the ring.

His lips tick up. "What's this, a bug?"

"No! No, it's..." Why can't I force the dang word out? "It's the ring, Oliver. Figured you'd want it back until you give it to me at the party."

Oliver's smile vanishes. "Yeah, probably smart if we're spending the day with Molly and Susan."

I bite my lip. "You don't have to do this, Oliver."

"Yes." His eyes meet mine, shadowed in the dim light of the hallway nightlight. "I do."

My eyes flick to his lips and suddenly he's moving closer, setting his hands on my forearms, not looking away. I gasp, my hand settling on his chest.

Holy cannoli, is he going to kiss me? Am I going to stop him if he does? I don't know this man—not enough to kiss him! Do I?

His chest rises and falls a touch too quick; his pupils dilate. He ducks his head, our foreheads touching. This is why leaving my room was a bad idea. I can't let him kiss me. I can't give in.

Guard your heart!

"Are you certain there's not a wife in the attic?" I whisper.

That breaks the spell. He steps back, tearing a hand through his hair with a mirthless chuckle. "You can check if you want."

I shiver, his actions causing nervous energy to course through me. "I'm good. I trust you."

He raps his knuckles against the doorframe, not looking at me at all now. "Glad one of us does."

What does he mean by that?

Before I can ask, he says, "Night, Emily." And then he's gone, the door closed firmly in my face.

I exhale sharply and hurry back to my room. Leaning against the closed door, I shake away any lingering thoughts about kisses, shirtless men, and falling for my boss. Crawling beneath the covers, I sip my tea, read, and then drift slowly off to sleep.

Charlie's scream wakes me up at two in the morning. I stumble from my bed, almost face-planting when my feet get tangled in the sheets, and hurry to her room. Only, when I get there, no one is up. Charlie's pacifier bobs and her fists are curled up by her cheek.

Another moan—or cry? I don't know what to call it—echoes and I realize it's coming from *Oliver's* room.

Quandary number one—does my job description give me the right to barge into his room?

Quandary number two—do I even care?

Another moan and I'm stepping through his door. There's no nightlight, making it hard to see. I left my phone in my room, so that's no help. I blink, letting my eyes adjust as only a bit of the hall light illuminates Oliver. He's tossing in the middle of a king size bed. The blankets are twisted around his arms and legs, and even with only the faint light, I can see he's sweaty.

"No," he moans as he rolls to his stomach. "No, I'm not the right one."

My chest aches. "Oliver?"

"No!" He sits up, his eyes open, but unseeing. "No, I'm not the one, Gavin! I can't do it."

His words hold that tone—that sleepwalking cadence I know so well from Susan. He's shaking, clearly terrified of whatever he's seeing in his mind.

"Oliver, it's only a dream." I inch closer to the bed and when he holds out his hand, I take it.

Sleepwalking Oliver is strong *and* persistent! He pulls me forward and wraps his arms around my waist. His forehead rests against my shoulder as his body shivers. "I can't do this."

Supremely uncomfortable but also...not, I rub my hand in small circles against Oliver's back. "You'll be okay. You've got people all around you. We'll help you."

His arms tighten, pulling me closer as he somehow manages to swing his legs over the bed's edge. "I can't do it."

I smooth my other hand against the back of his head, tears pricking my vision. Will he even remember this? Do I want him to?

Slowly, I tip his face up to meet mine, pressing a kiss against his forehead. "You can, and you will. You'll never be alone, Oliver."

For a moment, I think he's woken up. But then his eyes roll back and he's asleep again. Carefully, I help him lay down. Smoothing out the covers, I tuck him in. For a few heartbeats, I wonder what it would be like to be the one to comfort him after every nightmare. Wonder about what it would feel waking up tucked against his side. Wonder about raising Charlie with him, being the shoulder to cry on, the listening ear.

And then I let all my wonderings pass away, like a beautiful dream that splinters and turns to dust when the sunshine touches it.

Because that's all this can be. A dream. A beautiful dream, but a dream, nonetheless.

I'm pouring cereal the next morning and stifling a yawn in tandem. I didn't sleep well after calming Oliver down from his nightmare. My lips tingle when I think about pressing them against his forehead. Holy buckets. I can't do this. I shouldn't have done it in the first place, but in that moment it felt right.

Now, a million moments later, my brain is wondering what *Oliver's lips* would feel like against mine.

So much for no feelings. A fat lot of good that contract was.

"Morning."

I look up from my bowl of granola as Oliver walks over. He's dressed in a green sweater with khaki dress pants. His hair is artfully disheveled, and he smiles when he sees me.

Does he remember last night? Well, I'm certainly not asking him! Nope.

"How'd you sleep?" I ask, gesturing to the cereal.

Oliver nods and I pour him a bowl as he says, "I slept okay. Had some dreams though."

I look up from stirring my cereal. He's staring at me, a peculiar look on his face. "Oh?"

"Yeah." He shakes himself, smiles, and spoons a bite of granola into his mouth.

Buckets. He remembers. But does he think it's a dream? Oh please, no. Which is worse? Oliver remembering me in his *bedroom* and *kissing* him, or thinking it was all a dream? Suddenly I'm no longer hungry.

Charlie squeals, dragging my spiraling thoughts from Oliver to her. "Hey, big girl! All done eating?"

She claps her banana covered hands.

Oliver chuckles. "Charlotte!"

She looks over at him and Oliver runs his fingers through his hair.

"Oliver!" I cry when Charlie mimics him.

He laughs, and Charlie grins, clapping her hands again.

I want to throttle Oliver, but a look at his face, with his green eyes sparkling with joy that Charlie copied him, I can't be angry. A smile of my own appears and I shake my head. "Guess it's time to clean you up, Charlie! Otherwise, we're going to miss everything in town."

"Are they lighting the tree in the daylight?" Oliver asks, taking another bite of his breakfast.

"No, but we've got to go shopping for all the decorations for the tree we're getting tomorrow. Plus, have you ever been to Yellow Submarine?"

"No?" Oliver's brows raise. "What in the world is that?"

I laugh. "It's only the best sandwich shop in the Midwest."

"Is it now?" He's teasing me, I know from the little smirk.

"Yeah, it is." I jut out my chin. "And if you continue to be a turd, I'm not paying."

He chuckles. "Emily, let me pay for lunch today, okay? We're dating, after all." He winks and my stomach sinks.

I should probably warn Molly and Susan. But another part of me doesn't want to. Telling them means it's only a ruse. And even though I know this isn't real, I want to live in my blissful delusional state for a while longer.

Chapter Eighteen

Oliver

"I can't do it."

Emily's lips against my forehead.

"You can, and you will. You'll never be alone, Oliver."

What a dream that had been. At least, that's what I think it is. There's no way on earth Emily came into my room to calm me down.

Part of me wants it to be real. Her whispered promise of me not being alone on this journey warms me, like cocoa on a frosty morning, sliding through me and spreading out into my limbs.

I watch Emily head out of the kitchen, Charlotte held an arm's length away as she hurries to the bathroom. I should probably help. Maybe I can get the kitchen cleaned up?

Connecting to the house speakers, I pump out "Wonderful Christmas Time" by Paul McCartney. Judging from all the Beatles attire I've seen Emily wear, I imagine she'll be appreciative.

"I love this song!" she screams down the stairs.

"I figured!" I holler back with a laugh.

The dishwasher is loaded and running by the time Emily comes back. Charlotte is propped on her hip, diaper bag and massive purse over her shoulder, and coat draped over her arm. A blush pink hat is on her head, her short hair framing her face adorably.

"Ready?" She looks up at me then quickly looks away. Her cheeks color to match her hat.

I grab Charlotte from her arms. "Yep! Let me drive today."

She looks up, brows pinching together.

"If we're dating, it's normal, Emily." I really hate that she won't let me call her *Em*, but I'll abide by her wishes. For now. Once that ring is on her finger, hopefully she'll tell me why she won't let me call her *Em*. I'll get her to tell me whatever is hiding behind those hazel eyes.

"I know it's normal." She huffs like I'm being completely ridiculous. "But do you have a car seat base?"

"I do. The seat I bought came with two, because I figured I'd need one and so would Lottie's nanny."

"Good." She hikes the straps of the bags further up her arm. Charlotte squirms, her little beige overalls making it hard to get a grip on her. They're warm, I can feel the thickness of them, and I'm guessing they might be fleece lined.

"Where did she get these?" I ask as we head toward the door.

"I bought them." Emily grins. "I have an obsession with baby clothes."

I chuckle. "She looks adorable."

Emily's smile grows as she pulls out a hat that matches her own and tugs it onto Charlotte's head. "Now she's ready to explore Cloverfield!"

Emily opens her car door and grabs the car seat.

As she does that, I press a kiss to Charlotte's forehead. She looks like a mini-Emily. Emily has on overalls today—although they're jeans instead of canvas. Both girls have on green thermal shirts, and Emily has cuffed her pant legs to show off her rubber ankle boots. Charlie has on little black socks that sort of look like Emily's boots.

"Ready?" Emily asks, holding the seat on her hip.

I punch in the code for the garage door, and it opens to my sports car. Emily sets the seat on its base. "Want me to buckle her in?"

I nod, unable to form words. The dream from the night before plays in my mind as I slide behind the wheel. This is ridiculous. I need to shake it. I'm spending all day with Emily and cannot let my sleep-addled brain get in the way. She's a friend. My friend. A good friend and that's all I'll let it be.

"Are you trying to strangle the steering wheel?"

I jump a little, turning to see Emily has joined me in the front of the car.

"Sorry." I smile and start the car, pulling onto the road as we head for Cloverfield.

"You okay?" she asks, leaning her elbow on the arm rest and inclining her body closer to me. I can smell her body spray.

You'll never be alone, Oliver.

Won't I? If she knew the course of my thoughts—the truth I won't even admit to myself—I guarantee she would run. I'd run. Because barely four months of knowing someone isn't enough to *know* someone...is it?

"Oliver? You're spacing out again and that combined with driving makes me very nervous."

"Sorry! Sorry, I guess I didn't sleep as well as I thought." I flash her what I hope is a convincing smile.

But if anything, Emily seems to look more concerned. "Why is that do you think?"

"I don't know. I told you I had some weird dreams." Dreams that would cause her to up and quit if she knew about them.

Her lip catches between her teeth for a moment before she asks, "Want to share them?"

I tap my finger on the wheel. "Not really. I don't want you to think I'm crazy."

She laughs, but it sounds airy, like she's run a marathon and is now trying to catch her breath. "I doubt I'd think that."

Should I tell her? She's trying to get to know me, but will this fact be too much? That I dream about her isn't *that* weird though, is it? Because besides my coworkers, whom I barely talk to on a good day, and Charlotte—who doesn't really count because she's an infant—Emily is the only person I interact with on a daily basis. It's normal to dream about her, right?

"I was dreaming about Gavin giving me Lottie and it wasn't great." I rub the back of my neck, keeping one hand on the wheel as we enter the more populated areas of Cloverfield. "In the dream, you showed up and calmed me down."

Emily leans away, turning to look out the window.

"Emily?"

"I—It wasn't a dream," she whispers, pressing her hands to her cheeks.

"What?" I ask, slamming on the brakes at a red light so I can turn to look at her. "What are you talking about?"

"I heard you crying out. Thought it was Charlie." She won't look at me. Her face is hidden by her hands. Hands which are trembling. "I came in and tried to wake you up, but you wouldn't so I said that it would be alright."

Wait...is she saying what I thought was a dream actually *did* happen? Did she...kiss me?

Nope, I don't want to know. Because the fuzziness of the dream is also layered with the memory of hugging her, pressing my forehead against her shoulder, feeling her hand rub my back—my bare back.

"Well, thank you for helping me." I clear my throat and startle when a car horn sounds. The light turned green while I was distracted by this conversation. We pull forward and find a spot to park at the edge of town.

"You're not mad?" she asks, twisting the hem of her scarf around her fingers.

"No, you were trying to help."

"How much...how much do you remember?" She won't look at me.

For the love, she did kiss my forehead, didn't she? Is this the reason for the awkwardness? Should I admit I remember it, or will that make it worse?

I go for a half-truth, though my conscience hates it. "It's all fuzzy. I remember that I hugged you."

"Sorry." She winces. "I won't let it happen again."

She reaches for the door handle, but I grab her arm. "Emily. It's fine. You helped me, and I appreciate it. More than you know."

Her face turns tomato red. It's adorable.

Hold up, nope! Not adorable. It's cute. No, that's Charlotte. Emily is...well, *adorable*. I can't ignore it. I'm attracted to this woman. More so than anyone else in the world.

And this is supremely problematic when I'm supposed to be fake dating her and eventually faking an engagement.

Should I tell her I don't want it to be fake? No, because she's been abundantly clear that a real relationship is not in the cards.

I'll have to be happy with friendship. Make it work. Because the thought of losing Emily is too much for me. And not just because I'll be out a nanny for Charlotte. No, this has gone so much deeper than that.

"Well, you're welcome." She pats my hand, dragging my thoughts back from the precipice I was standing on, and I let go of the death grip I had on her hand. "Let's get out there! There's a lot to see and do!"

I smile and climb out of the car, though my heart feels heavy. I shove away my morose thoughts and take the bundle of fabric Emily shoves at me.

"Put that on. You're going to carry Charlie today."

"Okay." I stare at it. "How do I do this?"

Emily rolls her eyes and takes it. She unfurls the bundle. I realize it's one giant piece of cloth. She finds a part with a tag and pushes it against my stomach "Hold it there."

I obey, and she gets up closer, wrapping the ends around my back and then over my shoulders.

"You cross it in the back," she explains, coming around to face me. "Then you cross it in the front."

She's close. So close. Heaven help me, I want to keep her this near forever.

Nope. Friends only, Oliver! Only friends.

My mouth goes dry, my ears ring, but I try my best to listen as Emily finishes explaining how to tie the sling.

"Then you tuck it into this part." She tugs on the tag and motions for me to follow her instruction. I obey. "Finally, you wrap it around the back, tie it, then bring it around the front and knot it."

She does it for me, and I am so thankful. If I had to do it, I would be fumbling with the knots forever.

"There!" She smiles. "Now to stick Charlie in!"

Emily turns toward the car, and I draw in a shaky breath. It's like ten degrees out, but I'm hotter than Hades. I wipe the sweat on my forehead with the cuff of my coat.

Get it together, Oliver. No time to have a mental breakdown.

Emily turns back with my baby girl and motions to the sling. "Tug that side out."

I pull on it and then Emily is back in my space along with Lottie's butt. Emily maneuvers Lottie's feet through the straps, then wiggles the baby down into the sling. The fabric goes up, tucking over her legs while leaving her arms free. Emily then tugs the fabric up on my shoulders to give Charlotte a bit more wiggle room.

It is strange, having Lottie attached to me this way. But I also like it. Emily smiles and I return it, reaching out to grab her hand.

It feels like an ice cube. How are her fingers not dead?

"Holy cannoli, your hands are warm!" She declares, curling her fingers into a fist so my hand completely envelops them.

"And yours feel like they should have frostbite."

She shrugs as we lock the car and begin to stroll toward main street. "They've always been that way. I've been told poor circulation ran in my dad's family, but that's from my very bitter mom's side so—" She abruptly cuts herself off with a shrug.

Interesting. That's the most she's talked about her family. I don't think I've learned anything new about Emily in the many months she's worked for me besides that she likes romcoms and the Beatles. And that's just from deduction, not because she shared it with me personally.

"What's something I don't know about you, Emily?" I ask now as we reach the center of town. The roundabout has a massively tall pine tree at its center. Its point, topped with a star, stretches up into the sky. Hydraulic lifts are around it, a couple people placing ornaments on the branches as people bustle down the sidewalks, clearly getting ready for the lighting that night.

"I'm nothing special." She swings our hands, stretching out her fingers so that they interlock with mine. "I'm a nanny. Former preschool teacher. I like kids, want to be a mom, and teach my kids at home. I want to just...love and be loved."

Are her cheeks red? From that admission or the cold, I'm not sure.

"Sounds like a worthy dream," I comment as we stop in front of a boutique.

"You think so? Sometimes I feel like..." she pauses, looking up at me for a long moment. I don't move, I want to know what she's thinking. "Sometimes it feels like the world frowns at it."

"And? Why should you care what the world thinks?" I chuckle. "The world has no room to judge you. It's a mess."

"True." Her hold on my hand tightens. "But it's hard when so many people in my life seem to voice my innermost thoughts. The negative ones."

"They're not worth listening to, Emily."

"They're family," she whispers, staring into the window display.

"Who—"

"Emily!" We turn to see a woman running down the street, a man at her heels. She's petite but carries herself like a force to be reckoned with.

"Molly!" Emily drops my hand and pulls her friend into a hug. "I've missed you!"

"It's hasn't even been a week." Molly laughs, meeting my gaze over Emily's shoulder.

The man—who I know to be the one and only Tanner Bradshaw—catches up and rubs at his knee. "Mols, I can't run like that without warning."

"Sorry!" She doesn't sound the least bit sorry as she wraps her arm around his waist.

"Oliver." Tanner nods my way, which I return.

"You know him?" Molly asks.

Tanner drapes his arm around Molly's shoulder. "He was part of my PR team. Speaking of"—he looks at me and smiles a touch sheepishly— "Not to bring up work on a day off, but I was approached by a baking contest. Once our engagement pictures were posted online, *Sweet'o'Rama* asked if we would be interested in being the award for their contest."

"How can you be the award?" Emily asks. Her arms are crossed, meaning I can't recapture her hand.

"Cakes, cookies, and cupcakes for our wedding!" Molly claps. "We were thinking it could be good publicity for the town."

Tanner nods. "Cookies as favors that are hockey themed but elegant, to fit Molly's vision."

"A cake for us that strictly fits the wedding theme." Molly interjects.

"And then specialty cupcakes, with a flavor we love, for all the guests." Tanner finishes.

"Wow. You've thought this all out." My head is spinning just *hearing* about this undertaking, let alone being the person who has to create it under all that pressure. No thank you. The thought alone sucks all the air from my lungs.

"We have." Tanner somehow tugs Molly closer. "But both Molly and I know a few bakers and cooks. It could be fun, too, if a few of our local bakers join the contest. Make it a Cloverfield and surrounding towns audition thing. That's why I want to talk to you about it, Oliver. As a marketing specialist, you'd know if this would help my image or not."

"Does your image even matter anymore?" Emily asks. "You're a high school hockey coach."

"It matters a bit, yeah. I'm still a hot topic." Tanner rolls his eyes. "But I am fading. I'd like to jump on this before I'm irrelevant. Also, a number of my teammates and staff are going to want to come so this will save Molly and me money too."

"Not that it's a huge point of contention." Molly chuckles. "You are relatively loaded."

"Hey, now! No need to go blabbing that around." Tanner laughs. "But yeah, I'll need to talk to you about that at some point, Oliver."

"Sure. Mother will be ecstatic that you're going to keep us on for a while." I laugh, but even I can hear the pinched edge to it.

Emily edges closer and slips her hand into mine. I squeeze it.

"Okay!" Her tone is cheerful as she turns toward the coffee shop. "Christmas decoration shopping can't happen without Sweetie's cocoa."

She tugs me forward. Molly and Tanner fall into step behind us.

"Is this a hard and fast rule, or just one of yours?" I ask.

Molly pipes up, "It's an Emily rule. Anything for hot chocolate."

"Always! Summer or winter, spring or fall." She grins up at me and I smile back. Charlotte waves her arms as *Rockin' Around the Christmas Tree* blasts out from the town speakers.

Emily dances a little shuffle down the sidewalk, and I spin her under my arm. She laughs and Charlotte squeals, making my smile grow. This is...fun. When was the last time I just had fun on a Saturday? I'm embarrassed to admit I can't remember.

I don't want to forget this feeling. This joy. Emily helps me relax, to enjoy the time I have and not worry about the next project, the next deadline, the next step. I can step back and breathe and know that it's okay.

"Productivity doesn't equal my worth, does it?"

Emily stops abruptly.

Oops. I hadn't meant to say that out loud.

Emily's eyes flash as she turns. She steps in front of me, keeping me from escaping into Sweetie's. "Molly, get us two candy cane hot chocolates, please?"

"Yep." The little bell jiggles as Molly and Tanner disappear inside.

"Now." Emily crosses her arms and glares at me. "Please repeat the question, Mr. Markel."

Chapter Nineteen

Emily

Oliver's mouth opens and shuts a couple times before he looks away. His chin rests on top of Charlie's head as she squirms.

"Oliver. Ask the question again, please."

Angry heat rips through me as he finally whispers, "Productivity doesn't equal my worth, does it?"

"No!" I stomp my foot, righteous indignation hitting me square in the chest. "Who's telling you this bull crap?"

"I—well, I grew up that way, that's all." He blows a raspberry as he exhales, making Charlie laugh and a little of my temper fade.

"Mother and Dad wanted me to work hard and excel. If I didn't, it meant I was doing something wrong. I had to be at the top. Do the best."

"And that equaled your worth?" When he nods, I snort. "Ridiculous."

He smiles sadly. "Yeah. It is."

"But..." I hesitate.

"Ask. Please. I want to share this with you, Emily."

Butterflies erupt in my stomach. I turn to look out over the street, unable to meet Oliver's gaze.

"Emily?"

"What made you realize this?" I blurt.

Silence is the answer I'm given. Stupid question. Ducking my head, I turn toward Sweetie's. Out of the corner of my eye, I can see Oliver's hand creep out to clasp mine.

"Don't," I whisper, not understanding my head nor my heart right now. I'm honored he trusts me, but I'm not sure I'm worth it. Not sure I deserve it. I'm playing along with this, but am I playing with our hearts? They're not an easy thing to fix. If I share too much with Oliver, give away a piece of myself, what's to say it doesn't get ground to dust? It's happened over and over. Each new home, each new relationship, each new school. I'm not ready to get messed up even more.

I need one hundred percent or nothing. This halfway limbo is killing me. I'll be friends, but friends with limits and boundaries and walls. I'm not letting Oliver sledgehammer his way into my heart. He may be attractive. I may like teasing him and love his goddaughter to pieces. But I will not, cannot, love the man before me.

Not doing it.

"It was you, Emily."

"No. Oliver, forget the question." I yank open the door and meet Molly at the counter.

Sweetie grins at me, but it slowly melts into a frown of concern. "*Stai bene*, Emily?"

Are you alright, Emily?

No, no I'm not. I don't understand this sadness in my heart, this longing to open up to my boss, of all people. A man who could just as soon cut and run as stay and care. Sure, Tanner ran from Cloverfield and Molly then came back, but this is different. That was a one-time thing and now they're getting married.

I've been left behind over and over. There's something about *me* that drives people away. So, if I just don't give any of myself—my true self—to them, they won't leave.

Simple.

Lonely.

But I'm not willing to risk it. Not willing to let loose despite my outward façade of nonchalance and goofiness.

"*Sto bene.*" I force a smile and gesture to Oliver who's come up behind me. "*Questo è* Oliver."

Sweetie doesn't look like she believes me. Neither does Molly if the lowered brows are any indication. But Sweetie turns her smile toward Oliver and Charlie and greets them. "*Benvenuti da Sweetie's, signore* Oliver."

He turns to me for a translation.

Although, embarrassingly, I'm not one hundred percent on all the words. "I think that means, *Welcome to Sweetie's, Mr. Oliver?*"

Sweetie claps, her bright smile making her dark brown eyes dance. "*Molto bene!* You've been practicing, I see."

"*Sì.*" I chuckle. "But I'm not *molto bene.* I'm not even sure I'm *bene.*"

"*Buono,*" Sweetie corrects.

"See? Horrible." I flinch when Oliver's hand brushes my arm. "Cocoa ready yet?"

Sweetie's astute gaze flicks between us before she slides two cups toward us. "Candy cane cocoa or in Italian, *cacao di canna da zucchero.*"

"Yeah, I'm not attempting that," I state wryly.

It earns me a chuckle. "Have fun shopping."

"Thanks, Sweetie!" Molly smiles and waves. Then, she breathes into the hole on the lid of her caramel latte. "Heavenly."

"Nope," Tanner disagrees as he sips his vanilla latte. "This is the divine beverage of choice."

They begin to tease and play bicker as we step back into the frosty air and toward Vintage Vestige. I frequent this shop a lot. The owner—Mary McCaw—created a store that is rustic in feel but still modern. Homemade candles, lotions, and body sprays that are warm and cozy sit on shelving that Mary refinished and weathered herself. T-shirts with original designs that say things like "Here Comes the Sun" and "Let It Be" (fellow Beatles fanatic, anyone?) are proudly displayed in frames along the top of the shelves and on racks throughout the shop. She has antique books and records in cool old crates while canvas totes and macramé hang on hooks mounted to the walls.

Walking into Vintage Vestige feels like a hug! It is warm and inviting and perfectly cozy. I pick up a little basket by the door as I breathe deeply of lavender, vanilla, and pine.

"Wow, it smells like..." Oliver trails off when I kept walking further into the store.

I make a beeline toward the candles and perfume shelf. Scanning the offerings, I grab my favorite body spray. I squirt a sample pump onto my wrists, before placing the bottle into my basket along with my favorite candle. With a sigh of contentment, I turn toward the Christmas tree in the center of the small shop. Homemade macramé ornaments and hand-painted designs on wooden disks decorate the tree. They range from cream-colored to reds and greens.

"Pick some, Oliver. They'll brighten up your living room."

He chuckles and plucks one off the tree that says, *God bless us, every one* and has a black silhouette of Tiny Tim on Scrooge's shoulder. He tosses it into my basket.

"I like it, even if it is black." I state. He shakes his head when I grab one that has the Grinch in leg warmers and a sweatband and says, *jazzercise* in sparkly silver paint over his head.

"Classic." He finds a glass ball that has the National Lampoon house with its millions of twinkle lights painted on it. Inside is glitter that Mary has somehow glued to the sides of the ball so that it sparkles just as brightly as the house from the movie.

I grab one with the *Home Alone* house and Marv and Harry's blue van in the drive.

"You're going to buy me out, Emmy Girl."

Mary stands beside us. She can't be a day over sixty, with faint age lines around her mouth and eyes. She's a widow, I know. Her husband had a massive heart attack five years ago and passed away at the young age of fifty-eight. But he'd left her enough money to start her dream—a boutique that hosts all her crafts and passions. She's a natural at running it too. Everyone loves Mary McCaw.

I wrap her in a hug. "How are you doing?"

The holidays are rough for Mary as they are for a lot of people—something I relate to but don't let affect my celebration. It's hard, but each year I'm alone, it gets a bit easier.

Mary smiles, her brown eyes glassy. "This year has been the best yet. Especially since you're here!" She gestures to Oliver. "And who is this handsome stranger?"

Before I can reply, Oliver holds out his hand. "Oliver Markel, ma'am. I'm Emily's boss."

I raise a brow. Not boyfriend this time? Are we only pretending for his mother then? I'm confused, but I don't have the emotional bandwidth to deal with that right now.

"Oh right! You're Charlie's godfather!" Mary grabs Charlie's hand and shakes it. "Glad you finally brought in Daddy Ollie."

Oh, just kill me now! Mary wasn't supposed to tell Oliver the nickname I'd given him! I only used it like twice with her around and even then, I was saying it to *Charlie* not Mary!

"*Daddy Ollie*, eh?" Oliver's grin is wicked.

Oh, buckets! This isn't good.

"Yep! Easier than *Oliver* for Charlie." I smile, and it feels large, fake, and painful. "Are there any other ornaments you want?"

Oliver is still grinning—meaning I wasn't as successful in changing the subject as I'd hoped—when he turns to Mary. "Do you do custom ornaments, by chance?"

As Mary launches into her spiel, I circle the tree. I find an ornament that says *Baby's First Christmas* and lay it in the little basket on my arm. A red macrame ornament with pearl beads woven into the design is next on the pile.

My eyes catch on a ball that's a blush pink. Mary has painted two pinkies locked together. Over the top, it reads *I'll Love You Forever,* while below the hands is *Our First Christmas*. Both are painted in a pretty swirly font. I look at Charlie and then over at Oliver. Mary still has her hand in Charlie's and the baby is being surprisingly docile. Oliver looks up and meets my gaze. It softens before he turns back to Mary, and I'm shocked that I can identify his expression so easily.

Tears—something I haven't dealt with in ages—attack me, and I suck in a sharp breath. *No, I will not do this. Not today. Not in front of my friends.*

I turn and thumb through the t-shirts, struggling to pull myself together.

A hand lands on my shoulder and I stiffen. "I don't want to talk about it, Oliver!" I hiss.

"Well, I'm not Oliver," Molly says in her worried voice. "And if you're that adamant, maybe you should?"

"No, I can't. And he keeps pushing and—" I groan. "Why did I think it was smart to move in?"

"I'm pretty certain a few of us voiced concern," Susan says, appearing at Molly's side. I'm not sure when she got here, but I'm glad to have her, even if she is scowling at Oliver and Tanner as they chat with Mary.

"I know. But I want to help Charlie." I bite my lip.

"Just Charlie?" Molly cocks her head to the side, her honey brown hair pouring over her shoulder. "Or Oliver too?"

I cross my arms. I wanted to help Oliver. I wanted to help him find his confidence, that heart of a father I see in his eyes every time he looks at Charlie. He just has to get past his insecurities and grab hold of it.

Is that my problem? Am I so scared to be hurt that I won't grab hold of any good thing that crosses my path?

Ugh! No, this is no time for introspection. I'm *fine*. I'm fine being Oliver's friend. His support and cheerleader. I don't need these annoying feelings to muddy the waters.

We're fine, everything is fine. Fine and dandy for the win.

Chapter Twenty

Oliver

Something is wrong, but I can't tell what with Emily's back to me. She gave me a look earlier, one of absolute terror. Low key panic is crawling up my spine. My relationship with Emily has to be on solid ground. I can't handle another problem right now, on top of everything else.

"So, what do you want on this ornament, Oliver?" Mary has her pen ready to jot down my idea.

"Can it say "Wonderful Christmas Time" across the top and the silhouette of the Beatles walking across Abbey Road?"

"Of course! Although it was just Paul who wrote that, you know."

I nod, not truly caring because I have a feeling the Beatles obsessed nanny will love it regardless.

Tanner leans with his hip against Mary's counter and nods toward the girls. "Sue looks like she's going to impale you with a stake through the heart."

I glance at the girl I've known since I was seven. "Yeah...we may have attempted dating in high school."

"Wait, really?"

"Yeah."

"What happened?"

"Nothing." I shake my head. I'm not telling Tanner about how my parents all but demanded I end things with Susan. While they were friendly with the Fentons, I wasn't to date their *daughter*. Of course not.

"Sure." Tanner draws out the words with an eye roll. "Well, paste on that marketing smile, Oliver. Here they come."

Emily won't look at me as she places the basket on the counter. I catch Mary's eye and press my fingers to my lips.

Mary winks at me before turning to Emily. "Ready, Emmy girl?"

"Yep."

A t-shirt lays on the top. It's gray with a yellow submarine on the front.

"That's cute." I point to it.

Emily smiles but it doesn't reach her eyes. What happened in the last twenty minutes to make her lose that sparkle? Frustration is mounting in me, but I don't say anything. It's not my place, is it?

Susan taps my arm and nods toward the door before striding out. I follow her.

Her hands are shoved into the pockets of her purple windbreaker, a floppy cream-colored beanie on top of her blonde hair. She glares at me. "What did you do to her?"

"What are you talking about?"

"She's been at your place one night and already she's falling apart. I'm no expert, but the common denominator is you."

"Are we talking about Emily or us? Because you still seem angry about senior year."

Susan's breath puffs from her lips in a scoff. "Of course, I am! I was going to *marry you*, Oliver! Oh, but one word from Mother dearest, and I'm not good enough."

"I never said that."

"No, you just dumped me."

I wince, hugging Charlotte to my chest. She's fallen asleep, her head tucked up by my shoulder. She's a comforting buffer between Susan's accusations and myself.

"So, what are you doing to my friend? Because I swear, Oliver if you hurt her like you did me, they won't be able to find your body."

"I'm not going to hurt her. I'm pretty sure she's hurting me." I mutter the last part but it's loud enough for Susan to catch.

"You like her?"

I nod, feeling like an absolute heel for admitting this to my ex-girlfriend. "She's ... different. Different in the best way. But I've already screwed this up, Sue. If you only knew what we're doing..."

"And that is?"

"Oliver? What are you doing out here?" Emily shivers as she steps out the door. "Holy cannoli! It's so cold."

I smile at Emily, surprised when she sidles up to me and slides her hand in mine.

Susan's brows go up.

I gulp.

I'm dead meat.

● ● ● ● ● ● ●

A few more boutiques later, and too many homemade ornaments to count, we're all piled into the Yellow Submarine sandwich shop. The place holds a yeasty scent mingled with the salty savory aroma of melted cheese.

Emily has relieved me of Charlie and is changing her in the bathroom as I place our order. Susan keeps sending me death glares, but Molly and Tanner are managing to rope me into conversation.

That band in my chest is back, drawing itself tighter and tighter around my lungs as I stand and wait for our sandwiches.

Susan slips to my side when Molly and Tanner wander over to the soda machine to get drinks. She hugs her coat and hat to her chest. "Our conversation isn't over. Are you two dating?"

"Sort of."

"*Sort of?* How does one *sort of* date?" When I flinch, Susan's mouth falls open. "Wait, are you *fake dating* one of my best friends?"

I shush her. "Yes! Alright? Mother caught me at the store with Emily, made assumptions based on a fake girl I fabricated to keep her off my back, and now Emily and I are a fake thing."

There is absolutely no need for her to know about the fake engagement plan, right? That will only make her angrier than she already is. I mean, her scalp is turning tomato red. If I mention that other factoid, she will erupt in a fiery mess. Yep, nope. We're not going there.

"And if she has real feelings?" Susan pokes my arm. Hard. "She falls hard and fast! Oh, Oliver, you're a heel, a tool! Absolutely horrible!"

"And if I have real feelings, too?" I hiss, done being accused. "If I'm falling for her even though she made it very clear there weren't to be *any* feelings? If Emily has feelings, and that's a big *if*, then this isn't one-sided, Susan. I like her. A lot. And I'm going to keep pretending to be *just friends* with her because that's all she wants, okay?"

Susan's eyes are very wide. She doesn't say a word, simply opens and closes her mouth a few times. Then she shakes her head. "Okay. But if you're smart?" She grabs her sandwich from the top of the display and cuts me a sideways glance. "You won't let *this* girl go."

We eat the absolute best sandwiches in the world. Warm, melty cheeses, savory meats, and the freshest tomatoes and onions.

I groan and pat my stomach. "You're right, Emily. Yellow Submarine is fantastic."

"Hear that, Dan?" she hollers at the owner, who is currently slicing some fresh bread for a customer ordering grilled cheese. "Oliver is in love!"

Heat climbs into my face at how accurate those words are.

Emily licks the crumbs off her lips and looks at her watch. "It's two o'clock. The tree lighting is at five."

"Want to come back to the house?" Molly offers. "We could watch a movie, Charlie can nap, and then we can head back here at five."

Emily looks at me and I shrug. "I'm game."

Susan is looking between us, but I can't make myself meet her gaze. Because I admitted it. I like Emily. A lot. And somehow knowing that someone other than myself knows that truth makes it more...real.

I stand and pick up Charlie. The little girl nestles down against me, her chubby fist grabbing the fabric of my jacket as her eyes start to slide shut.

"If we're doing this, we'd better hurry." I chuckle. "She's already half asleep."

"Aw, how precious!" Molly coos. "Okay, let's go."

We all head to our vehicles and Emily directs me to her old house.

It's quaint, and stepping inside, I see marks of all the girls. The sweet scent of fresh cookies from Susan, the stack of books and the leather briefcase that are Molly's, and the baby blanket and toys on the bench that were left here by Emily one time when she brought Charlotte over.

I smile as I shrug out of my coat and set the diaper bag by the door. Emily is already hurrying up the stairs with Charlotte, a diaper and wipes in her hand.

"Come into the living room, Oliver." Molly invites.

The living room is cozy. A television stands on the low table against the wall, a couch positioned before it with a love seat to the left. A fireplace takes up the far-right wall. They have a small Christmas tree in the left corner between the TV and the love seat and in front of one of the three windows that run along that wall.

Tanner presses a knob, and the fireplace turns on.

"Electric," Molly offers as she sits on the love seat. Tanner settles beside her and wraps his arm around her shoulders.

"What movie?" Susan asks as she crouches in front of the TV.

Molly and Tanner offer a few suggestions. I agree with Molly—the newest version of the Grinch with Benedict Cumberbatch is the best. Tanner wants the live action one with Jim Carrey and so does Susan.

So, it's up to Emily to pick.

Susan checks her watch. "I have to be at my booth by four so she better hurry."

I chuckle. "That's up to little Miss Lottie."

"Lottie?" Molly asks.

"My nickname for Charlotte."

"Cute," Tanner says, but he's staring at Molly.

Gross. Is that what I look like when I stare at Emily? It's kind of annoying if I'm being honest.

But it also shows how much Tanner loves the woman at his side. He can't stop staring at her. It brings a small smile to his lips, a light to his eyes. What would it be like to have the right to look at Emily like that? Not stolen glances that I feel guilty about, but long, lingering looks that mean I get to call her mine?

I rub my face and sigh. This isn't right. I shouldn't be thinking this. But I can't stop.

"Ready!" Emily calls as she skips into the room. She plops onto the couch by me and crosses her legs. Her knee brushes mine and I dare to set my hand on top of it. "What are we watching?"

"That is up to you," Molly states. "It's a tie between *The Grinch* with Benedict—"

"Cummerbund!" Emily claps. "Yes, that one!"

"You didn't hear the other option!" Susan protests, but Emily holds her hand up with a flourish.

"Nope. Don't need to. I want Benny Cucumber-Patch."

I snort. "Do you even know the poor man's real name?"

She sniffs. "Benedict Cumberbatch, thank you kindly. And messing up his name will always be an endearment to the Cumber-Community."

"Aren't they called Cumber—" Tanner starts before Molly slams her hand over his mouth.

Emily presses her hands against her cheeks. "That is not a word to be uttered in this house, sir! How dare you!"

"Sorry," he says through Molly's hand.

"You should be!" Molly wipes her hand on her jeans. "You just licked me, you little punk!"

Tanner grins, not looking at all repentant.

"Okay, so *The Grinch*." Susan rolls her eyes as she finds their digital copy and hits play. "I'm going to go make some popcorn."

"No! Let me." Emily jumps to her feet. "Oliver will help."

"He will?" When she gives me a glare, I grin and follow her out to the kitchen.

But when I reach her side, she has braced her hands against the counter, staring off into space.

"Emily?"

"What are we?" she whispers, her shoulders hunching. "Like, are we friends?"

"Sure. We're friends."

"Nothing more?"

My heart races as I inch just a bit closer. "Do you want us to be?"

"I don't know." Her voice catches and I see a sheen of moisture over her beautiful hazel eyes. "I don't want to let my guard down, but I should. I've told you things I've never told anyone. I'm scared that—"

I cup her cheek. "Emily, I'm not going to leave."

"You can't promise that." Her chin dips, her lip quivering. "My parents said that. And then there was the car crash."

I let my thumb drift over her cheekbone, relishing the smoothness of her skin as I struggle to put my words together. "I'm sorry, Emily."

"It's fine."

"No, it's not." My other hand ghosts up to cup her other cheek. "I don't understand. Not fully. But I've seen the void losing a parent causes. Lottie's parents left her, too. But there will always be someone to love and support you, Emily, just like you told me."

"Not for me. I've been alone for a long time." She knocks my hands away as she dashes away a tear. "Let's make popcorn."

She grabs a bag and shoves it into the microwave. Her arms cross and she angles so I can't see her face. Do I want to?

"Emily, what if I do want something more than friendship?"

The words are out, floating in the space between us—a space that feels supremely large even though it's less than a yard. I want to turn her around, kiss her slowly, show her this isn't fake. Not for me. Not anymore.

"You don't. Not with me, Oliver."

"How can you say that? You don't know me. You can't know what I like and dislike, Emily."

"That's just it! These feelings? They're from the emotional roller-coaster we've been on the last couple months. They'll fade. You'll get bored and I'll be cast aside again."

"Again?" I lay my hands lightly on her shoulders. She tenses. "Emily, what happened to you?"

"I can't—"

The microwave timer goes off, signaling the end of the first bag of popcorn.

"We'll talk later?" I ask.

She nods, grabbing the bag out and handing it to me. "Take this to everyone in the living room."

It's a dismissal. No ignoring her lack of eye contact and the stiffness to her being. I want to scream. It's obvious that the feelings are mutual. So why is she erecting a wall between us with the bright neon sign of *just friends* plastered to its side?

Chapter Twenty-One

Emily

"You don't know me. You can't know what I like and dislike, Emily."

My hands shake as I pull the second bag of popcorn from the microwave. Oliver doesn't know what he's talking about. He can't like me. His mother clearly doesn't. I'm not prim and proper and I'm nothing like what a multi-millionaire should have in a significant other. Not even mildly close.

I'm loud, I dance in the kitchen, I spill food all the time. I love kids and finger painting, sidewalk chalk and bubbles. I listen to the

Beatles loudly enough to break an eardrum, and I sing off key. I inhale romance novels and watch cheesy romcoms.

Why would Oliver ever want to date *me*? Better question: how can he even *pretend* to date me? And why would he claim to want something more?

I shove away the thoughts and flop into my spot on the couch. Only now, I'm squished between Oliver and Susan. Neither are comfortable, but it's better than sharing the loveseat with Tanner and Molly. They're not exactly watching the Grinch as he recalls his emotional eating trends.

I try to enjoy the movie, I really do. But all I feel is Oliver next to me. His shoulder brushes mine and electric tingles race down my arm and up into my chest. I don't want my stupid body to react this way. Not to Oliver. Not to *anyone*. I'm not ready for this. I don't want the walls to come down. Do I?

I glance at Oliver out of the corner of my eye. What if Oliver is worth letting my walls down for? What if he isn't going to shove me off onto someone else when things get hard? What if…what if he really wants to work at this?

My phone buzzes and I glance down.

Uncle Lewis?

"Excuse me." I stand and move toward the kitchen.

"Want me to pause it?" Susan asks.

"No, it's fine." I retreat to the kitchen. "Hello?"

"Emmy? This you?"

"Yeah, Uncle Lewis." I try not to think of the last time I saw him. He basically said he and Aunt Pricilla no longer wanted me to live with them and that I was going to go live with Nanna. I was fourteen—my third home in as many years since my parents had died.

"What's wrong?" I ask. He wouldn't call me unless it was an emergency.

"Nanna died last night."

My knees buckle and I fall hard onto the yellow barstool. "What?"

"Yeah, she's been on the brink for about a week. Old dame finally kicked the bucket."

I close my eyes and will my emotions to settle so I don't go off on my uncle. Not that he deserves my respect. Not with a comment like that.

"Why didn't anyone call me? Did no one think that maybe I'd want to say goodbye?" My voice cracks and I clear it. "When's the funeral?"

"The funeral will be Monday. We thought it best not to bother you. Nanna mentioned you'd been caring for a little girl, and we know how much you adore kids."

"Still..." I trail off, not certain where I was going with the conversation anyways. "I'll try and make it. What time Monday?"

He gives me the details. The location, what to wear, when to be there. I feel numb, like I'm not really hearing this. How is Nanna gone? She was pivotal in my teen years, the one relative who hadn't shoved me off on someone else when I got to be too much. She kept me grounded; she raised me. How her sons turned out so absolutely horrible when she'd been a ray of sunshine is beyond me.

I hang up and stay perched on the barstool. I can't move, can't find it in me to make it back to the living room. I just sit there, silent tears blazing trails down my cheeks. She's gone. I didn't get to say goodbye. Didn't get to say thanks. Didn't get to hold her hand.

"Emily? What's wrong? Are you okay?" Oliver's voice wraps around me like a hug, and I suddenly don't care that I'm not what he needs. Not perfect. Not what he should want.

Because right now, he's exactly what I need and absolutely what I want.

I fling myself at him. Hold on like he's all that's keeping me on the ground. A great sob explodes when his arms slide around my waist, tight and solid, and he hugs me back. He doesn't know what's going on, but he doesn't seem to care. He holds me while I cry.

And boy, do I cry. I breathe in his scent. He smells like a forest—mossy, woody, fresh. His light stubble brushes my temple, and he draws me closer as my sobs taper off into the occasional hiccup.

"What's wrong?" His words rumble in his chest, and I let my eyes slide closed, not ready to face reality.

"Nanna died. And no one bothered to tell me she was even sick." My voice shakes, like one more word will have the tears pouring out in in fresh, unending waves.

"Emily." My name sounds like an apology that I'm so glad he isn't saying. I don't want platitudes that are what you're *supposed* to say. I just want him here, holding me. I don't want him to let go.

We stand that way for a little longer before Oliver eases me back. "What do you need?"

"Monday off. The funeral is at eleven in Highland."

"I'm coming with you. You shouldn't be alone for this, not with your family."

"But someone needs to watch Charlie."

"I will." I turn to see Susan standing there, her lips pressed into a thin line. "Oliver's right. You shouldn't be alone."

"But what about your cookies? Don't you have like ten dozen you have to make for that Christmas bazaar?"

"Yes, and they can wait for an afternoon. Besides, Molly will be off work soon for the holidays and I can rope her into helping."

"I really can go alone, you know."

"I know." Oliver's hands are still on my waist. Somehow, I didn't noticed until just now. "But you're not going to. I'll be there for you, Emily. No matter what."

No matter what. Does he really mean that? Or are they just pretty words that will be revoked the moment he realizes how much work I really am?

The tree lighting that evening is fun, but a bit depressing with the news of Nanna hanging over me. She's gone, and I can't bring her back.

Oliver tangles his fingers with mine. He keeps looking at me like I may combust at any moment. It's possible, but it will be in a flood of tears rather than flames. Although I am righteously ticked at my uncles. None of them could bother to call me and tell me that Nanna was sick and *dying?* Of course not.

Charlie is quieter than normal too. I wonder sometimes how much empathy the little girl holds in her. She seems to know things she shouldn't at only six months. She watches as the town counts down and the tree lights spiral to life. It starts at the lowest branch and spirals to the star, bathing the roundabout in the soft yellow glow of the twinkle lights.

"Beautiful." I breathe out.

"Yeah." Oliver agrees, but when I turn, he's staring at me. "Really beautiful."

Holy cannoli, Oliver is looking at me the way Flynn looks at Rapunzel in the lantern scene. He's not allowed to do that! He's real—flesh and bone. But I can't ignore the way his green eyes reflect the lights, the way his blond hair seems even brighter in the glow.

"Stop that." I tug my hand free and hurry toward Susan's cookie cart.

Susan's brows hop up when she sees my flushed cheeks. "You okay?"

After having my meltdown in the kitchen, I came back and told everyone what had happened to Nanna. It was hard, but Oliver kept his arm around my shoulders the whole time. Somehow that helped me through.

And now he's being so sweet. So attentive. I don't need it, but I like it. I don't deserve it, but he's giving it anyways.

I'm the one who's supposed to be helping him, so why does he keep breaking down all my walls and wrapping me up in what is basically a hug for my emotions? They don't scare him. If anything, he keeps getting closer and closer with each one he sees. But what happens when he sees my anger? It's ugly, large, and every now and again involves a flying breakable. Or how I retreat when I'm scared? I can be both bold and terrified in turn, and it's not easy to keep up with.

"I'm fine," I say to Susan. "Four of your sugar cookies, please."

"Buttercream frosting?" she asks, already picking them up and putting them in the white paper bag with her hand stamped logo.

"Yes. Sugar cookies without it are a travesty."

Susan chuckles and hands me the bag. She doesn't let go when I take it. Instead, she makes me meet her eyes when she says, "Oliver is a good man. He's trying to help you and I believe he could love you a lot if you let him."

I can feel my hands start to shake. "I'm scared."

"You want to help Charlie. I think that may mean helping Oliver." Susan looks over my shoulder and I know she's looking at the man in question. "He's been hurt too, Em. But I know he loves big and hard and beautifully when given the chance. Besides, if anyone can stand up to Pricilla Markel, it's you."

"I can't do this. I live with him and what if—"

"What ifs? They're not worth it." Susan leans her forearms against the counter of her booth. "I think the very best things in life happen when we jump in, feet first, running. I think it's choosing to make the best of it, regardless of the outcome. And that it can be really beautiful. You weren't looking for it, but it found you. Accidentally? Maybe. But what an adventure you'll have if you choose to embrace it."

"When did you become so wise?" I grumble.

Susan chuckles. "Spinsterhood, I suppose."

"You're not a spinster. There's someone out there for you."

"Maybe." She smiles but it doesn't reach her eyes. "But what are you going to do, Em?"

"There's the question of the hour." I huff a sigh.

And the frustrating part?

I have absolutely no idea what the answer may be.

Chapter Twenty-Two

Oliver

Emily is walking back toward Charlie and me with a paper bag. "I got cookies for us."

"Thanks."

She won't look at me as we munch on the sugary treats. Her eyes stare out at the tree as people mill around the booths. Her mind is a million miles away. I want to lasso it, bring it back to the present and to me.

I finish my second cookie and dust the crumbs off on my pant leg. Emily still won't meet my gaze as we throw away the bag and then stand awkwardly by the trash can.

Finally, I ask, "Emily, what's wrong?"

I mean, besides the obvious fact that her grandmother died, and her *lovely* family didn't bother to tell her. That'd upset anyone, I'm sure.

She stiffens. I brace for a scathing retort, and am flabbergasted when she says, "You—you can call me, Em, Oliver."

"Okay." It feels like a step in the right direction—if only I knew what that direction was. Am I heading up, down, left, right or somewhere else entirely? I feel like I'm swimming in the ocean at night, completely lost in a riptide of emotions that make no sense.

I reach out and take her hand. She doesn't pull away, but lets her hand hang, limp and cold, in my grasp. "You still haven't answered me."

"Let's go get the tree tonight. We can decorate it tomorrow." She turns and tugs me after her.

I follow as the frosty air begins to fill with fluffy white snowflakes. They swirl around, adding to the enchanted feel of the downtown district. Soft instrumental Christmas music plays through the speakers and the conversations around us seem hushed as we weave our way to the empty parking lot that's become the tree lot.

"Okay. Big or small?" Emily drops my hand and props her fists on her hips.

"If we're setting it up in the living room, taller." I shrug. "But I don't know if we have enough ornaments. Or lights."

I'm not even certain I have *any* lights. I wince. Way to win over the Christmas loving female at my side.

But this is who I am. I'm not big on decorations. I'm not used to celebrating *anything*, so I've never learned how to deck my halls with anything but what Mother tells me to. Life has always been about work and in a lot of ways, I fear it will always be work unless I can break out of the mold my parents have forced me into.

"Then a smaller tree." She walks through the paths and looks at each one. The overhead lights are catching the snowflakes' shadows and swirling them in the breeze. Emily's short hair blows about her face. She pulls her hat tighter on her head and continues moving.

She doesn't simply *walk*, though. It's as if she dances, gliding down the pavement and spinning with her partners, the trees. The snow in the streetlight's glow is a spotlight on her, illuminating the woman I'm beginning to fall for—her spirit and joy and inner glow that comes from doing what she loves.

"This one!" Emily holds her hands out like the old Will Smith meme to reveal the tree she has selected.

It's a short, white fir. Emily leans in and breathes deeply. She smiles—for real, this time—and turns toward me. "I know they're expensive, but it's sturdy and smells so good—"

"We're getting it." If only because *she* picked it out. "Money really isn't an issue, you know."

She looks away, fingering the soft needles of the tree. "I know."

"But..." I wait her out. I'm getting an answer.

"But I still like to be smart. It may not be an issue now, but it could be someday. I'm just..." She bites her lip.

"Just...what?"

"Oliver, what's—"

"Hello, Emily!" A portly older man all but waddles up and crushes Emily in a hug. His grin is wide enough that I can see it under his bushy white beard. The man could be Santa Claus.

Emily hugs him back, saying, "Hello, Kris."

"Kringle?" I ask.

The man rolls his eyes. "Haven't heard that one before. But the name is Spencer. Kris Spencer."

We shake hands and I say, "We'd like this tree please."

"Right away." He smiles at Emily. "Where's your car?"

"Oh, I actually rode with Oliver." She hesitates before slipping her frigidly cold fingers into mine again. "I'm helping him pick out his tree."

Kris's bushy brows raise. "Is this a boyfriend?"

I nod, not able to voice the lie. And is it, really, when I don't *want* it to be? I want to be Emily's boyfriend. Heck, I'm ready to propose for real and make her my wife. I've never felt this way about a woman. I've never felt this way about *anyone*.

But does *she* feel the same way?

"Okay, well, bring the car around and I'll get it tied up. Payment is up by the front too, so we can work it out there." Kris shoves his hand into his red Carhartt overalls and wanders off toward the front.

I fish my keys out of my coat pocket. "Why don't you go get the car? I'll pay Kris and help him get the tree to the front."

"Want me to take Charlie?"

"Sure."

We unwrap the sling and I hand her the little girl. Emily smiles and kisses her cheek. With Charlotte tucked in the crook of her arm, she heads off toward the road we parked on.

My heart warm and head full, I grab the tree and head off toward the front of the lot.

"That'll be $120." Kris fluffs his beard as I pull out my wallet and hand him six twenties. "You're Oliver Markel, aren't you?"

"Yes." I shift, not loving that people know who I am. It's weird. Zero out of ten, do not recommend being semi-popular. I can't even imagine what it's like for Tanner.

"Hm," is all Kris says in reply, wandering back off among the trees.

Weird. I turn and wait for Emily.

And wait.

And wait.

Fifteen minutes pass and I start to worry. With shaking hands, I pull my phone out and try calling her. Nothing. I try again and again, but it goes to voicemail each time.

What if something is wrong? It's busy down the road. What if she got mugged? Or hit? Or hit someone? What if something is wrong with Charlotte?

Or what if, like Gavin, the universe plans to take her from me? I can hear the crunch of twisted metal, can almost picture her broken, bloodied body on the side of the road.

My pulse roars in my ears, and I'm moving before I realize it, running around people. I try to not panic—and fail horribly. My palms are sweaty; I can barely see straight. The world has tunneled to one purpose—get to Emily and Charlotte and keep them safe.

I reach the spot where we parked to find Emily shutting the back door of the car. She turns when she hears my steps, but I don't slow my approach. Crushing her to my chest, I hold on with everything in me. She's here. Not bleeding, not broken. Whole and healthy and fine.

She is fine.

I will my heart to calm, my vision to clear of the fuzzy wetness of tears. I suck in a sharp breath and mumble, "You're okay."

Over and over, it's all I can think to say. I can't rid my mind of the image of twisted metal, blood, and carnage.

She is fine!

"I had to change Charlie." Emily eases back but doesn't step out of my embrace. She lays her hands on my chest, likely sensing I need to know she's standing here and not, you know, *dead.*

Embarrassment shoots through me at how I threw myself at her. What a moron. I can't look at her. I'm still shaking from the panic induced adrenaline rush. Even my voice is wobbly when I say, "Sorry. I jumped to conclusions when you didn't pick up your phone."

"It died." She stares at me. I can feel the heat of her gaze. "Oliver, this is about more than me not picking up the phone."

"I—" I cup her cheek, dragging my eyes to hers. I don't try to hide the tears that blur my vision. "I thought of Gavin. I panicked."

"Oh, Ollie." She's hugging me again, and I don't try to choke back the sobs. Why now, after everything, am I *crying*? I shouldn't be crying. Nothing is wrong. And even if it were, this isn't the time nor the place to break down.

But Emily doesn't chide me. Doesn't scoff and walk away. She doesn't tell me I'm an idiot for jumping to conclusions. She just holds me.

"I'm sorry I scared you," she says at last.

I sigh. "I'm sorry for freaking out."

"No, it's okay." She tightens her hold on me. "It was actually a little sweet."

"Don't patronize me." I find myself chuckling, not quite ready to step away from her. I like her hands around my waist and her head nestled under my chin.

"We're both a little bit of a mess today, huh?" she whispers.

"Yeah."

She looks up and our faces are so close. She's studying me, eyes full of worry and concern. How can she be so gentle with me? How does she tolerate a man on the edge of a nervous breakdown who flips out over not being able to reach his *nanny*?

But she can, and she is, and I am falling in love with her with every second that ticks by.

I lean my forehead against hers. "Emily?"

"Yes, Oliver?"

"If you don't stop me, I think I might kiss you."

"I think I'm not going to stop you if you do."

A gust of wind swirls around us, snowflakes twirling in a tiny snowstorm that contains only us. But I'm not cold. No, it's like there is fire rushing through my veins as I press my lips to Emily's.

She tastes like buttercream frosting and peppermint. Her arms slide up around my neck, pulling me closer as *she* deepens our kiss. If I was lost in a dark ocean before, I suddenly feel like I've been blasted into space. And unlike the ocean, I know right where I am, and I'm ready to explore.

It could have been hours, or minutes, or days, but finally Emily brings us back down to Earth as she breaks our kiss. Her cheeks are a pretty pink while her hazel eyes glow in the faint light. Gosh, but do I ever want to kiss her again.

"Oliver?"

"Yeah?"

"Is this real?"

"Yeah, Em. It's real." I press a peck to her forehead. "So, so real."

● ● ● ● ● ● ●

After we grab the tree, I drive us home. Emily holds my hand as she stares out the window. Her thumb absently traces over my knuckles, and it takes a severe amount of self-control to stare at the road rather than her.

"Oliver?"

"Yes, Em?"

"Are we actually dating?"

My heart jumps into my throat. "Do you want to?"

"Yes, but I also think…" She pauses. "But I think we need to get to know each other more too."

"I agree." I squeeze her hand. "But that's what dating is for, right?"

She slowly nods. "Okay."

"So, I can call you my girlfriend, now? The contract is null and void?" I can't help but tease her as we pull into the driveway and park the car.

"Absolutely not!" She tisks her tongue then laughs. "I will still have my own room and days off. The only thing null and void is the feelings." She leans over the console and grins. "Because I have caught feelings for you, Oliver Markel."

"Oh, you have, have you?" I lean closer, our noses almost brushing.

"Mhm." Emily's smile widens and then she turns before I can claim her lips. "I'll put Charlie to bed while you bring the tree in."

"Rude!" I call after her as she slams the door.

She comes around the front of the car and if Charlie wasn't snoozing, I would have honked the horn.

Emily knocks on my window. I glare at her as I unroll it. "What do you want?"

She giggles. "What do you think?"

"Oh, no! You lost your chance missy!"

I go to roll the window up, but Emily is already opening the door. She leans in, wrapping her arms around my neck but loses her footing. She falls into my lap—something I don't mind at all—and squirms around to regain her footing.

"I got you now, don't I?" I tease.

She stills, huffing as she glares up at me. "Will you help me?"

"Gladly." I chuckle. Managing to get my hand around her back, I get her into an upright position. But then, our faces are level. She's in my lap. And far, far closer than she ever has been before.

Chapter Twenty-Three

Emily

Holy cannoli. I'm sitting on Oliver's lap. Sure, it's not super comfortable with the steering wheel digging into my side, but...*I'm sitting on Oliver's lap!*

Warning bells and sirens are going off. We're supposed to be taking things slowly. Getting to know one another before throwing ourselves down the mountainside like Buttercup and Wesley in *The Princess Bride*.

But it's Oliver. I'm sitting on his lap, my hands pressed against his chest. I can feel his heart racing through his peacoat, and his emerald-green eyes are glowing in the faint overhead lights of the garage.

Holy buckets, I'm going to kiss him. Again. My hands raise so I'm cupping his cheeks, and he winces.

I freeze, suddenly worried he doesn't want me to close the distance and press my lips to his—mine are already aching for another taste of his.

"Your hands are cold," he whispers.

"Sorry."

"You don't sound sorry." His nose brushes mine. "But I don't really care about your fingers."

Oh dear. His voice has dropped further. I thought husky whispers were made up along with the plethora of other things fictional men do. But apparently, I've been dating all the wrong sorts of men. Oliver's husky voice? Yes, please, all day every day.

"You going to sit there staring at me, or are you going to kiss me?"

"We need to get Charlie to bed." I reply, already playing with the hair at the base of his neck. "Plus, the wheel is digging into my side."

He smirks, pulls my face to his—like the scoundrel he is—and kisses me thoroughly.

"Oliver." I breathe. "Charlie. Bed."

He hums, his lips grazing my cheeks and nose before he presses a final kiss to my forehead and helps me wiggle out of the cramped space. It's freezing in the garage after being curled up against him for who knows how long. His lap is where I want to be. I don't want to leave his side and that's...dangerous.

I ease Charlie out of her seat. She curls up on my shoulder with a tiny baby sigh. Oliver grabs the diaper bag and I follow him inside. He sets it by the door then takes Charlie from me.

"I'll put her down."

"Are you sure?"

"Yeah." He cups my cheek. "You deserve a night off."

I chuckle. "I've only had one night on."

"Doesn't matter. Especially if you're waiting for me when I come back down?"

"Maybe." It's my turn for my heart to sound like a runaway train as he smiles and disappears up the stairs.

Holy cannoli. My legs start to shake, and I plop onto the barstool. What in the world was today?

Nanna died. That reminder is like a punch to my gut and it's hard to swallow past the lump in my throat. I'm sad but also angry at my family. I really don't want to go to the funeral on Monday, but it's not like they really gave me a choice either.

I rub my face, ignoring the makeup that I'm sure is horribly smudged already from crying and kissing.

Kissing.

I smile. I've kissed Oliver Markel. Not once but *twice* and heaven help me, I want to do it over and over again. Forever.

Heck, if he does propose to me at the Christmas party next week, I'll make him marry me, fake or not.

Woah, hold up! What am I thinking? I can't marry him! I don't know Oliver well enough to marry him, do I?

A memory I'd forgotten about springs up. One of my mom. A few years before the accident took her and Dad. I let my mind drift as it slowly takes over.

● ● ● ● ● ● ●

"Mommy, when did you know you loved Dad?"

I'm eleven and sitting on the counter as Mom makes chocolate chip cookies. The melodic tones of the Beatles croon softly from the radio as a cinnamon candle burns in the center of the table.

Mom hums "Something" along with George and Paul as she finishes smoothing out the dough in a jelly roll pan.

"Mom?"

She turns and hands me a spoonful of batter with a smile. "Well, we didn't date very long. We were friends first, and I dated his roommate, Franklin, when we were in college."

"Fine, but when did you *know* you were going to marry him?" I ask, insistent.

Mom pauses and leans her hip against the counter. "Emmy, it's different for everyone, you know. There's not a magical formula. Some people never fall in love. Never get married."

I bite my lip for a minute, thinking over her words. "But I will, right?"

Mom smiles as she slides the pan into the oven and licks the little bit of dough still clinging to the spatula. "I think so."

"And you and Daddy?"

She tips her head back and laughs. "Oh, my little romantic. I knew Daddy was the one the first time we kissed."

I lean closer, voice full of awe and whisper ask, "Really?"

"Really." Mom mimics me. "And we were married a few months after that first kiss."

"Woah."

Mom tweaks my nose. "When you know what you're looking for, when you know *who* you are, then someone will fall in love with the real you, Emmy girl. And then it's easy to weed out the fakers, the double talkers, the ones who want to use you and throw you aside. A man who will stick with you through the ups and downs, a man who leads and loves you well, who's gentle with that wild and beautiful soul you have. That's a man worth loving."

"Is that what Daddy did for you?"

"Yep."

The front door slams and Dad's voice echoes down the hall. "Hey! Where are my girls?"

"In the kitchen, Luke!" Mom calls back.

Dad appears, his brown hair ruffled, his tie and first couple buttons on his shirt loosened. He looks like superman in his black framed glasses and bright smile. "Hey beautiful ladies."

"Daddy!" I set my licked-clean spoon on the counter and jump into his arms. I'm small for my age so Dad hugs me and spins me around, much to my delight. He draws Mom into the hug, and we do our family group hug for a long minute. "How's my Em?"

"Great now that you're home."

He chuckles, it rumbles through his chest and into my ear, as warm and sweet as the cookies in the oven. This is my family. My beautiful family whom I love so very much. I'm happy and safe and loved. And that's never going to change.

● ● ● ● ● ● ●

"Emily?"

I turn, bleary eyed, to see Oliver standing at my side. I'm not in the apartment kitchen anymore, but in Oliver's.

"Sorry." I wipe at the tears but more come. "Sorry!"

"Why are you apologizing?" he asks, taking my hand in his. "What were you thinking about?"

"My...my parents," I mutter as more tears leak out of my eyes. "Buckets! I hate crying!"

He chuckles. "So do I, but I did it today. Therefore, it's your turn."

I shake my head. "I haven't thought about my parents in ages. It's been almost fifteen years since they passed."

"There's not a time limit on grief. Trust me." He tightens his hold on my hand. "Tell me about them, will you?"

"You don't—"

"Hey." His tone is the slightest bit sharp, and I jump. "I've told you; you don't know what I like and don't like. Not yet. And if I say I want to hear about your family, I mean it. Tell me about them. Please?"

I bite my lip. "Let's go sit on the couch."

He nods and doesn't let go of my hand as we move into the living room. I settle beside him on the couch and then take a deep breath.

"My mom stayed at home with me while Dad worked with a finance company. I don't understand it all, but they left me a trust that I was able to access at twenty-one. We lived in a modest apartment. Mom taught me at home, and I loved it."

"I wish my mom would have done that." Oliver admits. "I was…well, I was bullied a lot at school."

"Why?" I sit up and look at him.

"Rich kid. One of the richest. And I stood out, even in a school that's basically Ivy League for elementary schoolers."

"I'm sorry, Ollie."

"It is what it is." He leans his head against the back of the couch. "Keep going. What else should I know about your parents?"

"We loved old Disney movies, chocolate chip cookies, and the Beatles. We would dance to the Beatles music while making the cookies then watch a Disney movie all snuggled up on the couch with popcorn and warm, gooey cookies."

Oliver squeezes my hand.

"Dad hated Ursula, loved *The Lion King*." I smile at the memory, leaning my head against Oliver's shoulder. "Mom loved *The Fox and the Hound*. My favorite was *One Hundred and One Dalmatians*.

"Christmas was our favorite holiday. The first Saturday of December was always tree getting day."

"Hence this?" Oliver asks, gesturing to our bare tree in the corner.

"Yep." I snuggle closer. "And we'd blast classic Christmas music and decorate after eating a breakfast of French toast and orange juice. I had a whole box of ornaments, one for each year of my life along with some I made or that Mom made for me."

That box got lost in the shuffling from house to house to house. One of my uncles probably threw it out. My heart pinches at the thought and another tear slips free.

"What...what exactly happened to your parents?" Oliver asks in a whisper.

"Car crash. Drunk driver ran a four way stop and totaled the car. First responders said they were dead when they arrived on the scene."

"Is that why you applied to be Lottie's nanny?"

"Yeah. I understand, even though I was a lot older when I became an orphan. I hate the idea of a child growing up alone. Been there, done that."

"I'm sorry, Em."

"Like you said, it is what it is." I sigh, my eyes feeling gritty and heavy. "I can choose to be bitter or to find joy in the fact that they're in a way better place."

"Sucks they aren't here, though. Or that you didn't get to say goodbye."

"Yeah, well." I shrug. "After that I got shuffled from one uncle's home to another. Three uncles and three years later, and I'm fourteen and living with my wheelchair bound Nanna.

"By then, I was fairly self-sufficient and didn't spend much time at home if I didn't have to. She loved me the best way she knew how, even if she was harder on me than Mom and Dad were. Once I moved out, it became a little clearer that she was proud of my career taking care of children and she was always there to talk to. Knowing that the three people who loved me—or tried to, at least—are gone is really hard."

"Em, you're not alone. I—I lo—"

A Charlie wail interrupts Oliver, and I'm only too eager to leap to my feet. "I'll get her."

"Yeah, okay sure." Oliver runs a hand through his hair, leaning his elbows on his knees as I dash up the stairs. I pick up the little girl, holding her to my chest as I breathe hard.

"Was he going to say what I thought he was going to say?"

I hope not. I don't know how to respond. My head knows the logical thing to do, but my heart—that lonely, bruised thing that's felt far from useful in the last dozen years—insistently beats what I don't want to admit.

I'm in love with Oliver Markel.

I'm in love and it scares the absolute crap out of me.

Chapter Twenty-Four

Oliver

After about a half hour of waiting for Emily to come back down the stairs—surprise, she doesn't—I head up to my room.

I pause at Charlotte's door, catching sight of Emily in the rocker. Charlotte is curled against her chest and the pair breathe in tandem. Something catches in my lungs. I can't make myself move from my spot by the door.

Is this love? Do I even know what that word means? But as I watch my girls—yes, *my girls*—I don't want to retreat to my room. I don't want to be alone. Rather, I want to scoop them up, hold on tight, and never leave my home again. Home would be with them. Whether in this monstrosity of a house, in a one room apartment, or in the back of a van. I want to do life with Emily and Charlotte. I want to be the person who's there for them in the highs and lows. I want to celebrate the accomplishments and the successes and mourn the failures and disappointments.

Creeping into the room, I find a blanket and drape it over the pair. Gosh, I don't want to go. I glance around and see the window seat. Grabbing a blanket of my own, I curl up on the cushioned seat. It's not comfortable. At all. But it's near *them*. And tonight, I don't want to be alone. This is more real than anything I've ever felt before, and I want to enjoy it. This moment. Right now. Before it disappears like a lot of good things seem to do.

● ● ● ● ● ● ●

I wake up with a stiff neck, but it's worth it when I open my eyes and see Emily staring at me.

"Morning," I say, my voice still thick from sleep. I clear it and sit up with a groan.

"You did not sleep there all night." Emily's face is slack from shock. She shakes her head, stands, and settles Charlie in her bed.

I grin as she sits beside me. "What answer will get me in less trouble?"

"You're not in trouble." She stares at her hands.

"I sense a *but* attached to that sentence."

"But why?" She looks up and her lip is between her teeth.

Will she push me away if I admit the truth? She ran last night. She's been putting up roadblocks all along our path. But if I push toward her, crumble the defenses, fight for what I sense between us, can I win? Am I able to do that?

"Because I wanted to be near my girls."

"*Your girls.*" Emily's pinky curls around mine.

"Yeah. My girls." I duck my head and kiss her—morning breath and all.

Her cheeks flare pink and she stands. "Breakfast?"

"Let me." I jump to my feet and bolt through the door. With a grin over my shoulder, I say, "I have a plan!"

● ● ● ● ● ● ●

Apparently, my plans suck because breakfast is not working the way I envisioned. The French are monsters to their food. I cannot for the life of me figure out what I am doing wrong as I attempt to fry the egg drenched bread on my cast iron griddle.

The first six slices are still covered with raw egg. But when I turn up the heat, I burn the next six slices.

I am going to war with the shrieking fire alarm when Emily appears at my side, Charlie on her hip.

"What are you doing?" she asks above the annoying beeping.

I hit the reset button and almost fall off the stool as I jump back down. On solid ground once more, I wave my spatula in the air. "I'm attempting French toast. But I'm desecrating it rather than creating a culinary masterpiece."

Emily chuckles as she hooks Charlie into her high chair. "French toast? For me?"

"Well, you said it was a favorite so..." I shrug. "Although I'm showing that I'm more of a takeout kind of guy."

"This is really sweet, Ollie." Her eyes are rimmed with red, but her smile makes up for it as she looks up at me. "Want some help?"

"I want you to show me how!" I declare.

She nods. "Alright then. The Fitzpatrick School of Breakfast Foods is now open for business. First lesson: French Toast."

I scoot up behind her, tucking my hands behind me to keep from grabbing onto her waist as I watched her dip the bread in the egg, milk, and cinnamon batter like I had but she lets a bit drizzle off before she sets it on the griddle.

"You have it at a good temp, but you have to watch it," she explains.

"Watch it. Got it." The temptation is too great. I settle my hands on her waist, and she gasps but leans back against me. "Is the batter good?"

"Yeah. It's great."

"Good."

Emily flips the bread, the underside golden and perfect.

As soon as six pieces are plated, I turn her around and claim her lips with mine. She leans into me, her arms twining around my neck as she kisses me good morning. It's sweeter than the syrup on the counter, richer than fresh cream, stronger than the best coffee.

For the love, if this is drowning let the current take me. I never want to come up for air again.

Emily pushes me away, but she's smiling. "You're a bad influence, Oliver Markel!"

I chuckle as we slide onto the stools.

She cuts into the toast after dousing it in syrup. "The moment of truth!"

I watch as she places it in her mouth and chews. She tips her head to the side. Chews some more. Swallows. Grins. "This is the best French toast I've had in a long time."

"Really?"

She grins sheepishly. "Considering I haven't eaten it since the accident, yes, it really is."

I pause with my bite halfway to my mouth. "You haven't."

"Nope. But I'm glad the first time I tried it again was with you."

"I'm sorry, Em." I set my fork down. "I should have thought—I mean, I didn't know—"

"It's fine, and how could you have known?" She shakes her head. "Not everything is your fault, Ollie, and I'm not mad at you."

"Why are you calling me that?" I ask, catching that she's called me that a couple times since yesterday.

"Ollie?"

I nod.

She takes another bite. "I've called you that to Charlie since I've started working here and it just sort of...fits. Besides, I only nickname people I care about."

Care about. Not love. Does she not feel like me, as if my heart beats solely for her and her alone? Right now, it's thumping out that we're not close enough to each other. That I want to scrape back her layers like wallpaper in an old house. Layer by layer, piece by piece, until I find the heart of Emily Jane Fitzpatrick and lay claim to it.

Forever and always.

● ● ● ● ● ● ●

After we clean up breakfast, we move into the living room to decorate the tree. Emily pulls out the bags of decorations we bought, and I turn *Home Alone II* on the TV. Charlotte bounces in her exersaucer as Emily begins wrapping the tree in a strand of pretty white lights we bought yesterday.

"What color lights did you have on your tree growing up?" I ask.

"White." Emily steps back and eyes the tree before moving forward to adjust some things. "They are elegant and simple and then you can enjoy the colors of the ornaments even more."

"I wish my family would have decorated more for the holidays," I admit as Emily gives me the go ahead to start hanging ornaments.

I grab one and unwrap it. I hold it up, the tree lights reflecting off the red ball. *Baby's First Christmas.* I smile and turn to Charlotte. It is her first Christmas. I never thought about that. Not really.

"You alright?" Emily crouches beside me and I hold up the ball. "I saw that yesterday at Vintage Vestige and had to get it."

"Thank you." My throat is tight. I sigh and shove my hand through my hair. "I don't know what I'd do without you, Em. I really, really don't."

She smiles, grabs an ornament, and turns back to the tree. "You'd manage."

Would I really? I mean, sure, *probably*. But do I really want to? No. I don't. A life without the sunshine of Emily isn't one I want to live.

Chapter Twenty-Five

Emily

Monday morning, I roll out of bed and spend a good five minutes staring at the black dress draped over the chair. I don't want to go to the funeral. In fact, I would rather stare down Goliath, or one of the scary serial killers Molly and Susan love to listen about in their podcasts, than go see my uncles.

Getting to my feet, I throw off my jammies and pull on my dress. It hits right above my knees, with quarter length sleeves and a scoop neck. It's black. Boring. Not me at all.

But it's for Nanna. I can do this for her. I shove my feet into black flats and pull a chunky gray cardigan over my dress. I apply minimal make-up—I'll cry it all off anyway—then grab my purse and open the door.

Oliver is standing there, hand raised as if he was preparing to knock. His eyes sweep over me, warm, concerned, and far too intimate.

"Hey, Ollie." I cross my arms over my chest. He said on Saturday he'd be coming with me. Is he really? He's dressed in his usual gray business suit, a black dress shirt underneath with no tie this time. The top button is undone, which is unusual for him.

Maybe he really is planning on coming.

"Susan is here to watch Charlotte for us." He stares at me. Doesn't reach or ask if I'm okay—which I'm not. Is he even breathing?

"Good."

Oliver opens his mouth. Closes it. Looks away. "Emily, do you want me to come?"

"Yes. No. I don't know." I rub my temple, a headache already pounding. "My family is a mess."

Oliver snorts. "Mine isn't much better. You've met my mother, which means you know we only pretend to have it all together."

I can't argue with that.

"Besides." He reaches out now and lays his hand on my upper arm. "I want to support you like you've supported me in all of this."

"All of what?"

"Gavin's death. Charlotte coming to live with me. Fatherhood?" He chokes on the last word and drops his gaze. "It's been hard. But you've been here. A silent support that I didn't realize I needed but that I got anyways."

I hug him, leaning my forehead against his chest. No words spill out. No sage wisdom. I just hold onto him. He's my anchor in this storm of loss. I can't be strong when thinking about going back into the war zone that is my family. Not ready to be crushed and manipulated and tormented all over again after five years of freedom. But if Oliver is at my side, I'll be alright. I can face the hurricane of death because I know he's entering the fray with me.

"Em?"

"I'm okay. Just...don't let me go, Ollie."

"Never." He presses a kiss to the top of my head. "I'm never going to let you go."

It's a promise, a vow, and for whatever reason, my heart jumps at it. Lurches toward Oliver, not away. His whispered reassurance makes me draw close, dares me to open the locked gate that I've only now discovered built into the walls around my heart. My heart is screaming to invite Oliver into my deepest self, to trust him, and see what happens next.

But am I brave enough? After years of being torn down, I'm not certain I know what to do when someone comes along to build me up.

"Let's take Charlotte down to Susan and get some breakfast before we leave."

"Okay." I step back, wiping at the two tears that have already leaked out of my eyes.

Oliver takes my hand as we head to Charlie's room. She's kicking her feet and sucking on her hands. Sweet baby noises greet us as we lean over the crib. For a long moment, Oliver and I stand there, staring down at her. She smiles at us.

Holy cannoli, we feel like a family.

I take a step back, shaking my head. I can't do this. Can I?

"Emily?" Oliver turns and leans his hip against the crib.

This mental back and forth is getting old. I don't know what I want and then I do. I want to trust Oliver with my heart until I don't. I want to have a family—to be part of *Oliver's* family—and then I get scared and want to run.

"Em." He grabs my arms, forcing me to look up at him. "Stop it."

"Stop what?"

"Stop retreating from this."

"But what if I lose it?" I cross my arms and close my eyes, scared of what I might see in Oliver's gaze.

Oliver's hands slide down and clasp my hands. "Then you lose it. The beauty of living? Of loving? I'm learning that it's knowing there's always the risk of losing it all. But if we hold everyone and everything at arm's length, is life really worth living?"

"I'm scared." Admitting it hurts. Like a knife plunging into my chest.

"I know." He tightens his hold on my hands, pulling me closer. "I am too."

"I don't want to lose someone else I've grown to care about." Oliver nods.

"But..." I swallow, my throat tight as I suppress my tears. "But I could lose people by never letting them in, too, couldn't I?"

"Yeah." Oliver cups my cheek, forcing my face up to look at him. "But not me. Push me as hard as you want, Emily. I'm not leaving you."

"You can't promise me that."

"Yeah, I can. Death can take me, but I'm not walking away. I'm not leaving. You're stuck with me for the long haul, if you'll let me stay."

The long haul. He means it, I know. Oliver doesn't make promises he won't keep. There is so much we don't know about one another, but we know the important stuff, don't we? We are broken. Messy. Our families are far from perfect. And yet, we have good friends by our sides. Lots of love to give one another. We might put up walls, but we are willing to work over, around, and through them to get to one another.

"Thanks." I hug him again before he can think about kissing me and then we turn back to Charlie.

I scoop her up and change her diaper. Oliver picks out a cute light blue overall set with a ruffle-sleeved white shirt. I give Charlie a tight hug and press a kiss to her forehead that makes her giggle. Oliver's arms come around us both, his eyes glowing in the pink light filtering through the curtains.

"Will you let me?" he whispers.

I lick my lips and his eyes flick to them. "Let you what?"

"Let me stay. For the long haul?"

"Yeah, Ollie." I smile, my eyes feeling wet again. "For the long haul."

He smiles, kisses Charlie's head then my forehead before turning toward the door. "Susan's waiting."

And ... my legs are weak again. Holy cannoli, this is going to be one interesting day.

● ● ● ● ● ● ●

A few hours later, we're sitting in front of one of the many funeral homes in Highland. I'm shaking. Not because it's a funeral but because beyond those elegantly etched doors are three men who hurt me greatly. Who shoved their only sister's child from one person to the next before leaving her with their mother. Alone. Broken. Scared. And they still don't care.

"It'll be okay." Oliver reaches over the console and clasps my hand in his. "So, I'm your boyfriend. Real or not real?"

"Are you quoting the *Hunger Games* at me?" I chuckle, unable to look at him.

"Yep." He squeezes. "But also, please answer the question."

"Real. If you want me."

"Emily Fitzpatrick! You had better know by now that I don't often let people see the messy parts of me."

I glance at him. "Is that why you asked me to move in? To see the messy parts?"

"Yeah. Because you don't judge people."

"Oh, I do." I squeeze his hand back before letting go to unsnap my seatbelt. "Just not you."

"I'm not people?" he asks, a teasing glint to his gaze.

"You're the best kind of people. You're one of the people I ... trust."

"You trust me?" he asks, reclaiming my hand once we're out of the car and heading up to the funeral parlor.

Despite the riot that's my heart, I nod. "Yeah. I do."

Oliver's smile is bright enough to chase away the storm clouds overhead and warm enough to thaw my frozen fingers. He's so happy. So full of joy that I'm scared to take him inside to the family that'll snuff it all out like a fire denied oxygen.

The foyer is papered in tans and creams with burgundy carpet and seating. Gold accents cover the furniture and the walls. A sign points the way to Jane Coaly's funeral.

I draw on my rage. My anger dries up the tears as I march down the aisle toward the casket. It's open. Nanna looks like she'll pop up at any moment, hand me a bowl of fruity rings cereal, and ask how school was. I stop halfway down the aisle. Oliver stops beside me, looking down like he wants to say something but presses his lips thin.

"Emmy!" the low voice of Uncle Lewis—Mom's oldest brother and the first person to shove me away a year after Mom and Dad's accident—stalks over. His dark brows are lowered over equally dark eyes. He crosses his arms and rests them on his large stomach. "Wasn't sure you'd come."

"My problem wasn't with her. It's with you, Lewis." I can't find the desire to admit I'm related to him by blood.

"I took you into my home."

Yeah, sure. And then nagged on everything I did. Every time I cried, he told me to suck it up. He didn't care that his sister was gone, only that I took up residence in his home. Out of all my uncles, he is the one I hate most. He pushed me away in my deepest grief. He hadn't loved me at my lowest, so he doesn't get to tear me down now.

"I'm going to go say goodbye to Nanna." I try to step around Lewis, but he grabs my arm.

His breath reeks like he was drinking before showing up for his mother's funeral. "Listen to me, *Emily*. You're not getting a dime of Mom's money."

"What are you talking about?"

"She may have left everything to you, but you're never going to get any of it. I'll see to that."

"She left me money?"

"As if you don't know!" His grip tightens and I hiss in pain.

"Get your hands off of her." Oliver's voice is even. Cold. He grabs Lewis' wrist and shoves him away. His arm wraps protectively around my waist, and I shiver, thankful he came despite my misgivings a few hours before. "Let's go, Em."

Lewis stares at us. "Who's this?"

"I am her boyfriend, Oliver Markel. Perhaps you've heard of me?" Oliver's brow hops up when Lewis' mouth falls open. "Ah, so you have."

"How—what—Markel?" His voice squeaks.

Oliver smiles and in it I see a trace of the ruthlessness his mother has, but I'm not concerned about it. Like, at all. I know the man behind it, and he has a heart of gold.

"Yes. Markel. And you should know that means I have the best lawyers in the tri-state area, and that also means they'll be at Emily's disposal. You contest the will? We will fight and we will win." He inclines his head toward Lewis. "Good day, Mr. Coaly."

His hand against my lower back, Oliver guides me up to the casket. Dozens of flower baskets surround Nanna. She would have loved it. Her lips are turned up ever so slightly in sleep and I let a few tears slide. Oh, goodness. I didn't think it would be this hard. I reach out and lay a hand against hers. They're cold.

My breath catches. Oliver's arms come around me and he holds me close. "I'm sorry, Em."

"I wish they would have let me know she was sick. Or that she would have reached out. She knew I needed space, but she called every so often. I—I should have picked up the other day."

"Emily, *should'ves* and *could'ves* don't help anyone."

"I know. But—" I shake my head, falling silent as we move to our seats, letting others say goodbye.

"We'll have to look into the will thing," Oliver whispers, his thumb rubbing against the back of my hand. "It could be important, especially if Lewis is that upset about it."

I nod, my voice refusing to work. Oliver squeezes my hand as the pastor gets up and starts the service.

We're a few rows behind my uncles. They and their wives glare at me, but I ignore them. I'm the only person left that represents my mom. I know none of them liked their baby sister and they really didn't like my dad. But I couldn't care less. I don't need their approval and what's more, I don't want it.

Oliver's arm goes around me as the pastor talks about Nanna and her life. A few family members get up and recount stories, and then the pastor asks if any other family members want to speak.

An awkward silence settles, not one of my uncles moving to talk. Before I can really process what I'm doing, I stand and make my way to the podium. "Hello. I'm Emily Fitzpatrick, Jane's granddaughter."

A few people whisper, but I ignore them.

"I lived with my grandmother in my teens. She cared for me as well as she knew how, even though she should have been free to do whatever she wished in her sixties and seventies. She was always willing to help me with a school project or with something to take to a potluck with friends. She wasn't planning on raising a fifth child, but she did. And I think she did pretty well."

Lewis snorts, but my eyes land on Oliver, who smiles and nods.

"She may have screwed up when it came to her sons. They pushed me away. Sent me to Nanna when I'd just lost my *family*. But Nanna took me in. And for that, I say thank you. Thank you, Nanna, for caring, even when no one else would."

Another silence—this one stunned—wraps around the room as I return to my seat.

Oliver leans close, his breath brushing my ear. "Well done."

I lean my head against his shoulder, listen as the pastor prays, and watch as the pallbearers carry the casket to the cemetery across the street from the funeral parlor.

After that, Oliver and I slip away, deciding to forgo the dinner at the church.

"Do you want to go home now?" he asks as he starts the car.

"Not really." Going back to the house means too much time to think. I don't want to think. I want to escape my mind, and for that I need a distraction. "Do you have something in mind?"

"Well, you need a dress for the party this Saturday." His cheeks darken.

"Yes. And?"

"I thought that maybe...well, let's go get one."

Chapter Twenty-Six

Oliver

I look at my watch as I sit on one of the couches that faces a three-sided mirror wall. This isn't a place I ever thought I'd be caught dead in—a fancy dress shop in downtown Highland.

But I so loved the way Emily's eyes lit up when we walked through the doors. She browsed for an hour before retreating to the dressing room to try on the massive pile of dresses she pulled from the racks.

Now, this is something I am enjoying—maybe a little too much. I know some guys would be bored out of their brains, but not me. Emily is a masterpiece in each of the gowns she's modeled. Personally, I think she looks pretty great in leggings and a Beatles t-shirt. But the selfish part of me wants to see her in a party dress, too.

The first dress she tried was pale blue with sequins on the bodice. It looked nice but that was all I could really say. It didn't scream *Emily* to me.

The second was a low-cut, short-skirted red one that had my protective instinct flaring. She looked hot as heck, but the thought of Ethan or any of the other guys seeing her in it made me want to wrap her in a blanket and hold on tight to her.

"You okay in there?" I ask. It's been fifteen minutes since the last dress, and I need something else to think about other than the sexy red one.

"Yeah, I'm fine. It's just…I think I really like this one." She sounds puzzled and I wonder if she has on one of the dresses I slipped onto the pile when she was distracted with the sales clerk. I'm no fashion expert—far, far from it—but I can appreciate colors and her lovely figure.

And speaking of, I am dying to see Emily in another dress. "Come on out. I want to see it!"

The curtain parts and her head pops through. "Did you pick this one?"

I grin. "I won't know until you show me."

Her lip pops between her teeth as she slowly steps out and in front of the mirrors.

I can't help it; my mouth falls open. The plum-colored fabric looks almost metallic, iridescently shimmering around her legs in an ethereal motion. It brings out the hazel color in her eyes—eyes that are glowing as she turns this way and that before the mirrors. The gown hugs her hips in all the right ways, cinching at the waist while flattering her torso with the sweetheart neckline. The bare shoulders of the gown with off-the-shoulder sleeves pulls it all together.

"Wow." I can't say anything more.

"Do you...like it?" she asks nervously.

"You looked pretty great in the other gowns, but this one"—I stand and come up behind her— "Emily, you are absolutely the most beautifully stunning woman in all the world."

She laughs and drops her gaze to the gown. "It's expensive."

"I'm buying it."

"No! You can't!" She meets my gaze in the mirror. "Oliver, you've done enough for me."

"Don't tell me I can't, because I will always prove to you that I can." I grin and kiss her cheek. "You're getting this dress, if only because I'm selfish and want to stare at you all night in it. It's perfect on you."

"Oliver—"

"Emily!" I turn her around and kiss her, not caring when the sales clerk lets out a surprised squawk at the PDA happening in her dress parlor. When we break apart, I whisper, "Stop arguing. You're going to lose."

"You're bossy." She chuckles. "But I'll give in this time because I want this dress, too."

I snort a laugh and sit back down as she disappears into the changing room. "Do you need anything else for the outfit?"

"Shoes, but Susan has a shoe fetish, so I can probably borrow a pair from her."

"Jewelry?" My brain hops to the ring in my desk. My mouth goes dry, my hands clammy. Am I really considering…?

"Ready!" Emily steps out of the dressing room, the gown draped over her arm and a large smile on her face. "Thank you, for this."

"You're worth it." And oh, do I ever mean that. Worth the fight, worth the pain that brought us together, worth chasing her down when she retreats into that complicated mind of hers.

She interlocks our fingers. "I'm not, but thanks for thinking so."

I'm not going to argue with her. I know how special she is, and come Saturday, Emily will know how I feel, without any room for doubt.

● ● ● ● ● ● ●

Tuesday, I'm pacing around and around my desk at the office. Work is pointless. Mother will harp, but what else is new? The little black box sits in my pocket. I shoved it in there this morning before leaving the house.

I kissed Charlotte and Emily before leaving this morning. If you told me a week ago that would happen, I would have said you were crazy.

Now, I'm the crazy one. We talked about a fake engagement, but now I want it to be real. Really real. No strings attached, no contracts, straight up marriage. Heck, I'd marry Emily tonight at the courthouse if I could.

A knock sounds on the door and Ethan pops his head in. "Hey, how are you doing?"

"Get in here." I hurry to the door, yanking him in before slamming it and turning the lock.

"Woah, guess you're not doing great." Ethan adjusts his glasses. "Was having Emily move in a bad move?"

"No, it was great. In fact, we're really dating now."

Ethan's brows shoot up under his hair. "Well, that escalated quickly. Should you really, you know, be living together then?"

"Probably not." I rub the back of my neck, fish the ring box out of my pocket, and turn it toward Ethan. "Which is why I think I'm going to propose at the Christmas party and see if she..." I gulp. "See if she'll elope."

"Elope." Ethan's voice has zero inflection, like I hit the reset button and he's frozen in a loop.

"Yeah. If Mother finds out we're engaged, she's going to try and stop a full-blown wedding. I also don't want to involve Emily's side of the family. They're money hungry and they know we're dating. If they find out we're getting married, I don't doubt they'll try blackmail or something worse to get a cut."

Plus, there is still the mess of Emily's inheritance from her nanna that I need to figure out. I jot down a note to do that either tonight or tomorrow.

"So you're going to ask her to marry you in like, what? A week?"

"Do you think we can?"

"Maybe, but she's going to have to know to get the marriage license."

"It only takes three days to be valid." I began to calculate. "If we go to the courthouse Monday, we can be married on Friday."

"Oliver, she hasn't said yes yet."

I look away. That is my biggest fear. That Emily doesn't feel the same way as me. Or at least, not strongly enough to rush into marriage. But the thought of her moving back in with Molly and Susan, of her not being there in the morning or greeting me with a smile when I get home from work each day hurts. It scares me. I don't want to live alone anymore, not after getting a taste of doing life *with* someone.

"I know, Ethan. I do. But plans never hurt, right?"

"I suppose not, man." He chuckles. "This means I was right. You love her?"

I gulp. I haven't straight up said those words to Emily. The scary *ILY* that bares reciprocation. Because what if she doesn't? What will I do then?

A knock on the door saves me. "Oliver?"

"Buckets."

Ethan looks at me with amusement. "Yep, you're in love."

I shush him as I unlock and swing the door open.

"Hello, Mother."

Her expression is pinched as she sails in. "Out," she orders Ethan, who nearly trips over his feet as he hurries to obey.

I move around my desk, taking the ring box and sliding it back into my pocket before Mother can ask about it.

"What's wrong now?"

"The report for the Bradshaw case?" Her brow arches. "He emailed saying he talked to you about some cooking contest and that he wants you to represent him."

"I'm aware, but the contest isn't set to start filming until after the new year. I'm working on it now. I am only one man, Mother." I can't help the bit of venom that coats those words.

Mother taps her manicured nail on my desk edge. "I made you, Oliver. Both as a person and as a businessman."

And here I thought she birthed me in a suit and tie. Actually, it wouldn't have surprised me at this point.

"Thank you for the history lesson."

"Don't you dare sass me!" She launches to her feet. "I can fire you, you know."

Would she though? Really? And destroy the beautiful illusion that we were a perfectly happy working family of three? It's why she hates Charlotte. It threw a kink into her curated world order.

"I'm not sassing." Turning to my computer, I say, "I'll finish this before going home."

Home. It is the best word in the dictionary, if I had to hazard a guess. Synonymous with *love* to me. It's the place you yearn for after a difficult day. The place where your family waits, open-armed and ready to hug you.

It's full of peace and joy.

The place you go to love and be loved.

My home is two very special people and not a place.
My home is Emily and Charlotte.

Chapter Twenty-Seven

Emily

The rest of the week is a beautiful blur. Oliver kisses me goodbye every morning and then again when he comes home from work. I work on learning how to cook more than just breakfast foods—although he never complains about it when I make French toast or eggs and hash browns. I quickly learn spaghetti and meatballs are super easy and I only burn them once, thank goodness.

All too soon and yet not quickly enough, it's Saturday morning. My stomach is a twisted mess when I roll over and see my gorgeous plum colored gown. The morning sun makes it shimmer as it catches a draft from the warm air blasting out of the floor vent.

I'm going to a fancy work party. With Oliver. As his girlfriend.

My mind conjures the lovely memory of him slipping the engagement ring on my finger a week earlier. That's not happening now, because now we're real. We're a couple. The engagement was to fool his mother and to keep Charlie safe.

"She doesn't have a leg to stand on," I mumble as I sit up and stretch.

My phone buzzes and it's Susan to our roomie group chat.

Susan – Molly and I will be there at 1 o'clock to help you get ready, okay?

*Me – *thumbs up emoji**

Molly – YOU'RE GOING TO A FANCY PARTY WITH OLIVER!!!

Me – Yup.

Molly – YUP?! JUST YUP?!

Me – What do you want me to say?

Molly – I thought you'd be more excited.

Me – I don't know what I'm feeling. This is a lot.

Susan – Are you two officially dating?

Me – Yeah. I'm his girlfriend.

Molly – !!!

Molly – Why wasn't I informed of this?!

*Susan – Did you not notice them last week at the tree lighting? They couldn't stop staring at each other like this *heart-eyed emoji**

Me – Were not!

Susan – Well, Oliver was staring at you like that. You were avoiding eye contact like it was the plague.
Molly – Is it smart to be living with him if you're not married?
Me – We're being good.
Molly – If my mom finds out she's gonna have a fit, Emily Jane!
Me – Then you better not tell her, Molly Elaine!

The dreaded dots of anxiety appear then disappear then reappear. I bite my lip and stare at the gown. Buckets, they're right. I know they are. But the thought of moving back in with them hurts. I like being here for Charlie when she wakes up screaming. To see Oliver first thing in the morning as he stumbles into Charlie's room with bedhead and bleary eyes. I want to be here. It's...it's home now.

What makes it home though?

I bite my lip, peace warming my heart when an image pops into my head. It isn't the house, or the large kitchen, or the unfairly comfortable white sofa in the living room. It isn't even Charlie, although she is a part of the puzzle.

No, the image that pops into my head is Oliver. It's Oliver dancing with Charlie to a bopping Christmas song. It's Oliver in the kitchen watching and helping me make a homemade meal. It's Oliver curling up with me on the sofa as we watch a cheesy Christmas romcom. It's Oliver and me talking together. It's his kiss. His hand in mine.

Home is now synonymous with Oliver.

And the thought of leaving him—even for a few days—breaks my heart in two.

● ● ● ● ● ● ●

When I get down to the kitchen in my yoga pants and an oversized sweatshirt of Oliver's I had totally stolen from the laundry, he is already there, making French toast.

"You didn't have to do this." I smile my thanks when he slides me a cup of cocoa across the counter. While I was learning dinners that didn't involve syrup and/or sausage, Oliver learned how to make the best homemade candy cane cocoa in the world (just don't tell Sweetie I said that.)

He winks and grins. "Hey, you have a full day getting beautified for our date tonight."

The party starts at five in a ballroom in downtown Highland. Molly and Susan declared that they wanted to do my nails, hair, and make-up for the event. Oliver took their side, basically telling me I was going to get the beauty treatment and declared that Tanner would keep Charlie and him company while my friends accosted me with beauty products.

"I don't need to look like a model," I grumble into my cocoa.

Oliver takes a sip of his peach tea with a chuckle. "You already look beautiful. Especially in stolen clothing."

I grin a bit too widely as I meet his gaze. "And don't you forget it!"

"Never." His eyes still sparkle, but his grin fades to a moony half smile and his tone is solemn. "I want you to steal my sweatshirts for the rest of our lives, Em."

It's too serious. Even though I love what he's saying, it also scares me half to death. So, I do the only logical thing, and begin eating the French toast he sat in front of me.

"Are you nervous?" he asks, turning back to the skillet.

I look up and swallow my bite of sweet and cinnamon-y food. "Should I be?"

Oliver shrugs. "No, but..."

"But?"

"It's going to be a lot. Mother is not happy about us dating, you living here, and...all of it."

"She seems like a delightful individual." I can't help but roll my eyes. "But you met my uncles and if you can deal with them, I can deal with her."

"Speaking of your uncles." Oliver scoops his breakfast onto a plate and joins me at the island. "I had one of my lawyers dig up your nanna's will."

"*Lawyers*? As in, more than one?"

His emerald eyes dance. "Yes, it's a large firm."

"Yeah, but *lawyers*!"

"Anyways." Oliver shakes his head. "Did you know what your nanna did for a living?"

"She was a stay-at-home mom. Raised Mom and my uncles."

"Em, she's Aria Jean Mcoyle—one of the most prolific mystery writers of this century."

My mouth falls open. "She's...Aria? My *nanna*?"

"Yeah. You've read most of her books, haven't you?"

Without reply, I turn and run up the stairs. There on the bookcase he's moved into my room is a whole shelf of Mcoyle novels. I grab five before hurrying back to Oliver's side.

"You're saying this one"—I thump down *Murder in the Churchyard*— "that she dedicated to *'my darling granddaughter'* was really to me? Or this one"— *Til Death Do Us Part*— "that is dedicated to *'dearest E'.* That was to *me*?"

"Unless you have an uncle named Everett or Edward." Oliver's arms are crossed and resting on the granite countertop. "But this explains the money. She really is rich. She got thousands in advances for each book and then royalties once they surpassed that advance. And with how many books she's published—"

"They undoubtedly surpassed." I fall hard onto the stool and lean my forehead against my palm. "She never told me. All those years and she never said a word. Wait." I sit up and glare at Oliver, even though it really isn't *his* fault. "She *gave* me my first Aria Jean Mcoyle novel! My nanna made herself my favorite author!"

Oliver snorts, pretends to cough, then finally gives up and flat out laughs at me. "Honestly, it's such a *you* situation to be in. And why are you complaining?" He slides the document across the counter and points to a number. "You're an heiress, Em."

My mouth falls open at the seven-figure number on the page. Yeah. *Seven.* I've never seen so many zeros with a dollar sign in front of them in my life.

"Wow."

"Also, look at her name." Oliver grabs the manilla envelope the document was in and writes out Nanna's name followed by her pen name. "It's an anagram."

I look at it, the letters rearranging in my head.

Jane Marie Coaly.

Aria Jean Mcoyle.

"Why wouldn't she tell me, Ollie?" I ask. Anger and sadness war for supremacy in my chest. I decide to lock them both in a mental closet until I have time to sort them out. But when I look at Oliver, his forehead divots in worry, my sadness breaks the lock and bursts free.

Which is swiftly followed by anger exploding out because I don't *want* to cry. I won't! I abruptly stand, hands shaking.

Charlie bangs her plastic spoon on the tray.

I reach for her when Oliver grabs me around my waist and turns me to face him. "What's going on in that head of yours?"

"Nothing. Let me go." I push against his chest but pause when I feel the solidness of it. His heart thumps a rhythmic beat against my palm. I close my eyes. What would it feel like to let my wall all the way down? What if I let myself cry, really cry? I did it the other day. Could I do it again? And again, and again until he's seen everything my heart holds? All my anger, fear, sorrow? My joy, pain, disgust, and every emotion in between?

The worry of loss—of losing the support I am currently leaning (very literally) against—begins to ease as I wrap my arms around him and let my head fall against his chest. His heart beats faster under my ear as he rocks me back and forth.

"It's okay, Em." He presses a kiss to the top of my head. "I've got you."

I find myself relaxing. "I know."

"Do you?" His breath catches.

"Yeah, and I'm learning to trust that you won't let go. You won't run away from me or push me away." I look up at him. "I'm going to push away, Ollie. I'm going to try and reconstruct my walls."

"That's okay, Em. I probably have some of my own that you'll smack into."

"Am I worth it?" I whisper, more of those blasted tears filling my eyes. "Can you look at the mess that's my heart and say it's valuable and worth the long haul?"

"Emily." He reaches up and tucks my hair behind my ears.

"No one has ever wanted me, Oliver." I swallow the bubbling panic that admitting that creates. "My friends here in Cloverfield ...they're my family now. And...well, you know why I stayed here."

"Charlie."

"Yeah. But I never planned on you. On noticing how lost *you* were and yet even then, you were trying to love that little girl. I found myself falling for the broken man who needed help."

"You're falling for me?"

"Yeah. I think I'm still falling for you, Oliver Markel."

"Well, that's good." His nose brushes mine as he leans closer. My toes curl in anticipation of our lips meeting. His green eyes fill my vision as he whispers, "Because I've fallen for you, Emily. Completely and totally. I lo—"

Charlie's scream ricochets through the kitchen and I yelp at the pain it causes in my head. Oliver heaves an exasperated sigh as he turns to little miss and fists his hands on his hips. "Really? Right then?"

Charlie throws her spoon across the room and pounds her hands on the tray with another squeal of rage.

"I'll go clean her up." I say with a chuckle. Picking her up I mock glare at her, but my lips won't stay turned down as her doe eyes look into mine. "You really know how to kill a moment, kid."

Oliver's laughter follows me up the stairs. And that, more than anything, warms me through and through.

● ● ● ● ● ● ●

"Hold still!" Susan's exasperated sigh forces me to stop my nervous fidgeting as she tries to apply my eyeliner. I never wear the stuff because with my luck I'd gouge my eyeball out trying to apply it.

Molly is behind me with a curling wand, making quick work of my short hair. "You're going to look stunning in that dress!"

"Thanks." I haven't told them that Oliver paid for it. Or that he helped me pick it out. They wouldn't understand.

"I still think you should move back in with us," Susan grumbles, but her lips twist into a smile. "Unless you're planning on marrying the man in the near future?"

"We haven't talked about it." *Lies*. We have. But as a farce, not a real *forever and always* kind of marriage. An engagement we could end as soon as Oliver got his daddy feet under him. "Besides, I barely know him."

"He's a good man," Susan states.

My mouth falls open. Susan *rarely* ever compliments men. There's something about her past that she's not talking about. Molly found out she once had a crush on her brother Ryder. But Susan never talks about it, and I don't push. Heaven knows I have enough walls of my own.

Susan smiles at my silence as she hands me the mascara wand. "Shut up!"

"I didn't say anything," I declare before doing my lashes.

"Yeah, you didn't have to." Susan sighs, leaning her shoulder against the wall. "I know, I know. It's shocking that I'm defending him. But I see the way he stares at you, and I would kill for a guy to look at me that way." Her brown eyes drop to look at her Christmas-socked feet. "Don't let him go, Em. He was always the nicest guy in school, and it got him bullied and picked on. But he was a good friend."

I nod slowly.

It's Molly's turn to exclaim, "Stop moving!"

With a chuckle, I hold still as she braids, twists, and pins my hair back. Looking in the mirror, I can't believe it's me. I feel pretty, worthy to go to a fancy gala on Oliver's arm.

You're an heiress.

I gulp in a breath as Molly zips me up and Susan hands me a pair of sparkly silver stiletto heels and a black clutch. In goes lip gloss, my credit card and driver's license (one can never be too careful), and my phone.

With a spin, I ask, "Am I ready?"

Molly claps. "You look like Cinderella!"

"Thanks to my fairy godmothers!" I declare and pull them into a hug. "Thank you, girls."

"Anytime." Molly sighs. "You will *always* be worth it, Em."

I step back and shake my head. "Nope! You will not make me cry and ruin this make up!"

Susan laughs and crosses her arms. "It's all waterproof."

"How am I supposed to take it off?"

"There is face wash in the bathroom." Molly rolls her eyes. "Honestly, we should have taught you makeup long ago."

"I rarely wear it." I laugh again and then look at the door. Oliver is downstairs with Tanner. The men have been entertaining Charlie while I got gussied up. Now it's time to go show him. Will he like it, like he kept telling me he would? Have Susan and Molly really been able to wave a magic makeup brush and create beauty from cinders?

Or am I still the frumpy nanny I've always been beneath all this fancy finery?

Chapter Twenty-Eight

Oliver

Molly comes waltzing down the stairs at three forty-eight, but who's counting? Not me. She grins and sits on the couch, wrapping her arms around Tanner's shoulders as he sits on the floor with Charlie on his lap. He's reading her the book he and Molly bought Charlie: a book about a little blue truck.

"She's coming." Molly's words drag my attention from the stairs to her and she meets my gaze with a smile. "She looks lovely."

"Good. The gown looked good on her when we bought it Monday." My gaze goes back to the stairs, willing Emily to appear.

"Wait." Molly straightens, though she leaves her hands on Tanner's shoulders. "You were with her when she got it?"

"Yeah. I...well, I actually bought it for her."

"That little stinker!" Molly jumps to her feet and runs back up the stairs.

Tanner laughs. "I'm assuming that there was a reason Emily didn't tell them about it."

A squeal reaches us, and I wince. "I imagine so."

My hand slips into my suit coat pocket and fists around the ring box.

"Are you okay, Oliver?" Tanner struggles to his feet, Charlie in his arms as he lifts and lowers his injured leg to stretch it out.

"Just nervous." I'm hoping he'll just assume it's about taking Emily to the company Christmas party—which nine times out of ten means a lot of drunk people and a late night.

But no such luck. Tanner's brow shoots up and he looks pointedly at the hand in my pocket. "Isn't it a little soon for that?"

"No." I shake my head. "I know."

"Do you, though?" Tanner holds his hands up in surrender when I growl. "I mean, I know you know yourself and what you want. I just mean...be careful with Em."

"I know. I am. This is...right, Tanner." I can't explain how I know, but I do. I want to spend every moment—waking and sleeping—by Emily's side. She makes me a better man, a better father to Charlie, a better employee. Knowing she's here, caring for Charlie and me, makes me *want* to stop work and come home.

I want to hear about her day—what books she's read, what shows she's watched, what Charlie has done, and everything in between.

But I can't vocalize that. Sure, it may seem fast. But for me, too much time has passed without my ring, my name, and my heart belonging to Emily.

"She's coming for real now!" Molly calls, thundering down the stairs with Susan on her heels.

I walk to the end of the stairs, watching as Emily steps from her room and almost skips to the top of the stairs. Carefully she side-steps down the stairs and to my side. She smiles, looking even better than she had Monday in the shop. Her makeup is light enough that I barely notice. A pretty pink gloss coats her lips, and I am willing to bet a million dollars it will taste like peppermint. Her eyes are shadowed with a silver dust that shimmers with each blink and a simple strand of pearls adorns her neck. Matching teardrop earrings complete the look.

"You look amazing, Em!" I declare, taking her hand and squeezing it.

"Good enough to be with you tonight?" She chuckles as she says it, but her eyes look genuinely curious.

"I would take you in that sweatshirt you had on this morning and show you off to everyone without hesitation. But this?" My eyes drink her up and I grin. "This will make every guy in the office green with envy."

Her cheeks darken and she ducks her head.

Susan demands photos—like we're headed to prom. We pose and smile (although I'm pretty sure Emily throws in some goofy faces) and afterwards they all hug us and promise that Charlie will be well taken care of.

Then it's out the door, into the car, and off towards Highland, Mother, and this ridiculous party.

My fingers tap against the wheel, and I find that I'm at a loss for words. That's never happened before. I glance at Emily who is staring at me with an arched brow.

"Stop that." I slip my hand into Emily's.

She laughs. "Stop what?"

"Looking at me like that."

"But you're just so cute." Her nose wrinkles up as she smiles. "You like the gown?"

"Nope." It's my turn to grin at her. "I like you *in* the gown."

Her cheeks flame red, and I can't help but chuckle as we head toward Highland. But like when I'm on my way to work, that invisible band of anxiousness wraps around my chest. My fingers tense around the wheel. I'm proposing. What if Emily says no? What if I make her mad and she runs out like Cinderella at the ball, and I never see her again? My grip tightens around Emily's. I can't handle the thought of losing her, so I definitely won't be able to cope if it becomes a reality.

Emily pulls her phone from her clutch, connects it to the car's Bluetooth, and turns on a song. What plays isn't a Christmas song, but a Beatles' song. "P.S. I Love You" fills the car—with maracas, the synth guitar, and thrumming bassline. Emily sings along, wildly off-key, but beautiful to me. Because it's her, throwing herself into something she loves.

As the song finishes, she turns to me. "So, what do you think?"

"Of the song?"

"Well yes, but I more meant what it's about."

"Love?"

"Yeah. You started to say something this morning, but Charlie interrupted us."

I lick my lips and rub my thumb over her knuckles. "It's not the right time yet, Em."

"When will it be, Ollie?"

In about four hours, when we're dancing after dinner and I can ask you, Emily Fitzpatrick, to marry me as I am completely, totally, irrevocably in love with you, you beautiful woman.

Any hope of escaping this relationship with my heart intact is now gone. If she says no, I don't know if I'll ever be the same.

Scratch that—I won't be the same. I'll be a shell of myself. Broken beyond belief. She currently holds all the power in our relationship. It's up to her now.

"Ollie?"

"Sorry. Soon." I smile at her, my chest tightening as we pull into the parking lot of the hotel that boasts the ballroom. "I promise."

"Okay." She looks a bit sad, but it quickly turns to a smile as I hurry around and help her out of the car. She slips her hand onto my arm, leaning close so that her snickerdoodle scent wraps around me.

"Em?" I look down at her. Snowflakes are falling as a bell jingles somewhere down the road. The parking lot lights are warm despite the chill, and I pull her closer. For all the reasons the car was wrong, this place feels perfect. Quiet, intimate, us together in a swirl of snowflakes and solitude. And now, I'm finally read to say the words. "I think...I love you."

Her eyes dance, browns and greens swirling together in that look only Emily can give. "Why?"

"Why?" I laugh and shake my head. "You're bold and tenacious. You love wholeheartedly. You care so well for those you love, and I can't begin to compete with you in that. You're funny and passionate. Gentle and kind. You're infinitely patient with this bumbling fool of a godfather and his inadequacies of raising a baby girl. And you're so open—"

"I'm not," she interrupts, shaking her head. "I'm not open, Oliver. I have so much in me that you don't know."

"And there's a lot you don't know about me either."

"But so much of who I am is...fake. Pretend. I'm scared to let people in."

"So am I." I cup her face in my hands. "But, Em, I'm not pretending with you. I've loved you since the day you stood up to my mother in the grocery store. You love my goddaughter like she's your own, you do my freaking laundry without a murmur, you listen to me and help me calm down when my thoughts are spiraling. You're the most amazing woman I've ever met, and I'd be a fool to let you walk away."

I'm ready to drop to one knee here in the parking lot but a voice breaks through my swirling thoughts. "Are you going inside, or standing out in the snow all night?"

"Hey, Ethan." Emily smiles at him and my irrational side roars to life. Jealousy, pure and simple.

"We're going." Although I would really love to run to a chapel in Las Vegas and get married right now.

Emily must sense the shift in my mood, because she squeezes my bicep as we pass through the revolving glass doors and into the lions' den.

Chapter Twenty-Nine

Emily

The ballroom is...a lot. It's a weird blend of classic and chic. Exposed brick walls reach to the base of raw wooden boards that make up the vaulted ceilings. Exposed wooden beams stretch across the whole expanse. Oliver's mother draped shimmering golden chiffon material and fairy lights over them all. Low lights, the tinkling of champagne glasses, and the quiet murmur of conversations are layered in with the string quartet's music, creating a beautiful atmosphere.

In my dress, on Oliver's arm, I feel a lot like Cinderella heading to the ball—a fraud. I'm not part of the social elite. I'm not even close to their status.

Or at least, I wasn't until this morning. I am...the heiress of Nanna's book empire. I've somehow fallen into a fortune. A secret fortune, sure, but...

"Ready for dinner?" Oliver asks, smiling down at me with such warmth in his gaze that it chases away the chilling thoughts of being lied to for years.

"Yeah, let's go eat food."

He chuckles and guides me toward the tables—at the far end of the room. Holy buckets, that was a clever move on his mom's part. In order to sit, you have to pass over the dance floor, around the crowds of people milling about. Every single one of them casts me judge-y looks as they very pointedly talk to Oliver and don't spare a word for me after introductions are made. I can see Oliver's jaw grow more and more tense with each second that passes. This is going to end badly if I can't get him away from these people soon.

Ethan slides up to us after about an hour of torturous small talk. We are so close to the table and chairs. My toes are pinching in these stupid heels of Susan's (seriously, who subjects their feet to these *willingly?*) and my stomach growls loudly enough for Ethan to hear and smirk at me.

"Hey, Oliver? Sorry to pull you away, but there's a gentleman over there who would like to speak to you," he interjects during a pause in the conversation with a Mr. Graham.

"Oh, thanks, Ethan." There's a wealth of meaning behind that *thanks*. Oliver shakes the man's hand. "We'll have to catch up Monday, Mr. Graham."

"Yes, yes, of course!" He smiles at Oliver, gives me a look-over, then wanders off to bore some other poor unfortunate soul.

"I hate that guy," I whisper.

"Same," Oliver and Ethan murmur at the same time, making me snort.

"Where's the guy, Ethan?" Oliver asks, following his friend over to the tables.

Ethan's smirks, his eyes narrowing and his glasses sliding down his nose. "Oh, he's right here." He gestures to himself. "He wants you two to get food before Emily's stomach gets loud enough to be picked up by the singer's mic."

I laugh, I can't help it. It's a little too loud and draws a lot of curious glances. "Sorry." I clear my throat and inch a bit closer to Oliver.

He's grinning though, so I must not have embarrassed him too much. "Thanks, Ethan. What would I do without you?"

"Oh, shrivel up and die." He clasps Oliver's shoulder, whispers something that sounds like "Good luck," to him and then he too disappears into the crowd.

Oliver pulls a chair out for me and helps me sit. "What do you want?"

I pick up the menu. There are three choices, and I choose the least fancy—filet mignon and whipped potatoes, julienned carrots in honey glaze, and herbed asparagus.

Oliver orders the same, then angles his chair so he can look at me and the people heading onto the dance floor. "So?"

"It's not the frat party you made it sound like," I say.

He shrugs. "We've only been here an hour. By nine, it gets…"

My nose wrinkles again. "Yeah, I could totally see Mr. Graham tearing it up on the dance floor."

"No, he's the one passed out on the table," Oliver admits, earning a laugh from me. "But I can point to at least four people out there right now that are here with someone who isn't their spouse."

"Gross." I thank the waiter who places my plate before me. He looks taken aback and then returns my smile somewhat hesitantly. "So, there's no side chick for you, Oliver?"

"You're really going to ask me that?" he asks, mock affront in his voice.

I giggle and take a sip of the sparkling juice I requested. I refused to drink when I turned twenty-one out of principle—I would not do to someone else what the accident had done to me. I wouldn't widow, orphan, or ruin someone's life because I chose to be reckless with my beverage choice.

We eat in moderate silence. The meal is delicious. The gravy is creamy, the potatoes salty and smooth, and the steak is medium well-done (the only way a steak should be). I sigh in contentment after wiping my lips on my linen napkin. "That was great."

Oliver looks over, his lips quirking, and asks, "Ready to dance?"

"Sure, but if I step on your toes, it's not my fault."

"Whose fault would it be?" he asks.

I open my mouth, close it, then shrug. "Okay, fine. It's my fault."

He chuckles but holds his hand out to me despite my admission.

I let him lead me out as the quartet begins to play one of my favorite instrumentals—"Mia and Sebastian's Theme" from *La La Land*.

Oliver's hands settle on my waist. He stares at me as if he's never going to see me again and he wants to memorize every nuance of my face.

We sway more than actually dance, lost in each other's gazes as the rest of the crowd swirls and waltzes around us like multicolored clouds in the twinkling fairy lights.

Needing to ease some of the tension, I say, "We haven't seen your mother yet."

"Way to kill the mood, Em." He chuckles, but his eyes dart around and his throat bobs. He's nervous—about his mother or something else having to do with this party, I'm not sure.

"Sorry. Are you okay?"

His gaze lands on me right before he stops moving, dips his head, and kisses me. It's deep, searching, a tiny bit desperate, and—holy cannoli—it's one of the best kisses in my entire life.

"Holy buckets, Oliver," I breathe out as we break apart. We're not moving now. Just standing amidst the swirl of the Christmas party. "What the *heck* was that?"

His hands on my hips tighten as he looks at me. His voice is soft as he whispers, "A question."

"And the question is?" I'm shaking. Is this...no, surely not. He couldn't—wouldn't...would he?

"Emily Jane Fitzpatrick." Oliver's hands fall from my waist, the space instantly cooling. His green eyes never leave mine as he drops to one knee and pulls the little black box out of his suit coat pocket. "Will you marry me?"

My hands fly to cover my mouth. "Are you kidding? This isn't funny, Oliver."

"I've never been more serious about anything in my life. I am madly in love with you, Em. I want to wake up to you every morning and fall asleep in your arms every night. I want to raise Charlotte with you, I want to be the father of your babies—*our* babies. I want to do life with you, every second of every day. I want to marry you and love only you for as long as we both shall live. And I want to do it soon." He chuckles, his face turning a bit red as people stop dancing and turn to stare at us. "So, will you marry me?"

Tears are sliding down my cheeks—it makes sense why Susan and Molly picked waterproof makeup, the traitors. I can't wrap my mind around this. He's asking me to marry him! Me! The nanny, the woman caring for his goddaughter and who was dirt poor at the point he started to fall for me.

But he's still kneeling, holding out his grandmother's ring, and waiting for me to answer him.

"Yes! I'll marry you, Oliver Markel."

He's on his feet faster than I think possible, swooping me up in one arm and spinning me around like every romantic comedy hero ever. "I love you."

Tears return as he slips the impossibly perfect-fitting ring onto my finger and kisses me again. The people around us clap politely but I don't care that they're here. I don't care that I'm at a party that makes me feel supremely uncomfortable. I don't care that they're staring at me. All I care about is Oliver and kissing him again.

He seems to read my mind and presses another kiss onto my lips as the quartet starts playing "Married Life" from *Up*. I chuckle as Oliver spins me, but it's cut short by a screeched, "*Oliver Tate Markel!* What the *hell* do you think you're doing?"

He freezes, his eyes widening even as his shoulders roll back. He slides his arms around my waist as his mother flies toward us. Her champagne-colored gown sparkles with each stalking step and her green eyes flash with venom. At her heels is a man I've never met, but with the way his eyes dart around and how close he's walking to Pricilla Markel, it must be Oliver's father.

"I proposed to the woman I love." Oliver's voice is surprisingly steady, his grip warm and reassuring on my hip.

I slide my arm around his back, leaning into him as his mother stops before us. She sneers at me, her face so much like Oliver's in looks but with none of his kindness and joy. "I forbid it."

"And I forbid you from forbidding it." Oliver's nostrils flare as he glares down at his mother. "She makes me happy, makes me a better man. She loves Charlotte. She's everything I want in a wife."

"She is a *nanny*. The *help*."

"And she's a better woman than you have ever been!" Oliver snaps.

Mr. Markel crosses his arms. "You have no right to speak to your mother that way, Oliver."

Oliver throws a hand into the air. "And she has no right to speak to Emily that way!"

The room is so quiet, all you can hear is the soft sound of the quartet seemingly soundtracking this argument as all the employees of the marketing firm lean in with rapt attention.

The beads on Mrs. Markel's dress shimmer as she shakes with rage. "After all I've done for you—"

"And what, exactly, have you *ever* done for me, Mother? You and Dad never really cared about me unless it pertained to the business or my education. I was a hiccup, wasn't I, Mother? An *oops* in your life's plan."

"Oliver—"

"I'm not finished!" He steps closer to his mother, dragging me along with him. "I'm an adult. You are done disrespecting me and my life choices. I don't care what you do to me. Fire me, for all I care. But I love Emily, and I'm going to marry her, no matter what!"

I squeeze his waist and it breaks the stare off he's having with his mother. He inhales sharply.

"Fine, then." His mother's eyes dart around at her gawking employees as she draws back her shoulders. "You're fired!"

I glance at Mr. Markel. His brows are lowered, but not in anger. He looks contemplative as he glances from Oliver to his wife and then, strangely, to me. There's a question there, as he searches my face. I don't know what he's looking for, but I hope the silent strength and support I'm giving his son is answer enough.

Oliver laughs. Full on guffaws in the middle of all the people around him. "Good! Thank you, Mother."

"What?" his mother splutters.

"Yeah, thanks. I've wanted to quit for months, but since you fired me—" he leans in close, a grin that rivals Loki's curling his lips. "Now I don't have to."

Somehow, I get the feeling that Pricilla Markel isn't one to be at a loss for words often, and seeing her open-mouthed and silent after Oliver's declaration is the best kind of petty revenge.

"Let's go." Oliver tugs me toward the door. "Since I'm fired, I'm not required to stay."

Before we reach the doors, Pricilla shouts, "I will stop this wedding!"

There is a slight note of hysterics in her voice. Now I know for certain that Pricilla never gets told *no*. Losing control of Oliver is going to drive her crazy.

Oliver pauses by the double doors, turns to stare at his mother, and declares, "I'd like to see you try."

Her mouth opens to argue, but he is already leading me out to the car. Once we get there, he presses me up against the passenger door, and begins to kiss me deeply.

"Are you alright?" I ask after we come up for air, a little in shock at the turn of events. I'm engaged. To *Oliver*. I look down at my hand but Oliver tips my head back up.

"I am fantastic." He laughs, sounding lighter and freer than he ever has. "I'm going to marry you."

I wrap my arms around his neck. "When?"

"When what?" he asks, his hands running up and down my side.

"What date are we tying this knot?" I bite my lip. "I think I should move out until we're married. I...this is playing with fire, and I want to do things the way my parents would have wanted."

"I do, too. You deserve it, Em, which is why..." He nuzzles his nose into my neck, sending shivers down my spine when he whispers, "What about this Friday?"

"Friday?" My eyes widen. "Are you serious?"

He chuckles and nods. "Yeah, I looked up how long it takes to get a marriage license. We can get it tomorrow and then be married Friday after the three-day waiting period. I already talked to Molly's pastor, he said he'd marry us. Molly says she knows the perfect place for us to do it. All we need is a dress, which the girls said they'd take you out to do tomorrow after we get our license. And after Mother's threat..." he shrugs. "Seems like the best course of action."

"You...you planned it all out. You didn't even know if I would say yes." My body sways closer to him of its own accord.

"Nope, I didn't. But I hoped you would. And that hope was enough to pull this harebrained scheme out of me." He presses a kiss to my lips before he's finished speaking. My fingers find the nape of his neck and play with his hair. He steals the air from my lungs, making me lightheaded as we stand out in the freezing cold, warming each other with a kiss that is more succulent than the best dessert ever created.

"Oliver?" I whisper when we finally come up for air.

"Hm?"

"I love you." My voice cracks. "I love you and I'm not sure I'm good at showing it. I might never be but—"

"You care for me Emily. You listen and support, take care of the day-to-day things. That's love. You look out for Charlotte and have her best interest at heart. That's showing me that you love not only her, but me too. You take the time to be there after everyone else walks away." He brushes the back of his hand against my cheek. "You're you. Amazing, wonderful, and yeah, a little broken. And every piece is precious. I love you, Emily."

And then *I'm* kissing *him*. Memorizing the feel of his lips against mine, the way he presses then eases back. The way his hands travel up and down my back, his thumb grazing the skin exposed at the top of the gown and making me suck in a breath.

A shiver races through me and we break apart. "Want to finish this somewhere else?" I ask.

His pupils are dilated, and he smiles wryly. "I don't know if that's the best idea. Not because I don't want to!" He hurries to reassure me. "But because I *do* want to. A bit too much."

A nervous laugh slips out. "Well, then—"

"Want to go show the girls your ring?"

I nod, although I really do just want to be alone with Oliver. But he's right, we don't want to do something we'll regret. So, we climb into the car and head for home.

"Should I move back in with Mols and Sue?" I ask, raising our clasped hands to my lips and pressing a kiss to the back of it. Now that I am going to marry him, it makes showing him I love him so much easier.

"That's up to you." He looks at me out of the corner of his eye. "I want you to be comfortable. But I promise I can be a gentleman for five days."

I laugh. "You've been a gentleman for a lot longer than that, Ollie."

He chuckles. I turn on my romance playlist. Suddenly, each song seems to fit Oliver and me. He loves me, I love him, and I'm going to marry him!

The ride back to the house feels infinitely long and yet far too short. He helps me out of the car, interlocking our fingers as he heads inside. It's only seven thirty, and Tanner, Molly, and Susan are standing around the counter, along with the surprise presence of Ryley Pruitt.

He has a camera around his neck and grins widely when we step in through the door. "It's the couple of the hour!"

"What are you doing here?" I laugh.

He waggles the camera. "I was roped into helping."

"You offered!" Molly rolls her eyes. "And Ryder offered to make a special meal for a reception on Friday."

I glare up at Oliver. "Did everyone know you loved me except me?"

"You should have known." He bumps me with his shoulder. "I was dating you after all."

"For a week! Seriously, this has got to be the quickest progression of relationship events ever."

He chuckles and obliges Molly, Tanner, and Ryley's chants of "Kiss, kiss, kiss!"

Holy cannoli, I'm not sure if I'll ever get over the sheer presence of Oliver Tate Markel, let alone his kisses and hugs and smiles. And I'm *very* certain I'm okay with that.

"So, dress shopping Monday?" Susan grins but her eyes keep flicking toward Ryley. Ah, right. There was a beef there, too. A stinkin' love triangle between the Pruitt twins and Susan. But I'm too blissfully contented to play matchmaker with Susan at the moment—even though I am fairly good at it.

"Yeah, after we get our marriage license."

Oliver squeezes my hand. "Want to take some pictures in the living room? We can get more outside soon, but—"

"Oh! Yes, please." I wrap my arms around his waist, grinning up at him and sighing contentedly when he presses a kiss against my forehead.

The camera clicks and Ryley smirks. "You're so cute, it's disgusting."

Tanner laughs, his arms looped around Molly, her back against his chest. "You said the same thing about us, you know. Wait until it happens to you."

"Nah, I'll embrace bachelorhood and cool uncle status." He chuckles. "Emily and Susan are already honorary sisters in our house. And you're going to be our brother-in-law, Tanner. Might as well keep adopting all the poor lost souls wandering around Cloverfield."

We all laugh, then Ryley gestures for us to sit on the couch. I settle onto Oliver's lap. His arms wrap around my waist and his breath is shaky as he presses his forehead against mine.

"Have I said how much I love you?"

"Only about three times tonight alone." I chuckle, my hands braced on his shoulders. "But you can tell me a couple dozen more times before I'm tired of it."

I close my eyes, relishing the rumble of the laugh in his chest, his warm hands against my back and the broadness of his shoulders. Holy cannoli, this is heaven, right? Because never in a million years did I think I'd get lucky enough to earn the affections of someone like Oliver. Someone so good and kind and caring. Uncle Lewis said no one would ever want me, and yet here I am in Oliver's arms, being looked at like I'm the most precious treasure in the world. I don't deserve it. Don't deserve him. And yet he gave his love to me anyway.

What an amazing thing grace really is.

Chapter Thirty

Oliver

After the engagement photo session with Ryley, all my brain wants to do is kiss Emily. Over and over and over. My body craves her like an addict in rehab. There is no way I'm ever getting used to her. Her kiss, her touch, her very presence is intoxicating and has been since day one. Now that my ring is on her finger and my heart is in her hand, I cannot wait to give the rest of myself to Emily.

Molly and Tanner left an hour ago and Susan is putting Charlie down as Ryley finishes our pictures. Emily's fingers are threaded with mine when her phone rings.

"Molly?"

A shriek blasts through the speaker and Emily jerks it away from her ear. Incoherent babbling echoes out of the phone as all three of us look at each other in shock before Tanner's calm voice breaks through the chaos.

"Calm down, Mols, it's not a big deal."

"It's a *huge* deal, Tanner! They're in my *house*!"

"What are in the house?" I ask, thoroughly confused.

Emily's lips twist and she says, "My guess? A mouse."

"No! Not *a* mouse. Mice! Plural!" I can practically picture Molly shuddering. "The little furry menaces!"

"Now you sound like J. Jonah Jameson from *Spiderman*," Ryley helpfully chimes in.

I chuckle. "Yeah, but instead of *wall-crawling menace* they're *wall-dwelling menaces*."

Another sob echoes from the phone.

Emily rolls her eyes. "Molly, do you need somewhere to stay? When can pest control get out there?"

"Not until Wednesday and we can't be in the house for twenty-four hours afterwards."

"Well, then this is actually perfect." Emily grins up at me. "We really shouldn't be left alone here, right?"

"Right." I draw out the word.

"So, Sue and Mols can move in until our wedding on Friday."

"Friday." I don't love the idea of Emily's roomies moving into my house, but neither do I like the idea of having her leave—even for few days. And I do have the room—five bedrooms, three and a half bathrooms, plus the three living spaces means my house is…well, ginormous. I can handle them living here for a week.

I nod and Emily turns back to the still sniffling Molly.

Ryley claps me on the shoulder. "Good luck, my dude."

I chuckle. "How bad can it possibly be?"

***

Turns out: pretty bad. I haven't gotten a moment of alone time with Emily today. With Susan and Molly helping with Charlotte and the elopement plans—because getting married this quickly, that's what it is—it's like they're *everywhere*. I can't get a moment of peace, and not working actually makes it worse.

By Sunday evening, I've had it.

"Em, let's go into town and get a cocoa. Please?" I'm halfway begging, but I really don't care. I need some alone time with Emily.

She looks up from the notebook she's been using to jot down the list of things that need to be done before Friday. Her eyes take me in—my joggers, Crocs, and sweatshirt. I'm sure I look rough, but I haven't had anything to focus my nervousness on.

"Sure." She turns to Susan who is feeding Charlotte. "Are you okay with watching Charlie?"

"Absolutely!" Susan makes a face and Charlotte claps and giggles. "Get out of here and enjoy your date."

"Thanks, Susan." I incline my head. It's still odd, our relationship. But she's pushing Emily and me together. I'm not going to argue about it.

"T-minus five days!" Molly sings as she dances into the kitchen with a stack of papers in her arms. "Have fun!"

"Thanks." Emily grabs her coat, her purse, and my hand in the span of two heartbeats then all but yanks me out of the door. As we round the corner to the driveway, she hugs me tightly. Groaning with her face pressed into my chest, she mumbles, "Why did I think it was a good idea to have them live with us?"

I hug her back, resting my cheek against the top of her head. "It was the smart thing to do, and they needed somewhere to go."

"But they're *everywhere*."

I laugh. "I was thinking the same thing. But it could definitely be worse."

"Worse?"

"Yeah. Tanner, Ryder, and Ryley could be here, too."

She shudders, stepping out of my arms and toward the car. "Yep. That would be worse. The tension."

"Tension?"

"Susan and Ryder don't..." Emily shrugs. "I don't know the full story, but something went down between them a few years ago and Susan can't even converse with him civilly."

"Interesting." And it is, but my brain is stuck on the fact that I want to kiss Emily. Nope! We're engaged but that doesn't give me permission to maul her face whenever I want to.

"What, is there something on my nose?" Emily wrinkles it as I pull onto the road.

"No, but I do want to kiss you." Although, if I wait until after cocoa, she'll taste like peppermint and that's a flavor that's quickly becoming associated with Emily in my mind. Peppermint and cinnamon. Spicy sweetness that perfectly captures the personality of the woman at my side.

Emily laughs. "Eyes on the road, Ollie."

I press a kiss to the back of her hand and then focus on the Christmas music playing through the car and her thumb circling my knuckles.

We reach Sweetie's and I pause by the side of the car as Emily steps out.

"May I kiss you now? I've only been waiting all day, you know."

Her eyes sparkle in the twinkling lights that Sweetie has wrapped around the awning. "Yes, you may."

I cup her cheek and press a soft, lingering kiss to her lips. Desire floods me. Five more days and she'll be my wife. Forever together.

Emily grabs my face and presses a quick peck to my lips then declares, "I want cocoa."

"Your wish is my command." I laugh, pulling her close as we stroll into the café.

Sweetie looks up and grins at us. "Now, you can't deny this is something, *mia cara*."

"No denying it anymore, Sweetie." Emily holds out her hand, the ring sparkling in the light.

I think we've really and truly shocked the poor lady. Her mouth falls open as she glances between the two of us. "You're serious?"

Emily nods. "The wedding is Friday in the park if you want to come."

"Outside in December?" Sweetie asks, her eyes still wide.

"Yep." Emily hugs my arm, her smile sparkling. "We want to get married soon because..." she trails off.

"My mother isn't happy. I'm afraid she's going to try something—she basically said so—so we want to be married quickly. Also, I can't imagine Emily not being in my house anymore. She belongs there."

"Well, I always knew there was a spark." She gestures between us. "I'm happy for you."

"Thank you." Emily is glowing and I can't find it in me to look away. I probably look just as disgustingly infatuated as Tanner does with Molly.

That thought prompts me to turn back to Sweetie. "Two candy cane cocoas, please."

"On the house for the almost-newly-weds." She winks and goes to make the drinks herself.

"If your mother gets wind of this ceremony, what do you think she'll try?" Emily folds her arms and leans against the pastry display case.

"I don't know." I shake my head. "I've never crossed her before."

"Ever?" Emily's brows raise.

"No. Not when she told me what school to go to, who to date, what projects I'd take on in the marketing firm."

"Who did you date that she didn't like? Besides me?"

Oh, for the love. This isn't a conversation I want to have. At all. But it's one we need to have, isn't it?

I clear my throat, staring at the massive cinnamon roll in the case. It takes every ounce of my determination to say, "Susan."

Emily straightens. "You dated Susan?"

"Junior year of high school." I can't look at her, the tightness in my chest is painful. I hadn't meant to keep this from her, but it scared me. Would she think less of me if she knew? Would she have walked away if she'd known I was her friend's ex? I brace my hand against the counter, dizziness blurring my vision.

"Ollie!" Emily grabs my shoulders, forcing me to look at her. "It's okay. Don't freak out on me."

"Is it?" I gasp. "This is something I should have said before, but I didn't want things to be weird. It's just—"

"It is weird. But that's okay because I like weird." She grins. "And if it was that big of a deal to Susan, she would have told me."

Some of the tightness loosens. "Are you sure you're okay with this?"

"I love *you*, Ollie. I don't care who you dated before, who your family is, what hardships come with marrying a multi-millionaire. I love you. I will keep choosing to love you, whether you deserve it or not." She grins and I tuck a strand of her hair behind her ear. "We'll give each other grace. We'll push back against one another. We won't give up on each other."

"No. We won't." I press a kiss to her forehead and then turn to take the drinks Sweetie hands over the counter. "Thanks, Sweetie."

"Of course! *Felicitazioni* to you both."

We slide into a booth, across from each other, and hold hands. We talk about the wedding. We talk about Charlotte. We talk about Christmas and what we're looking forward to. We talk about traditions—or lack thereof—and ones we want to create with our family.

And all the while, there's no panic. No fear. Just quiet contentment knowing that I'm not facing the future alone any longer. I have a partner. A helpmate. One I'm falling more and more in love with every passing second.

Chapter Thirty-One

Emily

Monday, we get my dress. Molly, Susan, Mrs. Pruitt, and I all cry over it. It fits perfectly—no alterations needed.

Then, I met Oliver at the courthouse, and we get our marriage license. Four more days, and I'll officially be Mrs. Oliver Markel.

The next thing I know it's Thursday night—the night before our wedding. We are sitting on the couch with Tanner and Molly next to us, and Susan in the recliner. We're watching *Leap Year*. Ryder and Ryley said they'll meet us at the venue tomorrow—the gazebo in the park—an hour before the one o'clock ceremony.

Ryder volunteered to take some photos and he also said he'd whip up some barbecue to be eaten at the rec center afterwards along with Susan's delectable cookies.

My brain is running laps, making sure everything is planned, everyone has everything they need, that I'm not forgetting a catastrophic piece of the puzzle.

Susan will watch Charlie at her place over the weekend so Oliver and I can have the house to ourselves for our "honeymoon". It'll be short, but sweet, and if I'm being honest, I'm ready to just start living life together.

We have the flowers—wooden roses from the craft store in Highlands. They're red and beautiful against the white snow and the green shrubbery around the park.

We've hung Christmas lights under the gazebo. They sparkle like stars against a pitch-black night in the countryside.

I have my ring and dress. Oliver got his ring at the jewelry store when us girls were dress hunting. He's going to wear his gray suit, and Ethan is his best man. I chose both Molly and Susan as my maids of honor—because I can't pick just one or the other.

"You alright, Em?" Oliver whispers into my hair.

I realize I've tensed my shoulders. Laying against his chest the way I am, he felt it. I force myself to relax. "Yeah, just thinking through my list."

"No matter what happens tomorrow, I get to marry you and that makes me the happiest man in the world." He kisses the top of my head and tightens his hold. "Tomorrow night, we don't have to sleep in separate rooms."

That has me flushing and I squirm. Not because I'm nervous! Okay, maybe I'm a little uncertain. Oliver is amazing, but…what will tomorrow night be like?

Nope. That's a tomorrow thought. Tomorrow, whether it's amazing or awkward, we'll work through it together. As husband and wife.

My mouth goes dry. My heart thunders in my ears and I bury my face against Oliver's chest. My hands shake, but it's with excited energy.

Wife. Tomorrow, I'm going to be a wife. My dream for as long as I can remember.

I smile when Oliver's arms tighten around me, and my tired eyes begin to slide shut. I'm safe. I'm wanted. And tomorrow, we'll vow to never walk away from one another.

With those happy thoughts, I drift off to sleep.

I'm sitting on the vanity stool in my room as Molly once again pins back my short hair.

Déjà vu!

But this time, she slides a comb veil into the pins. Because I'm getting married today.

"There!" Molly leans over, squeezes my shoulders, and smiles at me in the mirror. "You're a bride!"

Both Molly and Susan look stunning in their long-sleeved, dark green maxi dresses. Their hair hangs in soft waves and thick shawls wait on the bed to keep us warm when I exchange my vows with Oliver.

Just a few more hours!

"And you look absolutely perfect!" Susan declares, snapping the palette of gold eyeshadow shut. "We're ready."

I stand and slip on my heeled boots and turn to study myself in the full-length mirror Molly brought over. My lacy gown has a chiffon underdress that covers my skin. It keeps the itchy lace off me, but also acts as extra insulation from the cold. There's no train, and it barely skims the ground. I drape my white shawl over my shoulders as I descend the stairs.

Tanner is at the bottom, messing with cufflinks of all things, but pauses to grin up at Molly as she follows behind me.

"Here comes *my* bride." His blue eyes dance. "I've got Oliver and Charlie in the car, and we're heading out."

"You better hurry before Oliver gets too antsy and ruins the big reveal!" Molly declares.

"Yes, ma'am!" Tanner salutes, presses a kiss to Molly's lips and then runs out the back door.

"You nervous?" Susan asks.

I wring my hands and bite my lip. "Nope."

"Liar." Molly laughs. "But this is a *fast* engagement."

"Yeah, it is," Susan agrees. She grabs the box with our bouquets off the table and heads out the door.

Molly links her arm with mine. "I'm nervous about getting married and all that comes with that, but I'm also ready to be with Tanner every day and every night. Is that what you're feeling?"

I think about last night. How safe I felt wrapped in Oliver's arms. About every other moment I've spent beside him in the last four months. Laughing, crying, anger, pain. It didn't matter. He held me close and didn't let go. Yeah, today there are nerves. But that's normal on a wedding day. The bigger side of my heart—the side that is craving Oliver more with each minute—it's ready. Ready to jump into forever.

"Yeah." I smile at my friend. "But I'm ready. Let's get me married!"

It's a surprisingly warm day as we step out to Molly's car. The sun shines down, reflecting off the snow and making my eyes water. The girls help me into the back of the car, making sure to keep my skirt free of any muck. Then they settle themselves in the front. They chat about life, about Susan's cookies—she made a crap ton for after the ceremony—about Molly's final week of teaching before Christmas break, about the hockey team and how that is going.

I sigh and turn to look out the window. What's Oliver doing? What's he feeling right now? He's probably an anxious mess. I can't help but chuckle at that.

Holy buckets, I'm doing this. Really doing this! I'm marrying Oliver Markel!

We pull into the parking lot. Little lanterns with candles line the shoveled path up to the gazebo and everyone we love and care about is here, standing between the warm lights. Mr. and Mrs. Pruitt are first, Charlie cradled in her arms. Ryley and Ryder—both with cameras in hand. Sweetie and Nico. Rick Pruitt and his shadow, Owen. A few of the teachers from the preschool. Oliver, at the end with Pastor Frank. Even from the car, I see his beaming grin. Ethan stands at his side.

But most surprising of all, standing right next to the gazebo, is Oliver's father. He's not smiling, but he's not frowning either. It's neutral. Beaten. And it breaks my heart.

Susan opens the door and Molly adjusts my veil and shawl before smiling—bright and warm enough to melt the snow around us. "Here comes the bride. The most beautiful bride!"

"Until your wedding this May," I counter.

She laughs, shakes her head, and turns. Taking the flowers from Susan, she begins walking toward the gazebo as soft instrumental music plays from some hidden speaker.

Susan faces me now. "Make him happy, Em."

"Always." My voice catches. "And I'm sorry. About what happened between you two in high school."

Her voice is sincere when she says, "It's fine. I'm learning that everything happens for a purpose. I haven't seen what that purpose is for me, but for you?" She glances over her shoulder. "He's standing there, waiting for you to make him the happiest man in the world. So let's go get you started on your happily ever after."

"It won't always be happy. But it certainly will be forever after."

Susan smiles then turns and follows Molly down the path. I take a minute. Inhale. Exhale.

The music switches as I head down the twisting path. "Mia and Sebastian's Theme" from *La La Land*. The candles flicker in time, warm and bright in the gray daylight. But I don't feel the winter air against my cheeks. Don't see the people lined up down the path. Barely hear the music at all except for the fact that it fits this scene so well. Me, walking toward Oliver as he stands under the twinkling lights. Even as he smiles, tears glisten. Yet such joy radiates toward me that my heart jumps, hurrying me forward.

Oliver clasps my hands in his after I hand my bouquet to Molly. They're warm despite the cold. He leans his forehead against mine as he whispers, "You're stunning, Em."

Pastor Frank starts his short message, but I hardly hear a word. I don't hear the exchanging of the rings and certainly not my vows (it's a good thing I've had them memorized since I was five). I hear Oliver's but only just. My brain is on a loop, reminding me that we're doing this. We're getting married.

My smile doesn't falter as Molly hands me my flowers and Pastor Frank says, "I am pleased to present Mr. and Mrs. Oliver Markel!"

Ryder, Ryley, and Rick whoop a cheer and begin to clap. "Got to Get You Into My Life" by the Beatles blasts and Oliver and I dance back down the path to the handful of people clapping and laughing and cheering. We pause to give Charlie kisses on the cheek as she squeals in Mrs. Pruitt's arms. Then Oliver spins me into a dip, presses a deep kiss onto my lips. "I love you, Em."

"I love you too, Ollie."

He grins, straightens up, and continues heading down the path.

"Oliver, Emily! A word, please?"

Oliver stiffens but turns. "Hello, Dad."

Mr. Markel's brows lower. "I'm sorry for the way your mother and I acted last weekend, Oliver."

"But not sorry enough to call?" Oliver glares for a moment before he sighs and runs a hand through his hair.

His dad flinches. "Yes, well." He clears his throat. "Regardless of past actions, I want to tell you I'm happy you've found someone to love. And who loves you?"

I wrap my arm around Oliver's waist. "I love him very much, sir. He's a good man, your son."

Biting my tongue is the only thing that keeps me from tacking on, *Unlike you*. I need to try and respect his parents, even if I don't like them.

Mr. Markel nods. "I'm sorry your mother missed this."

"She doesn't care." Oliver's tone is laced with derision. "She's never cared about anyone or anything except for herself."

"No, Oliver, she cared. She just..." Mr. Markel sighs and runs his hand through his hair. The action is so much like Oliver that I can't help but smile. He may look like his mother, but a lot of his mannerisms are from his father, including his hesitant uncertainty. "Your mother has always had a hard time showing affection. Even with me. This isn't an excuse, but I think you needed love and affection in a way she wasn't able to give. She's upset at being out of control. She's mad at you. But I think she does care. She'll come around."

"I don't know if I want to invite her back into my life, Dad. I don't know if I can handle it."

Mr. Markel nods. "I understand. But don't give up on her, Oliver."

I bite my lip when Mr. Markel holds out his arms to embrace Oliver. I'm not sure my husband is going to move forward, and Mr. Markel begins to lower an arm so it's a handshake instead of a hug. But then Oliver steps forward and embraces his dad. A few back slaps and they break apart.

"I do love you, Oliver." Mr. Markel pulls off his glasses and wipes his eyes. "I'm sorry I wasn't better at showing it."

Oliver nods. "I love you too, Dad."

Mr. Markel smiles, nods to me, and then heads for the silver Mercedes in the parking lot.

I shake my head. "That was..."

"Weird," Oliver finishes. "Yeah. But also good."

"Ready for Susan's cookies?" I ask, grinning up at Oliver.

"Ready for a lot more than cookies." His eyes sparkle and the heat of his gaze has me melting like the candles along the path.

My smile is wide as we climb into the back of Oliver's car and Ryley drives us over to the recreational center.

Cookies and punch, barbecue, and potato salad. Laughing and chatting and celebrating.

I'm a wife. A mother. A partner to this amazing man. I'm Mrs. Oliver Markel. And there's no one else I'd rather be.

***

<u>One Week Later</u>

The unwanted alarm of Charlie crying stirs me from slumber. Oliver's arms are wrapped around me, my head nestled under his chin. I sigh, feeling warm and comfortable in bed with him spooning me. I *really* don't want to go get Charlie.

Another cry, and Oliver stirs, his whiskers rubbing against my hair.

"Good morning, my husband." I roll to face him, letting my fingers skim his cheek as he slowly rouses to wakefulness.

He smiles lazily down at me, taking in my horrific bedhead and pillow-creased cheek. "Good morning, beautiful."

Ignoring my morning breath, I kiss him. He returns it and for a moment, the soft humming of our fan and the birds chirping the only sounds in the room.

Oliver is deepening his kiss when another angry cry from Charlie reaches us.

He sighs, leaning back to trace my face with his eyes.

"She has always had impeccable timing," he grumbles, before rolling away from me. "I'll go get her."

It's decidedly cooler in the king-sized bed without him beside me. The week since our wedding has been marvelous. The three-day "homey-moon" was perfect—exactly what both of us needed to adjust to life as husband and wife. I moved into Oliver's room and we took some trips to some of the larger cities around Cloverfield for meals and sight-seeing.

Surprisingly, or maybe not, considering my hopes and dreams, being a wife and mother all at once isn't as daunting as I thought it could be. It's pretty much the same as being a nanny, but instead of leaving at the end of the day, I get to fall asleep in Oliver's arms and wake up to his smile.

My eyes are half-lidded by the time Oliver steps back into the room with Charlotte tucked under his arm. Dang, he's handsome.

I've discovered over the last seven days that Oliver prefers to sleep without a shirt on, and if this is my view every morning, I don't think I mind. Yes, his shirtlessness is still as distracting as it was a month ago, only it's a distraction that's mine for the taking. I can't help but grin at that.

Oliver yawns, runs a hand through his blond hair, and moves over to our bed.

Our bed. I shiver, pulling the navy comforter up to my nose and breathing in a long draw of Oliver. This is *our* home, *our* room, *our* little family, *our* life. And the longer I'm here, the more certain I am that I love this little life I've found myself in. With each passing minute, it seems to grow.

Oliver lays Charlie down beside me then climbs back into bed, pulling me against his chest. He sighs contentedly, as if he was holding his breath until he was once again tucked back into the warm cocoon of us. Charlie squirms beside me, soft baby babble escaping.

"Miss me that much, huh?"

"You're warm." He mumbles burying his nose in my neck and tightening his hold on me. "And yes. Every minute away seems like forever."

Seriously, the man is a walking romance novel. And I love it.

Charlie squeals, and we both look at her, a soft smile of love blooming on my lips. Holy cannoli. Between my past and the barricade around my heart, I never thought I could find love like this.

But I'd been wrong—thank my lucky stars.

Oliver tucks a finger under my chin, turning me to face him. He lets his thumb caress my jaw as he whispers, "I don't know how I found you, Emily Jane, but I sure do love you."

"I love you, too."

The words are barely out of my mouth before Oliver presses a light, lingering kiss to my lips. I sigh, fighting a smile because I've learned it's hard to kiss when you're smiling. Charlie laughs. Oliver grins, his green eyes dancing with such unbridled care and love that I think I might burst.

Yeah, I definitely was wrong.

It feels so good to let the walls fall. In opening up my heart, I found the chance to get folded in. Folded into family, into joy, into home. And yeah. Even into the grace and acceptance that comes with being loved for who you truly are.

The End

Acknowledgements

With each story I write, I realize more and more how many people it truly takes to craft a book into the best it can be.

Thank you to the team at Quill & Flame for taking a chance on my little town of Cloverfield and believing in it even when I didn't!

Thank you to my family—Dad, Mom, Andrew, Clara, Abby, Alex, Allison, and Azariah—for putting up with all my brainstorming and story ideas. I love you all 3000.

Thank you to my writer friends—Amber, Anna, Crystal, Nathanial, Rachel, Vanessa, plus everyone else who listened to me rant about this swoony blond millionaire and his nanny, who is the biggest Beatles fan. You all are the greatest!

And thank you to the Master Storyteller—the True Author of love, the only One who can knock through all our walls and inhibitions, the One who loves the orphan and the outcast and binds up all their broken hearts, the One who loves without measure.

Thank you for giving me the gift of storytelling, and for filling these pages with the evidence of your mercy and grace!

IF YOU LIKED *If We Do*

CONSIDER CHECKING OUT MORE QUILL & FLAME PUBLISHING HOUSE TITLES

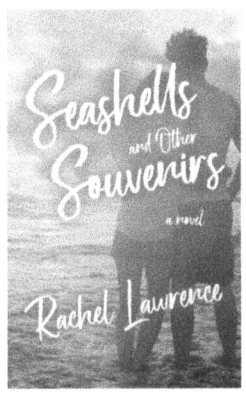

On Thin Ice — Anna Augustine

Seashells and Other Souvenirs — Rachel Lawrence

By Blood and Blade — Anna Augustine

Wishes (A Heartbooks Novella) — Brittany Eden

Hearts (A Heartbooks Novel) — Brittany Eden

By Light and Love — Anna Augustine

HEAT WITHOUT THE SCORCH

Quill & Flame
PUBLISHING HOUSE

WWW.QUILLANDFLAME.COM

Milton Keynes UK
Ingram Content Group UK Ltd.
UKHW021643011224
451755UK00011B/786